CAGE OF
DREAMS

BOOKS BY REBECCA SCHAEFFER

The Market of Monsters series
Not Even Bones
Only Ashes Remain
When Villains Rise

The City of Nightmares duology
City of Nightmares
Cage of Dreams

REBECCA SCHAEFFER

CAGE OF DREAMS

CLARION BOOKS
An Imprint of HarperCollinsPublishers

To everyone who gave *City of Nightmares* a chance

CAGE OF
DREAMS

1

My worst fear used to be that I would fall asleep and wake as a Nightmare, my body and mind twisted into something monstrous and unrecognizable, and I'd slaughter everyone I cared about.

Now, sometimes I dream of becoming a monster—at least then I wouldn't be so afraid of everything.

I crouch behind the bar of the speakeasy I've been working at for the past month as gunfire roars above me. There's a gang war going on because someone looked sideways at someone else, or made a remark about the upcoming mayoral election or some other equally inane nonsense. The patrons of the speakeasy are always getting into fights over *something*, and then they start shooting.

The bar, of course, is bulletproof, which is why I'm crouched behind it like the coward that I am. My only company are the bottles of various alcohols, which are also stored in the bulletproof bar—because servers can be replaced if they're shot, but the alcohol brings in the money. Heaven forbid something happened to it.

The waistcoat of my heavily starched uniform digs into my side as I curl into a ball, painfully aware of how incredibly fragile my body is, how easily a bullet could rip through me, shredding my internal organs into a bloody pulp.

But it's okay. Behind this bar, I'm safe.

Usually, I bring a penny novel to work with me for times like this. These shoot-outs can go on for a *while*. But I finished the last penny novel I was reading, and I haven't brought in a new one yet.

Which means my only distraction is my own thoughts.

I can't think of worse company.

The Friends of the Restful Soul always taught me that peace comes from within, that deep breaths and slow meditation can bring calm in even the most stressful of situations.

But the Friends of the Restful Soul also turned out to be a cult that lured people in by promising to help them and instead kidnapped them. So, I take all their advice with a grain of salt these days.

I try and think of the whole Friends situation in a positive light sometimes. Sure, they planned on kidnapping me too, but I escaped before they did—and I got several years of free food and rent from them before I got out. So really, who was getting conned here?

Me. It was still me.

Though I'd never admit it to anyone, there's a part of me that desperately wants to go back to the Friends. A part that dreams about my tiny little room there, its rough brick walls. A part that longs for the sense of peace and security as I lay on my bed, eyes closed, knowing nothing in the world could get to me, that for the time I was locked away from the world, I was *safe*.

I know it was all a lie. I was never really safe. It was just an illusion. I know that. I do.

But at times like this, with gunfire rattling above my head, crouched on the sticky floor of a speakeasy with shitty pay, bad hours, and constant risk of life and limb—well, that illusion starts to look pretty good.

The clatter of gunfire changes pitch, as the guns swing around toward something else. People yell, and the thuds of something heavy hitting gang members, followed by the thump of their bodies crashing to the ground, is a dark staccato amid the bullets.

After a moment, the gunfire ends, the thudding stops, and there's only silence.

I'm not dumb enough to peek over the top of the bar. Someone will come fetch me when the coast is clear. I'm not risking my neck out of curiosity. I'm perfectly happy to hide behind the bulletproof bar all night long. Or even longer. I could just live in this dark bulletproofed bar case, curled away from the dangers of the world. That sounds nice.

A head pops over the edge of the bar, looking down at me. "Hey, Ness!"

I blink up at my friend Priya. Her smile is cocky and bright, matching the neon bright turquoise ombré in her black hair. She has an athlete's frame, tall and long legged, and she's always dressed for a fight. Or a party. Preferably at the same time. Today, that means a variety of very illegal weapons pinned to a sequined belt, leather pants, combat boots, and a formfitting red turtleneck with a black waistcoat.

"You didn't mention how exciting your work was," Priya continues brightly as she swings herself onto the counter, legs draping over the edge. "Is it like this every night?"

"Mostly," I admit, continuing to crouch behind the bar.

"Sounds fun," Priya says amiably, and I roll my eyes. Priya and I have very different ideas of fun. I'm afraid of almost everything—she's afraid of almost nothing.

"Is the coast clear?" I ask.

"Oh yeah." Priya waves absently. "I took out the shooters. They weren't too much of a challenge."

Of course they weren't. Priya lives for the adrenaline rush of hunting down and killing rampaging Nightmares, from ten-story lizards crashing through office buildings to sea serpents eating boats. A few gang members are probably a walk in the park for her.

I wish I were like her. She takes action. She fights the things that go bump in the night, and she does it with a smile on her face.

I hide from them and fantasize about rejoining an evil cult.

How can she be so brave when the world is so insane? And why can't *I* be like that?

I rise and dust myself off. My once white button-up shirt is now as gray as my waistcoat from all the crawling around on the floor I did to get behind the bar.

Priya hops onto a barstool, ignoring the pile of unconscious—at least, I hope they're only unconscious, though I wouldn't actually care if they were dead—gang members behind her.

"One Newham Twist please," she orders. "On the rocks."

I start mixing her drink while the other staff members drag the bodies in the middle of the room outside. Some of them leave bloody trails that another staff member mops up. The gang shootings are always so messy. At least with a customer at the bar, I have an excuse not to scrub brain matter off the walls this time.

The only bad part about not dragging the bodies into the alley behind the speakeasy is that I don't get the chance to pick their pockets. Whoever tosses the bodies gets to pick them clean. That's at least half the income from this job.

I'm careful when I pour her drink to lean the tumbler against the glass. The extra support helps hide the faint shaking in my hands, the only remaining sign that five minutes ago, death was rattling through the building.

I pass Priya her drink, and she downs it in one go, then slams it back on the bar. "Another."

I raise an eyebrow. "You know those are pretty alcoholic."

"That's the point."

I shrug, and make her another.

She downs that too.

My eyes narrow. "You okay?"

"What, you think I can't take my alcohol?" she asks, as though this is a personal offense.

"No," I say slowly, trying to figure out how to phrase this. "But you don't usually drink so fast. Did something happen today?"

Priya deflates.

"Not really," she admits. "It was the same as every other day since I've started working for Nightmare Defense. We train in the morning, then sit around waiting for calls about Nightmare attacks that never come, and then we train in the afternoon, and then we go home. Rinse and repeat."

She swirls her empty glass. "It's just . . . not what I imagined." Her expression turns bitter. "I joined to fight dangerous Nightmares, to blow up dinosaurs ravaging apartment buildings and behead flying zombies."

"Well," I say carefully, "maybe it's just because you're new. All the missions are going to the experienced members."

She shakes her head. "You killed all the experienced members, remember?"

I wince. "*I* didn't kill them."

She rolls her eyes. "I'm sorry, I forgot, you got someone else to kill them for you. How silly of me to miss the nuance there."

A month ago, Nightmare Defense, the one place that I'd always thought *wasn't* evil in Newham, had kidnapped me and my friend Cy. We'd accidentally survived a mass assassination they'd arranged, and then riled them up by exposing it. In an effort to, you know, *not die*, I'd released the monster living in people's dreams. The one that turned people into Nightmares. The one that, with a single touch, had turned every

6

single member of Nightmare Defense into cockroaches and butterflies, then crushed them beneath his smooth black shoe.

I didn't regret releasing the Nightmare Phantom. Yes, I'd released a monster from dreams and he'd wiped out the city's defense force. But I'm alive. And Cy's alive. That's what matters.

I'm too much a Newham girl to regret staying alive, whatever the cost.

"Sorry," Priya says. "That was uncalled for." She rubs her temples. "It's just, the people who got into Nightmare Defense a week before me got to crawl into a dragon's eye socket and pour acid on its brain. Like, how cool is that?"

We have very different definitions of what "cool" is.

"Uh. That's nice." I lean in. "But you also did some cool things. Remember that sentient flesh-eating blob that you dissolved last week? And the week before, you had it out with a twelve-foot-long crocodile."

"That last one wasn't actually a Nightmare," Priya points out. "It was just a pet someone flushed down the toilet that became very large in the sewers."

"It was sure nightmare material, though." I smile encouragingly. "That's gotta count for something, right?"

"I suppose it was a good fight," Priya grudgingly admits. Then she sighs. "But ever since you released the Nightmare Phantom, the number of Nightmares has plummeted."

"That's a good thing, isn't it?" I say.

Priya looks away. "Yeah, of course."

It doesn't sound like she believes it though.

7

Every year, thousands of people forget to take pills to prevent dreams, or break prohibition laws—like we're doing right now—to drink alcohol, effectively neutralizing the Helomine in the tap water that stops people from dreaming. Because if you can't dream, you can't have a nightmare, and wake up having become it.

But now, the monster that turned people into Nightmares isn't in their dreams anymore.

Because I brought him into reality.

"What do you think the Nightmare Phantom is doing?" Priya asks, thoughts mirroring mine. "I figured now that he's out, he'd be, I don't know, turning people into Nightmares on the streets and causing chaos everywhere."

"Me too," I admit. "It's too quiet. It's unsettling."

"Like the calm before the storm," Priya agrees, tapping her finger in a nervous rhythm on the polished bar counter.

I thought, when I freed him, I'd be unleashing chaos on the world. But it's actually been *less* chaotic. It unsettles me, this quiet. I can't help wondering if he's planning something much worse.

The band has come back onstage now that all the blood is mopped up, and a rollicking jazz ditty starts up.

New customers trickle in, drawn by the music, returning now that the fight's over. A woman walks arm in arm with her boyfriend, the two of them giggling together. She's wearing a flapper dress that glitters with beads.

She's also a three-headed wolf with goat hooves.

She waves as she passes us, three grinning mouthfuls of

8

jagged teeth, and I force my hand to unclench from my tumbler, wipe my shaking sweaty hands on my trousers, and smile politely back.

I'm better than I was—I haven't set anything on fire trying to escape from a terrifying-looking Nightmare in almost a month—but I still have problems with really obvious Nightmares. Logically, I know it's not their fault they were turned into their worst nightmare while they slept, and that they're still people under that monstrous skin.

But logic has never had anything to do with my fears.

Priya looks mournfully at the Nightmare girl, as though hoping she'll go on a murderous rampage at any moment. The girl doesn't oblige, continuing to giggle as she leans against her partner, a dapper Black man wearing a top hat, enticing him to dance.

Priya downs her freshly refilled drink and slams the glass on the bar. "Another."

I eye her. "I think you've had enough."

"Are you cutting me off?" she says, clearly offended. "Just because you can't hold your liquor doesn't mean I can't hold mine."

"Oh, I'm sure you can hold your liquor," I tell her. "But bar policy has a cutoff limit, and you hit it. I can't serve you for another hour."

This is complete horseshit. The bar has no such policy. If anything, the policy is "milk the customer for as much cash as possible, then when they've fallen unconscious from drink, rob them."

I'd rather not see Priya unconscious and robbed.

Priya mutters under her breath, and then reels out onto the dance floor, grabbing a random person and pulling them into a polka.

I sigh. I'm worried about Priya. She spent her whole life dreaming about getting into Nightmare Defense, and now that she's there, nothing is at all like she imagined. Every time I see her, she's more miserable.

I just wish I knew how to help.

Bang.

I drop instantly, pressing myself to the ground behind the safety of the bulletproof bar.

Did the gangs come back? Are we going to have a second shoot-out tonight?

Priya was on the dance floor—was she shot?

For that matter, was I?

I paw myself, checking for wounds, in case the adrenaline and terror have kept me from feeling them, but I'm uninjured as far as I can tell. It's okay. I'm okay. Everything's okay.

"Ness?"

I look up to see Estelle leaning over the counter looking down at me. She's white, freckled, with a halo of bright red curls. She's the one who got me this job a month ago, mostly because I think she felt sorry for me.

"Ness, what are you doing?" Estelle asks.

I stare up at her. "What are *you* doing? That was a gunshot."

Estelle lets out a long-suffering sigh. "No, it wasn't. Someone dropped their beer mug. It broke."

Oh.

Well, now I feel stupid.

I stand slowly, dusting myself off, trying to play it off like nothing happened.

Her eyes crease in concern. "You okay?"

"Fine, fine, fine," I insist, my voice high and chipper. "Never better."

I mean, for someone living in Newham, I'm doing as well as can be expected. I'm alive, and still have all my limbs. No one has tried to eat me yet today. That's honestly better than most days.

Estelle considers me. "And how are things going living with Cy? He hasn't . . ."

I flush, turning away. "I told you, he's a friend. He's just letting me stay at his place until I get enough savings to rent my own place. I'm not a blood worker."

Estelle purses her lips, seeming to not quite believe me. She's been worried about me from the start, and I understand her concern. After all, vampires can be incredibly dangerous. And it's easy to end up dead from blood loss. But I'm not feeding Cy.

Well. I did once. But that was a one-time thing.

And anyway, Estelle has to know that I'm not feeding Cy—after all, she *is*.

"Seriously, Estelle," I insist. "I'm doing fine." I note her hollow cheeks and shadowed under-eyes. "Are *you* okay?"

"Fine, fine." Estelle waves me off and looks me over. "You seem a little jumpy, though. Why don't you swap with me. Take the rest of the trash out and start mopping down the kitchen."

My shoulders loosen a little, and I'm grateful, though I won't admit it. Cleaning the kitchen is safe, far away from the drama of the speakeasy itself.

"Sure." I smile. "Sounds good."

I waste no time grabbing the trash bag under the bar and heading to the back alley. Maybe I'll get lucky and someone forgot to pick the pockets of the dead gang members tossed out there earlier.

The air outside is crisp and a little chill, a reminder that we're going into autumn. Tucked in the alleyways and hidden nooks of the city, the homeless population is already preparing—not for the cold, though that always kills a few people every year, but for the scams that rise up every winter. The shelters that aren't actually shelters but covers for some mad scientist to experiment on a population that won't be missed. The monsters seeking human flesh to eat or wear or sell that roam the streets, luring people in with promises of warm food and beds.

I shiver, and not from the cold. That could have been me in the streets.

If I'm not careful, it still could.

I shudder at the thought. No. I have a job now. I'm saving money. Soon, I'll be able to afford to rent my own place, my own little cubbyhole of safety. I'll be independent and stand on my own two feet without any help.

And I definitely won't end up on the street.

My fingers tighten on the trash bag handles, and wish I believed my own words.

I toss the bag into the alley, then look at the pile of bodies, wondering if I should go through them for anything of value the other servers missed. We call the money we find "tips" because the patrons sure don't tip when they're alive.

I take a step forward, but stop when I see her.

Her uniform waistcoat has been stripped off, showcasing the bloody hole in her white button-up shirt. The glow from the streetlight bounces off her pale face and dark hair, and her eyes are mercifully closed.

I don't remember her name. Lesley? Lisa? Linda? She was new. Just started this week. She was supposed to be on door duty tonight, letting people into the hidden speakeasy. Which meant that when the shooting started, she was out in the open with nowhere to hide.

She hadn't been part of the fight. She'd been a regular girl, like me.

Now she's dead.

Thrown out in the back alley with the rest of the trash.

I stare at her, unable to take my eyes off her. Not because I care she's dead, people die all the time. Not because I liked her and am grieving, I didn't even know her well enough to remember her name.

But because it could have been *me*.

I've done door duty. I've even had fights break out when I was on door duty. It's only been luck that's kept a stray bullet from hitting me.

How long before I'm *not* lucky?

The shaking hands are back, but this time the shaking rises up, and I have to crouch, to ball myself up and wrap my arms around myself, hold myself before I shake my bones right out of my skin.

On the ground is a ratty newspaper with a large photo on the front page. The Director of the Friends of the Restful Soul smiles up at me, his lizard face familiar and welcoming. I can almost hear his voice, so soothing, telling me to come home, that my wonderful little room is waiting, my safe haven.

But it's not.

My room is gone, and even if I could get it back, the illusion has been broken. I know it's not safe anymore.

But I want it *back*. I want that feeling, that knowledge that I was safe. I want the life I had there, even if I didn't fit. I had to play at religion and pretend to care, but it was a small price to pay for the free room and board. And the jobs they had me do were so much safer than working in a speakeasy. I delivered mail, I dropped off flyers.

And yes, the last time I dropped off flyers a woman turned into a Nightmare and tried to murder me. And true, the last time I did a mail run the boat exploded.

I know these things. It wasn't really safe, even without the whole kidnapping scheme. But it doesn't stop me from wanting that life back, the overwhelming sense of security and stability that living there gave me.

I want it so bad it hurts, and if I thought that I could beg the Director for everything to go back to the way it was, then I'd do it. No matter what the cost was.

But I can't.

Because it doesn't exist. The safety was a lie, and I still don't know how or where to find the reality. All I want is to be safe. To not be afraid.

But how can I be safe in a place where wild gunfights are a normal part of the evening?

I can't.

That's the truth. This job isn't safe, this city isn't safe. And it's only a matter of time before my luck runs out and I end up dead in an alley somewhere too.

2

Whenever I tell people I live in a closet, they either think I'm exaggerating—I'm not—or make a joke about Newham's rental shortage.

None of them ever imagine that I *chose* to live in a closet.

My closet is small and cramped, but it's contained. I like contained spaces. I picked it because it reminded me of my perfect little room with the Friends, but the truth is that it's a poor substitute. The doors are slatted, which means light and noise from the main room slip through easily, disturbing the peace of it, reminding me every time I'm there that it's nothing more than a sham imitation of a broken illusion.

But that doesn't mean I'm leaving my closet. For one thing, then I'd have to sleep on the couch in the living room, and that's just too exposed. I already feel guilty that Cy is letting me stay in his apartment rent free while I get back on my feet. I don't want to take up more of his space than I have to.

All the way home I try to focus on how nice it will be to relax in my little closet, and not on the image of my coworker's dead body, thrown away like so much trash.

It doesn't work.

Cy's apartment building is in the nice part of town, all whitewashed buildings across from green, well-tended parks. The lobby is full of polished fake marble and crystal chandeliers, the kind of thing I'd only ever seen in films before I met Cy. The door guard, a burly ginger man over seven feet tall with arms as wide as tree trunks, looks up from his book when I enter.

"Evening, Ness," he says. His speech is always slow and ponderous, and I suspect it's part of the change his body went through when he became a Nightmare.

"Evening, Ronald," I reply.

I've never asked Ronald what kind of nightmare he had to end up so monstrously large, with exaggerated features and slow movements, but I suspect it was about a person. When kids are scared of someone, a bully, a parent, a teacher, they often have nightmares about that person where all the scary features are overexaggerated.

And then they wake up looking like that overexaggeration.

When I first met Ronald, I was scared of him, like I was scared of every Nightmare.

Now, I smile as I walk past him to the elevator bank.

Most days, I see this as progress. My fear of Nightmares, which once paralyzed me, often ending in full-blown panic attacks, is becoming less crushing. It's not gone—a decade of fear can't be changed in an instant—but it's much more manageable. I'm getting a little bit better every day.

Unfortunately, as today has reminded me, none of this

seems to have affected any of my *other* fears.

Seeing my progress with my fear of Nightmares should be reassuring. It's proof that I'm capable of change, that I have power over my mind, that I can conquer my fear. And most days, I even believe that.

But today, it just seems overwhelming. When I had one huge, overpowering fear, it overshadowed all the other things I was afraid of. Now all those fears are on an equal playing field, and it's overpowering in a completely different way. There are so many things in the world I'm afraid of, so many different ways I skirt death every day.

How can I possibly conquer *all* these fears?

The unpleasant truth is: I *can't*. I just have to live with them.

I just wish I could *fix* it somehow.

I get off the elevator and head down the hall to Cy's apartment.

It's huge by Newham standards. The front door opens into a spacious living room with a plush couch, polished wood coffee table, and broad window that offers a spectacular view of the nightscape of Newham. A door leads to Cy's bedroom, which is just as big as the living room and even more richly appointed, and a bathroom with a state-of-the-art shower and a deep, claw-footed bathtub.

I pick up the papers by the door as I walk in, checking the news.

ANDREA GROVIN, MAYORAL CANDIDATE, ASSASSINATED reads the headline, along with a campaign poster of a woman with sleek black hair, head at a three-quarters angle as she looks majestically at something to the side. The Newham Cathedral towers in the background.

I don't bother reading the article to find out who killed her. Probably another candidate. Good riddance. We all knew she'd been kidnapping children and literally bathing in their blood to keep her skin dewy and young.

I flip through the paper, checking the other stories.

KOVAL HEIR DISAPPEARS, STEPMOTHER MARISSA KOVAL SAYS SHE'S "HAPPY TO LOOK AFTER THE BILLION-DOLLAR INHERITANCE" UNTIL HEIR REAPPEARS.

Yeah, that heir isn't ever reappearing, except perhaps as a skeleton at the bottom of the river.

JUDGE WHO SENTENCED MAYOR TO JAIL TIME REVERSES DECISION AFTER TRAGIC DEATH OF SON.

Wow. Who could have seen that coming? Certainly not every single person in this city.

"You're home early tonight."

I startle, turning around. I hadn't realized Cy was home.

You can tell Cy's mother was a movie star. He has flawless skin and vibrant green eyes that he outlines with black eyeliner, making them pop even more. His thick dark hair is lush and often slicked and styled, though it's not tonight. He's wearing a black waistcoat and trousers, and a deep green shirt that brings out the green of his eyes even more.

I resist the urge to look away awkwardly—he's so attractive it's almost intimidating.

"Yeah, had a bit of a night," I tell him.

"Tell me about it." He mutters, walking around to slump on the couch. He stares up at the ceiling, head dipping back over the couch arm like a maiden in a vampire movie, waiting for the monster to bite her.

It's especially funny, because if this were a film, he'd be the monster.

"I've had a wretched night," he proclaims, arm draped over forehead, making him look even more like a swooning maiden.

"Oh?" I meander over. "Worse than when we were kidnapped and held in cages by Nightmare Defense?"

"Not that bad," he admits, turning his head to face me and grinning.

I smile back, and feel some of the tension of the evening ease out of my shoulders.

I'm more relaxed with him than anyone in the world other than Priya. It's hard to believe when I met him, I was completely convinced that he was going to drink all my blood and leave me in a ditch somewhere.

Obviously, that didn't happen.

Nearly being assassinated in a boat explosion, swimming to shore together, and hiking several days back to civilization really shows you the core of a person. Somewhere between then and being kidnapped and nearly murdered by Nightmare Defense, I realized I actually really like him.

More importantly, I feel *safe* with Cy.

"So what happened?" I ask. "To make it the worst night ever, but not quite."

"My father."

I envy Cy a lot of things. He has an incredible surplus of money, which means he'll always have the safety that affords him. He'll never worry about paying rent, or if he can buy food. He'll never walk around in holey shoes or pinch pennies to afford a new fridge. On top of that, because he's a vampire, he's got incredible healing. He can heal bullet wounds, his flesh will knit right back up without a scar even if it's been sloughed off to the bone.

The one thing I do *not* envy, is his father.

"Your father?" I ask, nervous. "Does he know where you live?"

Is he coming to kill us all?

"Not yet," Cy says, and I let out a silent breath of relief.

"So what's going on then?" I ask, taking a seat on the plush chair adjacent to Cy.

"He's got a new film coming out." Cy grimaces. "The world premiere is happening next week at the Royal Theatre."

"Here?" I ask. "In Newham?"

"Yeah."

I shudder. Cy's father is an entertainment mogul and film producer. After he had Cy, he found a vampire to pay to turn him into one too, so that he could live forever, young and handsome and rich, as his empire grew. Unlike Cy, he doesn't pay people for blood. He seduces young women and then bleeds them dry and says it was "an accident" and he "couldn't control himself." He drugs women and bites them, and says it's a kindness because they'll wake up with no memory of the attack.

And he uses his films to convince people that all these awful things he's doing are romantic. That he's a tortured, tragic figure who should be romanticized instead of reviled.

"I don't know why I'm so upset," Cy admits. "I mean, I do, but it's not like this is the first time he's released an awful movie that romanticizes awful things. But it's the first time since I ran away and I just feel like I should *do* something."

"Like what?" I ask.

"I don't know. Burn down the building."

I raise an eyebrow.

He snorts. "Yeah, I wouldn't do that. I don't want to hurt anyone." His shoulders slump. "And it wouldn't help anyway. The film reel is probably at half the cinemas in the country by now."

"Probably," I agree.

He looks down at his hands. "I just feel so *useless*."

"You're not useless." I put my hand on his shoulder, and lean forward, pulling his body against mine in a hug.

Cy's father is a rich, powerful man. What can people like us do against someone who runs an entire movie empire?

Nothing.

Just like I can do nothing to the Friends of the Restful Soul, who have been kidnapping people for decades, who planned to kidnap me too for unknown purposes. It doesn't matter what people like them do—this is Newham. Laws don't apply to the rich. Or the gangs. Or the Mayor. Or the police.

Or really, most people.

It doesn't seem fair that Cy's father can go on with murdering people and then making movies about how romantic it is, that the Friends of the Restful Soul can just continue on with their human trafficking scam. But that's the way the world is, and I have no idea how it could be changed.

Cy pulls away from my hug, fixing his hair, avoiding my eyes. He takes a breath and asks, "So what happened with you?"

I shrug. "Oh, you know."

"Hmm." He watches me with narrowed eyes. "Come on, Ness."

"What?"

"Spill it."

I groan.

"I can see the wheels turning behind your eyes. You're also home early." His eyes are kind. "Did you get fired?"

"No!"

Not yet, anyway.

He looks at me expectantly.

I look down, at my hands, no longer shaking. Of course not. I'm home, Cy is with me. I'm safe. I wish I could feel like this all the time.

But that would mean never leaving the apartment. And all

that would do would be turn the one place I feel happy into a cage. I'd ruin what little peace I have.

Finally, I admit, "I'm thinking of getting a new job."

"A new job?"

"One that's a little less dangerous," I tell him. "Hopefully with better pay."

"And you decided this in the middle of your shift?"

I clear my throat awkwardly. "Yes."

He gives me a sympathetic look. "Did something happen?"

"Not really," I admit. "I mean, nothing more than usual. There was a fight, guns were fired. One of the other servers got caught in the crossfire though, and I . . ."

"Couldn't help wondering if next time it would be you?" he finishes.

I nod, silent.

After a long moment, he says simply, "Well, I guess we should start perusing the job ads, hmm?"

A small smile cracks my face. "You're not mad?"

"Why would I be mad?" he asks, brow furrowing in genuine confusion.

"Because I'm living rent free in your apartment, and this will probably delay me moving out on my own," I admit.

He waves it off. "Don't worry about it. Seriously."

But it's hard not to worry about it. I worry about everything. It's sort of my thing.

The phone rings, interrupting us. Cy rises and picks up the receiver. Unlike everything else in the apartment, which is new, the phone is an older wooden model with a brass receiver. It looks very distinguished, but it is a bit bulky.

"Hello?" He pauses, ear pressed against the polished brass. "Oh, yes, Estelle, hi."

I lean back into my seat, making myself small, as if to hide from Estelle even though I know she can't see me.

"Yes, she's here." Cy glances at me a moment, then says, "Her injury?"

Cy raises an eyebrow at me.

"Lie," I mouth, then point to my arm.

"Yes, we're taking care of the injury now." He goes along with my lie easily. "It's not nice at all. The adrenaline from the gunfight must have dulled the pain quite a lot."

Cy is lying for me. I don't know if I should be flattered or embarrassed.

"Of course, yes, I'll tell her." He tenses at something she says. After a moment, he relaxes. "Oh, of course, I understand. That sounds good."

He hangs up the phone and turns to me.

"There are easier ways to get time off to go job hunting, you know," he says dryly.

"Eh, but this one was the least likely to get me fired."

And I don't want to lose the job I have before finding a new one. Job hunting is a full-time job in itself, and my nerves are too messy to go back to the speakeasy tomorrow so I'd just . . . told a little fib that would get me some time off to sort things out.

Honestly, on a scale of all the lies I've told, this is one of the most harmless, so I don't see why I should feel guilty.

"Thanks for covering for me," I tell him. "Even though you disagree with my methods."

He waves it away. "It's fine."

I run a hand through my hair, still surprised by how short it is even after a month. At least these days my hairstyle looks deliberate and not the result of a Faustian bargain with a dream demon.

"It sounded like something else happened too?" I say.

"Oh yeah." He shrugs. "Something came up and Estelle can't feed me tonight."

I stiffen.

Cy buys blood from Estelle. It doesn't bother me, because they have a mutually beneficial business relationship. He needs to eat. She needs money. They treat each other with respect, and honestly, it's probably the least predatory, most practical way I've heard of for a vampire to get blood. In Newham, people usually take what they want and don't care who suffers.

And, well—Cy needs to eat.

"Oh." I turn away, trying to look nonchalant again.

I'm not afraid, even though my body is tight. It's not fear, per se. Cy won't hurt me. I know that. He's not going to be like "you're dinner now" or anything.

But the thing is, I've fed him before. I offered, once, and it was fine. I was fine.

And now part of me is scared that he'll take that as invitation to ask again.

The thing is—I don't think, normally, I'd be bothered if he asked. I might say no. I might say yes. I don't know. I didn't mind the experience.

But things changed when I became homeless and moved in here. Now I'm afraid he'll ask, because I'm afraid of how to answer. Can I reasonably say no, when he's letting me live here for free? Should I just say yes to pay him back in blood, even if I don't want to?

And if I did say yes, then would I actually be saying yes because I was okay with it, or because my subconscious wanted to placate the person who has the power to make me homeless?

"We're going to reschedule to tomorrow, first thing in the evening," Cy says, interrupting my thoughts.

My muscles loosen. He didn't ask me. I don't have to face the awkward choice.

This time.

"You'll be all right until then?" I ask, just to be sure.

"Of course."

"Good, good," I repeat. "I'm exhausted, I think I'm going to go to bed. It's been a long day. Lots of near death and all that."

I walk to my closet quickly, trying to mask the weird feelings that have bubbled up.

Cy watches me go, his expression a little sad, and I know

27

I'm not successful. "You're safe here, Ness. You know that, right?"

"I know," I tell him gently.

And I do know. Cy will never hurt me.

But the problem is that he *can*. He has so much power over my life, and if anything, anything at all, goes wrong—I'm screwed. If we get in a fight, I'll be homeless. If he wants to hurt me, I have no hope of defending myself.

All I wish is that I could be on an equal playing field with him, so that these thoughts would leave. If we were on the same level, then maybe I could trust my feelings more. Maybe I could feel better about acting on them.

As I crawl into my closet bed, I wonder what the world would be like if I were as rich as the Friends, healed as quickly as Cy, or was as brave as Priya.

If I were anyone except myself, small, weak, and powerless in a city filled with monsters.

3

The next week is a series of job interviews, most of which go about as well as I expect.

I show up to the first one to find a disaster well underway. A dragon trapped in a basement is roasting anyone who comes near, and most of the building above it has already succumbed to the flames. Nightmare Defense is trying to shoot it from above, but they're held at bay by the roaring torrents of fire from both the basement dragon and the building it set on fire.

I double-check the address in my notes, and then pick my way through the rubble of what used to be the building next door, which looks like it was knocked down by the dragon's swinging tail.

The street numbers are still painted on the sidewalk though, and yep, this was where my interview was.

I cross it off my list.

As I walk past a police auto, a balding, middle-aged man in a charred tuxedo looks out from the bars of the back of the truck, blubbering as he watches the fight.

"I was just trying to feed Gramma," he pleads. "Newham is overpopulated anyway!"

No one listens to him.

I suspect this was my interviewer.

Like for any job in Newham, I'd done my research before going to the interview. I'd made sure the company did exist—there was a number you could call for that, though it was susceptible to bribes. I'd also checked the paperboy's weekly scam listings, but they can't catch everything. There's just so many of them.

My next interview is at a butcher shop, and when the door opens, a giant tentacled monster with eight mouths and a baby's face greets me, holding a bloody meat cleaver.

Screaming, I turn and run away.

Obviously, I don't get the job.

The following interview is much more promising, at a small café in the financial district, and I think my interviewer is about to hire me when he gets *shot*.

Shot. Right in front of me.

On the street outside the shop, the Mayor rides her pet pterodactyl a couple of stories above the street. The pterodactyl's iridescent scales reflect the neon lights of the buildings around it, and its long mouth is open wide in a threatening screech. The Mayor carries a machine gun in each hand, her long black hair blowing behind her in a ribbon, a wild grin stretching across her face.

People scream and duck out of the way as she soars down

the street, machine gun *rat-tat-tatting* as she chases a man on a motorcycle. He's got distinctive face tattoos and a mustache, his face familiar from his mayoral campaign posters all over town.

"Run, run as fast as you can," croons the Mayor, laughing wildly as she fires at the motorcycle. Her pterodactyl screeches in rage as she tugs the chain around its neck, forcing it to turn and follow the motorcycle down the street and around the corner, out of sight.

She leaves a trail of devastation and people hit by her wild machine gun fire in her wake, and as my interviewer crumples lifelessly to the ground, so do my job prospects at his café.

Covered in blood that could just as easily have been mine if the bullet had been a few inches to the left, I leave the café.

Maybe I should wait until after the mayoral election is over, I think numbly as I walk.

Mayoral elections only come around once every five years. The last time there was an election—my first ever election in Newham—I hadn't been prepared for the sheer scope of violence in the streets. I'd still been living with my aunt at the time, and she'd insisted I hide inside for the duration of the campaign.

Unfortunately, she hadn't taken her own advice. She'd still gone to work every day, and ended up trapped in her factory when it collapsed—a strategic financial strike on a candidate to take him out of the running. She'd survived the initial collapse, but inhaling all the toxic shit while trapped in the debris gave her chronic Howling Cough that killed her a year later.

I should take the advice she gave me then. I should hide until it's over.

Except . . . well, after the election for Mayor, the gangs usually have a big fight. A lot of people die in the elections, and then there's often power vacuums that need to be filled. So that might take a few weeks.

By the time that's all cleared up it might be New Year's, which is of course when annual corporate reviews happen, and companies start taking out rivals so that they look good for their board reviews.

I sigh. I can't just wait for a safer time to job hunt, because there's no such thing as a safe time to be in Newham.

I haven't been paying attention to where I've been walking, and I'm surprised when I look up.

I'm at the Friends of the Restful Soul building.

I haven't been back here since I fled, and the feelings that rise up at the sight of the smooth brick exterior and classic arches are a painful mix of nostalgia and hurt and peace. I spent so much of my life here. I was as happy as I've ever been here.

Even if it was evil.

I still remember the first time I came here, like it was just yesterday.

I was eleven, and my aunt held my hand the whole walk there. I'd been living with her for less than two months, two strangers forced together by the brutal death of my father by my sister's hands—legs? Fangs? I don't know what they're called on giant spiders.

My fears had been uncontrollable. My terror of Nightmares was debilitating, my terror of spiders was worse. I wasn't sleeping, because I was afraid I'd turn into a monster like Ruby and kill my aunt. When I did sleep, it was fitful and panicky, all flailing limbs and screaming sobs. I might not have been able to dream—the drugs saw to that—but even without bad dreams, my sleep was anything but restful.

My aunt didn't exactly live in the nicest part of Newham, and her apartment was tidied as best she could, but the spiders still got in. I'd flee the apartment, screaming at the sight of a tiny little bug, my mind snapping back to the sound of crunching bones and the image of that massive long hairy leg coming down the hall.

Reason left the building, and so did I.

Literally—I jumped out the window multiple times. I was lucky there was a fire escape outside it and not just empty air.

I, in short, was a mess. My aunt simply wasn't prepared to cope with a deeply traumatized child.

So she dragged me to the Friends. Their free Nightmare therapy programs were her last resort.

"I'm going to be right there with you," she told me, her lips pursed, hand tight on mine. "Nothing will happen."

I'd nodded, numb, not really understanding. Looking back, it's clear to me that my aunt was skeptical of the Friends and their motives, but she was at the end of her rope. She couldn't afford a real therapist for me, and something had to be done.

So together, we walked up the steps into the Friends' building.

I remember thinking it was the most beautiful building in the world.

The classic brick facade and the smooth stone floor gave it a feel of antiquity, of age and wisdom. It was the nicest place I'd seen at that point in my life, and I was in awe. Soft, tranquil music was playing in the background, and a gentle woman with a friendly smile had greeted us at the door. She smiled at my aunt, gave me a candy, and said the magic words.

"You're safe," she'd whispered, her expression gentle. "It's okay. Nothing bad will happen while you're in here."

And I'd believed her. I'd believed all of them. I'd believed so much in my safety there that after my aunt died, I'd up and moved in there, joining them as a disciple. Not because I believed in their saints, or any of their doctrine—but because they were the only place I'd ever felt safe since my family died.

What a crock of shit that turned out to be.

But even now, even after learning that everything was a lie, that they were kidnapping people, were planning on doing who knows what to me, when I look at the building, I can't help but remember all the good times. All the shared laughs with Priya, all the times I curled up in my room, feeling like life was going to be all right.

All my days were structured and ordered. Someone else decided what I'd do for the day, and I did it. Food was provided to me. I never had to hunt for jobs, never had to worry over money, or staying too long on my friend's charity.

Life there was easy. It was simple. It was comfortable.

I miss it. I miss it so much it hurts. I want that life of structure and safety. I want the security of knowing how each day will go, of not worrying about the future. I hate the chaos of living on my own, the uncertainty of my job, the tenuous nature of my existence, the fact that stray bullets can sweep through my life and ruin everything.

I'd trade anything for that feeling of order and stability I had at the Friends. Anything. Even knowing it was all a lie now.

Sometimes, I wonder if I'd ever have left if they hadn't been trying to kidnap *me*. If they'd just been kidnapping other people. If I'd found out the evil they were doing, and it never touched me, would I have just chosen to ignore it so I could keep my safe, ordered life?

I might have.

It's not something I like to think about, but the truth sits there, nestled in my chest. I'm not a good person. I care more about my own safety than I do about almost anything else. And if I knew I was safe there, even if others weren't . . . well. The real question is *how much* evil I'd have committed to stay.

I really don't want to think about that.

I used to see people come in through the Friends' doors, people who'd escaped abusive relationships. They'd talk about all the horrors they'd gone through, how they'd finally gained the courage to flee.

But then they'd go back.

I never understood it. How could you go back to something like that? Knowing how awful it was?

Now I do.

They say that absence makes the heart grow fonder. It's supposed to be a romantic saying, but it's not, when you think about it. What absence does is wash your memories smooth, polish them like a pebble on a beach. The bad doesn't seem so bad. And the change, the instability that you're currently facing—well, that's not smooth at all. It's jagged and sharp and present and so very *hard*.

And so you start to think fondly of the life you once had. It's not the person themself you miss—it's the familiarity, the order, the routine. The stability.

I can't fall into that trap.

I *can't*.

I turn away from the building, my fists clenched, pain radiating from somewhere deep in my chest.

I don't even know what I want anymore. I want things to go back, but not really. I want the Friends not to have turned out to be evil, but that's not happening. I want them punished for all the pain they caused me and others, but good luck with that. I'd have to do the punishing myself, and I'm no vigilante. I leave that kind of suicidal nonsense to people like the Chaos League, the notorious vigilante group.

So what do I really want?

What I've always wanted. Safety.

I want the feeling the Friends gave me, the sense of security and order and protections.

I just need to find it. Somehow.

I lean against the brick wall of the building beside me and look up at a movie poster. It's a poster for the exact film Cy was complaining about last night. It shows Dracuvlad, an elaborately dressed, much too pale vampire played by a forty-something actor about to sexily bite a swooning girl who can't be more than sixteen.

I shudder in disgust. I hate those movies—I hate them even more knowing that Cy's father specifically engineered them to excuse his own abuses of women and make them seem romantic.

But as I stare at the vampire on the fading poster, his fangs bared, I think of Cy's father.

He didn't become a vampire through a dream or an attack. No, he sought it out, paying someone to make him into a monster.

And why not? It makes him safe from violence, illness, age. A price his victims have to pay.

But Cy is a vampire too. He's just as hard to kill—and he doesn't have victims.

I want to be safe on my own terms. That's why going back to the Friends could never work, even if they decided to stop being evil. At the end of the day, I'd still be reliant on them. I'd still be using them as a place to hide from the world.

But what if instead of hiding somewhere safe, I became something unkillable?

Maybe I've been thinking of safety all wrong. For so long, I've been afraid of becoming a Nightmare, turning into a monster that destroys all I love. But now, becoming a Nightmare doesn't scare me the way it once did.

My sister became a Nightmare because she was weak and she needed to be strong. She dreamed herself into a monster to protect me, to avenge herself, to become something more powerful than the cards life had initially dealt her.

Why can't I do the same?

How much safer would I feel if I were something less vulnerable? How much of my life could I live then, instead of hiding away?

The idea tickles at me, teasing me in a way that surprises me. For so long, what happened to Ruby made me afraid of Nightmares, afraid of the death of self that I thought came with it.

But now, knowing the truth, knowing she chose to become that monster, there's a strange appeal to it. Something compelling about knowing that I could become something that is strong and scary and hard to kill.

Not that I'd want to be a giant man-eating spider.

I look up at the noon sky, the hazy smog that hides the sun. The sun that Cy can't come out and see. Does he miss it? I don't know that I would. What value do I get out of the sun, really?

Maybe I should ask Cy to turn me into a vampire.

If I became a vampire, I'd have superhealing. I'd have strength and endurance and speed. I'd never have to dodge stray bullets again, never have to be afraid of the random chaos of Newham. I could finally move through the world without fear.

Practicality sets in a moment later. As much as I want Cy's strength and ability to heal, I don't really want the problems that come with it.

For example, feeding myself.

Unlike Cy, I'm not rich. I can't pay for blood. Which means I'd have to become the monster, attacking people on the street. Aside from, you know, not wanting to do that, it would also likely bring me to the attention of Nightmare Defense, professional vampire hunters, and enraged Newhamites, all of whom would try to murder me. That sounds even *more* dangerous.

No, vampirism isn't the answer.

But that doesn't mean that some other kind of Nightmare isn't.

I just need to find the right one.

4

I finally get a new job.

I initially thought I bombed the interview, if I'm being honest. I mean, not as badly as the interview right before, where I broke the chair I was sitting on over the head of the interviewer's assistant when he snuck up behind me, but still. It's a job at a fancy restaurant, and I hadn't been able to get the blood from the previous interview out of my clothes before this one started. Not the most professional I've looked.

But they'd called back and told me I was starting this afternoon, and while I'm tentatively hopeful about the new position, I'm a Newham girl through and through, which means I take any good luck with a large dose of skepticism and a larger bucket of caution.

Which was how I found myself back at the speakeasy several hours before opening, talking to Estelle about backup plans.

"Of course you can come back if you don't like the new job," Estelle says agreeably when I finally confess what's going on. She's got a mop in one hand, and the water in the bucket is pink from whatever she's been scrubbing off the floor. "We're always in need of servers."

"Because they keep getting shot?" I ask, raising an eyebrow.

"Or just quitting." She pauses, then runs her hand over the bandanna holding her mass of frizzy red curls back, then admits, "But yeah, mostly getting shot."

I snort.

"I don't know why you need to work." Estelle laughs, nudging me with an elbow and grinning conspiratorially. "You have your sugar— I mean, Cy to take care of you."

My jaw clenches, and I move away from her touch. "You were going to call him my sugar daddy, weren't you?"

Estelle rolls her eyes, her voice light. "Look, there's nothing wrong with having a sugar daddy. It's a mutually beneficial relationship, where one party gets money and the other gets—"

"Sex? Blood?" I snap. "Because I'm not giving either of those to Cy."

"But you have in the past," Estelle points out. "I saw the bite marks."

I flush. "Once. I let him bite me once. It's not a regular thing."

"And there's something wrong if it is?" Estelle asks, hands on her hips, her own neck dotted with healing bite marks.

"I— No!" I backtrack. "I just meant—" I take a breath. "Cy is my friend. I don't want our relationship to change."

And it would change, even if we both had the best

intentions. The moment you add money to any relationship, it changes. Giving him blood once because he's my friend is a very different thing from trading blood for housing. Neither is wrong, but they *are* different, and that *would* change things between us.

Estelle's expression softens. "I understand. I'm sorry I implied— Well." She pushes a stray curl behind one ear. "And I admire you for trying to gain your independence instead of just settling into the easier role."

"Is it easier?" I ask quietly. "To be so dependent on the charity of one person? To put yourself so completely in their power?" I shake my head. "The more I rely on him, the more screwed I am if something goes wrong. And this is Newham. Something *always* goes wrong."

And that something doesn't need to be anything about blood. I don't think Cy would ever pressure me for blood, or at least, not intentionally. He's a good person. But it's possible he'll reach a point where he starts making noises about me finding my own place or contributing. Or something could happen to him—his father could find him and seize the property as stolen, since Cy bought it with money stolen from his father, technically.

I just feel like so much of my life is out of my control. And after relying so completely on the Friends that I was left destitute and homeless when my life there collapsed, I don't want to make the same mistake again. I don't have a backup plan this time if things go wrong.

I just need a safety net, something to catch me if my world blows up again. But I don't think the word "safety" and the word "Newham" can go together. Not unless you're rich or indestructible. Preferably both.

"I don't know if it's easier," Estelle finally says. "I don't know that there *is* an easy way. I work three jobs, and I'm still barely making ends meet. But at least I'm not beholden to anyone except myself." She sighs. "I suppose it depends on what you want out of life."

All I want is safety. If only it weren't so hard to find.

Estelle wishes me luck in my new job, and I pray to whatever gods or devils are listening that I don't mess this up.

My new position is at a restaurant at a swanky hotel, Château Newham.

Nothing about either the hotel or its restaurant is French, but everything sounds fancier with a random French word in the name. The hourly pay is about the same as my speakeasy job—that is to say, not much—but it's in the middle of the richest part of the city, which means the tips might be decent. Or not. I guess I'll find out.

The important part is that this restaurant is the kind of place no one would *dare* shoot up. The people who go there are the kind of people who could annihilate your entire family with one phone call. No bar fights, no gang brawls, no shoot-outs.

Which means it should be a hell of a lot safer than my speakeasy job. Right?

My new boss, Nigel, is a tall, slim Black man getting on in years, with distinguished gray hair, gold-rimmed spectacles, and dressed as classily as the patrons.

"Your shift will start at noon every day and end at eight in the evening," he's telling me as he guides me up into the restaurant.

The ceiling is high and airy, and the stained glass windows are just as tall, like this is a classic, pre-Nightmare-age church. Who knows, maybe it was, before it was converted into a restaurant.

The tables are spaced well apart, giving a sense of privacy, and some of the booths even have velvet curtains, like a theater, lending an air of mystery to those behind them. Large plates with small portions of expensive food are set with great ceremony on tables. I can't imagine paying so much for so little, but I guess when you're rich you can do whatever you want.

I wonder what the food tastes like. Is it worth the money?

Not that I'll ever get a chance to try it.

"Here's the bar." Nigel waves his arm, gesturing to a beautiful piece of intricately carved wood, a piece of art in itself.

I gulp slightly. I feel like if I so much as nick something that beautiful I'll get fired.

Nigel gives me a rundown of how things will work here.

I've been hired as a bartender, but of course they can't call me that, what with prohibition and all. So I'm called a "mixologist," which sounds like I've got a degree in chemistry when I didn't even graduate high school. I'm sure the police would see through it—I mean, there's a bar full of alcohol in the middle of the restaurant—but no one is worried about being reported. They pay good bribe money to ensure there's no trouble.

It might be prohibition for the rest of the city, but up here, in the velvet-carpeted, high-ceilinged Château Newham, laws like that don't apply. All that applies is money, and everyone in the restaurant has a lot of it.

The bar is stocked with every kind of alcohol I can imagine, and several I never did—one of them claims to be fermented dragon tears, which just sounds unsanitary. A dead baby sea serpent nestles in another bottle of alcohol, and yet another claims to be stegosaurus milk. I don't even want to think too hard about that one.

When Nigel finishes his spiel, he asks if I have any questions.

"Just one," I say. "Is there anything I need to be careful of?"

"Kid, you're working in the wealthiest restaurant in Newham," he says gently. "You need to be careful of every single person who walks through that door."

Charming.

At least he's honest about it.

My shift starts early enough that I have time to get a feel for how things work here before the lunch rush comes in. It's different than at the speakeasy, where all the orders are taken at the bar, and bartending was a social job. Here, primly dressed waiters come up and tell me that they want a corkscrew for table nine, or a Newham Splash for table twenty-one, and immediately upon finishing, the drinks are whisked away.

I sort of like it. I don't have to pretend to care about anyone's problems.

As the day wears on, I start to relax. The drinks are the same as those I mixed in the speakeasy, albeit with more quality ingredients. The atmosphere of the restaurant is relaxed, with smooth classical music putting me at ease.

No one picks fights over stupid things that end in a shootout. No one smashes a beer mug over anyone else's head and starts a brawl. Everyone is slow and steady and painfully put together.

I can do this.

I let out a long breath. All I needed was a different job. Something a little more chill, something low-key. Something *safer*. I finally feel like I have a chance of getting my life under control. I might never be able to re-create that feeling of complete security I had at the Friends, but I can at least live a life that's less chaotic—well, relatively less chaotic for Newham.

I can feel the layers of worry starting to peel off. Everything's going to be okay.

"I want to speak to the chef, *now*!"

I look up from washing one of the shot glasses, and do a double take.

Marissa Koval, CEO of Koval Enterprises, wealthiest company in Newham, stands imperiously in front of her table. She's much like her picture in the papers, tall and lean, in her late twenties or early thirties, with olive skin that may or may not be a spray-on tan, long, silky dark brown hair, and enough jewels around her wrist to buy this building.

The waiter, a short brown girl with huge frightened eyes and small feathered white wings poking out the back of her uniform, scurries away with a muttered, "Yes, miss, I'll fetch him now."

A moment later the chef, a balding white man in his forties with a sheen of sweat on his forehead, comes out of the kitchen. He's walking slowly, and his expression is perfectly polite.

"What seems to be the problem, miss?"

"The problem?" Marissa Koval snarls, then points an accusing finger at her plate. "There's a hair in this food."

The chef leans in to look. "Ma'am, no one in my kitchen staff has long dark brown hair."

Oh, bad move. Sure, it might be Marissa's hair, but you can't point that out. Even *I* know that.

Marissa raises one perfect eyebrow, and then opens her designer clutch.

She pulls out a gun and shoots the chef in the head.

I drop behind the counter on instinct at the sound of the gunshot, heart racing. This is how the shoot-outs start, a disagreement over something stupid, and then things escalate.

But no other gunshots come.

After a moment, I peer over the edge of the bar and see that a team of people is dragging the chef's body away, and another team is already getting rid of the blood on the carpet under my new manager's watchful eye.

Marissa Koval has been given a complimentary dessert, an apology for the inconvenience.

The other waiters have all gone back to work, and within another minute, there's no sign that a man died moments ago, his entire death scrubbed from existence, leaving only polished marble behind. A practiced erasure.

Which means this is normal.

This is what normal means here.

Disappointment slams into me like a train, crushing the air from my lungs. I'd been hoping this place would be safer than my last job, but I should have known better. Nowhere in Newham is truly safe. This city thrives on chaos and violence.

"Hey," I call to the nearest waiter, the girl who Marissa was yelling at earlier with the tiny angel wings.

"Yeah?" She trots over.

My voice is raspy and I fist my hands to hide their shaking. "I get a meal break, yeah? Do we have someone to sub in for me?"

The girl nods. "I can cover you."

"Thanks."

I slip out from behind the bar and go through the door into the kitchen. I pass people chopping food and standing over the stoves, their faces somber, no one looking each other in the eye. But none of them look shocked or surprised. And why should they? These things happen. They'll get a new head chef, a new face to replace the old one, a new person to help them pretend the man who was just murdered never existed.

I move through them quickly, hating every moment of being in that somber kitchen, and slip out into the curving hotel hall. To my left is a door to a balcony. Fresh air, beautiful city views, and freedom from the oppressive atmosphere in the hotel.

I turn the other way, opening the door to the cloakroom.

I crawl into the dark, cramped closet, letting the heavy air and the layers of coats cocoon me, wrap themselves around me.

Finally, here, away from the prying eyes of the hotel patrons and my new boss, I crouch down, curling my arms around my knees. I press my face into my legs and take long, shuddering breaths as the tentative hope I'd had that things here would be different is crushed like a cockroach beneath the boot of reality.

No matter what job I pick, I will never be safe.

No matter where I go in this city, I will never be safe.

No matter what I do, as long as I am myself, small and fragile and breakable, I will never be safe.

Never.

The door creaks open, and my head snaps up, eyes red rimmed from terror.

Outlined by the light of the hallway beyond stands the last person I ever expected.

"Ness," says the Nightmare Phantom, smiling slowly to reveal sharp, pointed teeth. "How lovely to see you again."

5

I haven't seen the Nightmare Phantom since I freed him from his dream prison.

He looks much the same as he did then. His skin is white, but unnaturally so, no blush in his cheeks, no peach in his lips, only gray shadows where the skin is thin over the bone. Silvery white hair, thin and silky, drapes like spiderwebs, fine and a little bit ethereal.

But it's his eyes that always unsettle me, black, end to end, no iris or pupil, only darkness shadowed by silvery eyelashes. Something about them reminds me of a black hole, a dark abyss, like something was scooped right out of the universe and all that's left is the absence of existence.

Last time I saw him, he was turning most of Nightmare Defense into hideous horrors from their worst nightmares, all the while laughing with unrestrained glee.

To be fair, I asked him to. Since, you know, Nightmare Defense was planning to murder me.

But it's not a memory that sits easily in my mind.

While I've wondered what the Nightmare Phantom was

doing since then, I hadn't expected to meet him again. After all, he'd got what he wanted from me—freedom. I didn't have anything else to offer him, so I'd assumed we'd simply go our separate ways.

Now that seems like wishful thinking.

"What are you doing here?" I ask, my voice hoarse.

"Just passing by," he says.

I can't help but snort. "Right. Because you often frequent closets."

"Everyone needs to hang their coat somewhere." His hands are spread as wide as his smile.

I stare at him blankly. "You're not wearing a coat."

"Maybe I'm picking it up."

I lean back into the coats around me, most of them velvet and wool, elaborate cuts and designer brands. There's something utterly absurd about hiding in a closet only to be interrupted by the Nightmare Phantom, of all people.

"All right," I ask. "Which coat is yours?"

His smile widens, sharp teeth gleaming in the light. "All right, you win."

"What do I win?"

"The truth." He shrugs. "I wanted to talk with you."

"So you waited until I was hiding in the closet."

"I waited until you were alone."

"That's not ominous at all," I deadpan.

He laughs, grinning down at me. "Yes, that does sound a little serial killer-y, doesn't it?"

"It does," I agree.

The Nightmare Phantom leans against the wall of the closet and absently wipes his long fingers on the leg of his trim black pants. He's wearing a matching black shirt and waistcoat, colors meant to blend into the shadows, while his face and hands seem to glow because of how pale they are, making them seem almost disembodied.

He rubs his fingers together after touching his pants, still smiling.

"What are you doing?" I ask, baffled.

His eyes are on his fingers as he says, "Do you know, there are no textures in dreams?"

I blink. "I hadn't really thought of it."

"Most people wouldn't." His hand reaches out and he trails his fingers over the fabric of a coat. "After a century trapped in other people's nightmares, I can't help but find I enjoy experiencing different textures."

I think about all the things I'm feeling right now. I'm breathing. I can taste the air, feel the flow of it as it goes through my nose and mouth. I'm clenching my hands and feel the sweat of my palms, the heat of my own skin. The starched collar of my shirt is digging into my skin, making me want to scratch.

Having none of those sensations . . . would you even feel *alive*?

"A century," I repeat, really thinking about how long that is.

"Yes." He's still smiling, but it's a little unhinged, a little too wide, a little too cruel. "A hundred years with no break.

52

No way to sleep, even as others dreamed."

I shudder.

He plucks a button off one of the coats and turns it over in his hands, seeming pleased by the feel of it. "Nothing concrete either. It's a world built on other people's subconscious delusions, so nothing stays for longer than the span of a nightmare."

He crushes the button.

A fine layer of dust falls to the floor, all that's left of the button. He tips his head, still smiling at it as he watches the powder mix with the air and vanish into nothing.

I shudder. What would it be like to be stuck in an endless loop of strangers' nightmares, with no way out? No food, no textures, nothing real or concrete. Ever shifting, ever changing.

Can you go through something like that, trapped alone, adrift in other people's dreams for a hundred years, and not lose your mind?

I certainly couldn't.

I look down at my hands, clenching them.

"So what? You turned people into Nightmares to punish them because you were trapped?" I ask.

"No," he says. "I turned them into Nightmares because I was bored." He smiles at me, teeth sharp and shiny. "And because I liked thinking of the chaos they'd cause here."

Right. Why did I ever feel even slightly sympathetic to this monster again?

I shake my head. "Why are you telling me this?"

He laughs. "You asked."

Right, I had, sort of.

"You haven't told me why you want to see me," I tell him, deciding that I should start asking the important questions.

The Nightmare Phantom's fingers still absently play with a feather he's pulled from one of the coats.

"I'm here," he says slowly, his voice syrupy like honey, "to see if you'd be interested in . . . doing me a little favor."

I blink. "A favor?"

"Yes."

I stare at him blankly. "What on earth could *I* possibly do for *you*?"

He laughs at that. "Ness, you underestimate yourself."

"I really don't think I do."

"All right then, you underestimate me." His fingers absently pull strands from the feather, shredding it. "I took twenty minutes out of my week to get you this job."

I startle. "What do you mean?"

"Well"—he smiles, close-lipped, as though trying to hide the extent of his mirth—"I saw you interviewing when I was . . . researching the hotel. And I realized how useful it would be to have someone I know here. Someone who might be inclined to do me a favor." He spreads his arms wide. "I simply ensured the other candidates were out of the picture."

"Out of the picture," I repeat carefully. "So you murdered them?"

"Murder is such a strong solution," he replies. The feather is nothing more than a stem now, all the fluff gone. "Let's just say I gave them the option to turn the job down or become part of the lovely insect life that's so important to the city."

I cross my arms. "You turned them into cockroaches."

"Only some of them."

Yeah. Because that makes such a difference.

A nicer person might feel responsible for his actions. I freed him, after all, let him out of his cage to do this. But I'm not dumb enough to believe someone else's behavior is my fault.

And besides, I have no regrets freeing him. I survived, didn't I? I'd trade my life for most anything.

"Firstly," he says, "I want to be clear that you can say no, and I won't be mad." He grins slightly at my disbelieving sound. "It would be poor form to force you into anything after you so kindly helped me escape. I still have *some* manners."

If you count not turning me into a cockroach as manners, then I suppose he's not wrong. But that is admittedly a pretty low bar to clear.

"So," I ask, tone flat, "what's the favor you want me to do?"

His eyes eerily focus on me. "Oh, it's simple. No trouble at all."

"Then why can't you do it yourself?"

He crushes the stem of the feather into dust. "Unfortunately, it wouldn't be quite as easy if I did it."

Well, that sounds not at all ominous or like I'd be in extreme and terrible danger.

I stare at him. This creature lived for a century, turning

people into their nightmares. He did it because he was bored, because he thought it was fun. He's the very definition of monster.

And he came to me for a "favor."

A more egotistic person would think that they had some sort of special bond with him, or that he liked them. But I'm not the main character in a corner-store romance novel. I'm a hardened Newham girl, and I know that any kind of attention needs to be interrogated—especially when it comes from someone like the Nightmare Phantom.

The truth is probably very simple—the Nightmare Phantom knows me. He knows my fears, knows my weaknesses, knows everything about me because he's lived my nightmares.

He probably picked me because that knowledge makes me easier to manipulate.

That's never a good thing.

I consider turning him down immediately, but that seems too risky. He's got me cornered in a closet. And I have a feeling I'm not leaving until I hear what he wants me to do for him, and agree to do it.

Sure, he said he wouldn't force me to do anything, but I feel like it's much easier to make him think I'm on board with his plan and then run away once he can't hurt me, rather than risk saying no to his face.

Maybe he'd take the no with grace. But I have absolutely no recourse if he doesn't.

So it looks like I'm going to have to play along with this. At least for now.

I eye him skeptically. "So what do I get for helping you?"

He spreads his arms wide, and he smiles magnanimously, like he could give me the whole world. "What would you like?"

What would I like?

I'd like to stop being afraid all the time. I'd like to walk down the street without fear of getting shot. I'd like to have a life where I don't have to worry about money to support myself all the time. I'd like a place to call home that's completely mine, somewhere I'm not beholden to anyone else. I'd like to not be afraid of everything and everyone, to not be a target of every cult and monster that passes by.

I'd like to be safe.

I stare at him for a long moment, and then, before my brain catches up with my mouth, I say, "I'd like you to turn me into a Nightmare."

6

The Nightmare Phantom and I stare at each other as though neither of us can believe the words that have just come out of my mouth.

I can't believe I asked him that.

That I *asked* to become a Nightmare. Asked him, of all people, the person most likely to take that request and fulfill it in the *worst* possible way.

"I thought you were afraid of becoming a Nightmare?" The Nightmare Phantom raises an eyebrow, as though he's questioning whether he heard me correctly.

"I was. I am, still," I admit.

I will always be scarred by what happened to Ruby. I'll always fear the crunch of bones, always fear the monsters with sharp teeth and hungry eyes. My grief over her death will always be tangled up with my fears.

But my sister *chose* to become a monster. She chose to become something larger than herself, something that could fight off the monsters in her own life.

So why can't I?

I slam the brakes on. What am I *thinking*? I'm not *actually* making a deal with him. I'm playing for time, just making him think I'm interested so he doesn't turn me into a cockroach.

I'm not seriously considering making a deal with an unpredictable dream demon.

Again.

Of course not. I'm just . . . curious what he can offer.

I clear my throat. "I mean, that is, I don't want to be *any* old Nightmare. I want to be a specific kind."

"What kind?" he asks, head tipped.

"I want to be safe," I whisper. "I want to not be afraid."

He shakes his head, amusement fading into irritation. "I've told you before I have no influence on people's minds."

"That's not what I mean." I hesitate. "I don't want you to change my mind. I just want—I want to heal as well as a vampire."

"Yes, I *could* do that." A smile begins to play on his mouth.

Oh, I don't like that expression.

I clear my throat. "Without the side effects."

He *tsks*. "Boring."

"So you can't do it?"

"Of course I can do it." He waves this concern away. "I can cherry-pick which fears I use. I don't have to include the blood drinking and such."

"Could you do other things too?" I ask. "Make me

superstrong? Bulletproof?"

"Yes," he says. "If you can fear it, I can probably make you into it."

Well, that's great, because I'm afraid of everything. He'll have a lot of material to work with.

What else could I ask for? The ability to fly? To conjure protective force fields? To . . . um . . . well, I'm sure there's lots of possibilities. I'm just not imaginative enough to think of them.

At the end of the day, all I really need is invulnerability. Everything else is a bonus.

Of course, this assumes he's telling the truth. Which he's not. He's definitely just going to turn me into an immortal cockroach. Things that sound too good to be sure usually are.

"You told me once in dreams that it was hard to control what people became," I say. "Does that not apply in the real world?"

His smile curls up in amusement. "My control in the real world is excellent. People become exactly what I intend." He waves a hand in a *so-so* motion. "In dreams not as much. Things get twisted by people's subconscious. By day they're probably not afraid of a man-eating zombie monkey that looks like their boss. But in the nightmare, they have an all-consuming fear of this monster their subconscious dreamed up on the fly."

That certainly explains some of the bizarre Nightmares people end up changed into.

"So you can do anything here?" I ask.

He laughs. "Not anything. I'm not a god."

His sharp teeth smile in a way that makes me feel like there's a "yet" tacked on the end of that sentence.

"So, what can't you do?" I ask.

"Too many things that don't work together would be hard," he admits. "If you want healing and superstrength together, that's very doable on most people's fears. They go together, you see. Most things people fear are strong and hard to kill, so the fears are easily meshed.

"But"—he raises a finger—"if you want, say, to be able to turn any object into gold with a thought, it will be *much* harder." He shrugs. "Most people aren't afraid of turning things into gold—it's something they rather hope for, actually—unless it's involuntary, the Midas touch, if you will. So unless you're afraid of accidentally turning your friends into very expensive statues, it's hard for me to make that change. Especially if you *also* want to add strength and healing and the like."

He considers. "I mean, I could try. That could be quite fun. I'm sure the results would be . . . enlightening."

"No thanks," I deadpan.

Anything he considers "fun" is something I'd rather avoid.

"Of course," the Nightmare Phantom cautions, "you still only get one shot. And you wouldn't be able to change your mind afterward. I can't change people more than once and I can't undo any changes I've made once done."

No pressure.

I frown. "I haven't used up my one chance, have I? When I freed you, I lost my hair and you appeared . . ."

"No." He looks amused. "That was a separate bargain I made with someone else. Technically speaking, they changed you."

I blink. How many people are out here making Faustian bargains with the Nightmare Phantom?

I look at my hands, small and fragile and weak. If I were like the Nightmare Phantom, impervious to bullets, would I finally be safe? Or like Cy, able to heal from any wound? Would I finally be able to let go of the fear that has dogged my whole life?

I've always been powerless, the lowest of low on the Newham pecking order, always careful, always cautious. I've skirted death by the skin of my teeth more times than I can count. I constantly have to rely on other people to save me.

I've managed to survive this long, but I won't always have someone there to save me.

What would it be like to not be afraid? To not worry about gunshot wounds? To not hide behind bars during gang fights, to not walk down the street with my money hidden and my fake wallet visible, to not grip the keys in my hand tightly to use as a makeshift weapon when I walk home at night?

What would it be like to feel *safe*?

I lick my lips, like the promise of safety has a taste and I want more of it.

I shouldn't even be considering this, not seriously. I'm just supposed to be making a deal and then running. I can't trust the Nightmare Phantom.

Except . . .

I made a deal with him before. And he'd kept his word.

I'd freed him from dreams, and in exchange, he'd rescued me from my cage, wiped out Nightmare Defense, and let me and Cy go free. Of course, he was also in the cage with me, so he had to break it to get out himself. And Nightmare Defense was trying to kill him, so he had to wipe them out anyway.

But he hadn't harmed me or Cy. And even if it benefited him too, he *had* kept his word.

Would he do so again?

I don't know.

That's the plain truth of it. I just don't know if I can trust him. It's a gamble.

But so is life. So is living in Newham. It's like living in a terrible game of Russian roulette, and you never know when your luck will run out.

I've survived an exploding boat. I've escaped an assassination attempt. I got out of a cult that tried to kidnap me. I've survived so many things that have killed who knows how many other people.

But what about next time?

And the time after that?

I live in Newham, and the truth is, there's always going to be something. This city is crawling with power-hungry maniacs, insane Nightmares, vicious gangs, and corrupt corporations. This city is full of monsters.

And me?

I'm just a regular, boring human.

But I don't have to be.

Life is a gamble. Some people are born with all the luck and power, and some aren't. And sometimes, you get a chance to roll the dice and change things. There's a chance you could lose it all.

But there's a chance you could win everything you ever dreamed.

The way I see it, it's only a matter of time before my luck runs out. I have barely any money. I'm living off the charity of a friend who wants to eat me. I barely escaped an evil cult that is probably still holding a grudge against me. And that doesn't even count the random near-death experiences that rain down on me daily.

Someday, it's all going to catch up with me.

So what do I have to lose by taking the gamble?

"Let's do it," I say. "I'll do your favor, you make me a Nightmare of my choice."

He smiles, slow and amused.

"I have one condition," he finally says, and his voice is low and serious, not the light, insincere tone he usually uses.

"Which is?"

His black abyss eyes hold mine, and suck me in like a void, almost as intense as his words. "I won't give you any power that can harm me."

I blink. I hadn't even *thought* of that. I'm not even sure

what *could* harm him. He's indestructible. I've seen bullets literally bounce off him.

Except.

Someone trapped him in dreams once. Who's to say it can't be done again? Perhaps he can be trapped in other ways too.

No matter how indestructible you are, it doesn't matter if you're trapped in a cage you can't escape.

I examine him, as though I can see what's going through his mind if I just look close enough. Of course I can't. But I remember the careful way he coaxed our conversation in dreams, trying to get me to figure out how to free him. I think of the way he ran his fingers over the coats in this closet, savoring every texture as he told me of how insanity inducing living in nightmares for a century was.

And I wonder if I'm not the only one who values their own safety above everything.

"Agreed," I finally tell him. "As long as you agree not to try and use it as an excuse to not change me at all. I want my invulnerability."

He snorts. "I don't care about your invulnerability. You can have it."

"Great." I smile. "Then do we have a deal?"

His eyes on me are dark and strange. His expression is considering, as though he's weighing some calculation I can't fathom.

Then he smiles, slow and wide, his sharp teeth on full display.

"We have a deal."

7

The remainder of my shift goes by in a flash, my mind on the strange deal I've made with the Nightmare Phantom.

And his even stranger favor.

When I'm finished, I head down to the lobby, a beautiful, open space, with crystal chandeliers and red velvet carpets. The stair railings are plated in gold, though not nearly as much as the people, who drip with more money than I want to think about. All the staff wear the same crisp uniform of black pants, red waistcoat embroidered with the hotel logo. Which we have to pay for, of course. The cost gets deducted from our first paycheck.

"Ness!"

Cy strides up to me, smiling. For a moment, I don't even recognize him, because I'm not expecting him, and he fits in so perfectly with the wealth surrounding me. He's dressed in his best waistcoat, hair slicked and parted neatly, eyeliner perfect.

"How was your first day?" he asks.

"I— Fine." I blink. "What are you doing here?"

"I wanted to see how your new job went. I thought we could walk home together, maybe catch the evening show of that new play you wanted to see. My treat."

Of course he did. Because Cy is the kind of person who does things like that for his friends.

And I'm the kind of person who schemes against strangers for their enemies.

My expression softens, and I let a little tension from the evening out as my shoulders loosen. Being with Cy always relaxes me.

"That sounds wonderful," I tell him honestly.

He brightens. I almost need to look away from the sheer force of his smile. No one should be allowed to be that pretty.

"Great!" He offers me his arm, like we're going to a ball.

All right, now I'm suspicious. He's just being so cheerful, so bright, so smiling. Cy is naturally a nice person, but this is going over the top.

Something is up.

"Did something happen today?" I ask.

"What makes you think that?" He avoids my eyes.

Oh, something definitely happened.

"I'm happy to be a distraction from whatever is bothering you," I tell him. "But it might make you feel better to talk about it."

He's silent as he leads us out into the streets, but that doesn't bother me. Whatever is eating at him, I know he'll tell me eventually.

He's not good at keeping things bottled up.

Finally, he sighs. "I read the write-up of my father's new movie."

I should have guessed. Nothing can put him in a bad mood like his father.

"How bad was it?" I ask.

He bites his lip. "Bad. Really bad."

I ask carefully, "Your father has made a lot of films."

"Yes."

"You hate a lot of them."

"I do," he admits.

I examine him. "So what makes this one different?"

He looks away, a single hair escaping and falling across his forehead. "You know he romanticizes abuse in his films. How he has the vampires bite unwilling people and then wipe their memory, and claim it's mercy and not assault. Or murder someone and only focus on how attractive the murderer is, while glossing over the person he killed."

I nod, shuddering a little. I've always hated the movies made by Cy's father for exactly that reason.

"Well." Cy looks up at me. "The premise of this one is that Dracuvlad murders his wife. It's an 'accident' but a vampire hunter comes to kill him. Dracuvlad escapes, but loses his castle and his money, sending him into poverty. He spends the movie finding a way to get back what's 'rightfully his.'"

"Sounds like every other Dracuvlad movie," I say. "And every other superhero movie."

"It is," he whispers, "except this one is real."

I frown. "What do you mean?"

"It's"—he swallows painfully—"it's autobiographical. Or close to it."

He runs a hand through his hair. "The actress they cast as Dracuvlad's wife is the spitting image of my mother."

Oh.

Oh no.

"And she dies in the same way—my father was just 'too hungry' and 'couldn't control himself.'" Cy snorts. "You know, I thought it was bullshit before I was a vampire, and now that I am one, I can confirm, it *is* bullshit. I've been so hungry I felt like I was dying and I never attacked *or* murdered anyone."

I've been around Cy in truly desperate situations, where we were both starving, and the only people for miles. The kind of situation where you could theoretically justify murder as a survival tactic. And Cy never once even *asked* me for blood.

And yet his father is out here murdering women for "food" claiming he "couldn't help it" and then making a whole movie to justify why, actually, he's the victim.

What an *asshole*.

"So," Cy says, his voice scraping and harsh, "this movie has a vampire murdering his wife, who looks like my mother. And the whole movie then goes and vilifies the person trying to get justice for her death."

His hands clench into fists at his sides. "I just— I feel so many things right now, I can't even put them into words."

I can't imagine. Watching someone make a massive

megahit movie about how, actually, murdering your mother was okay and the people trying to hold the murderer to account were wrong?

The sheer audacity.

I can't even imagine how angry Cy is right now.

"After my mom died, the police did investigate." His mouth twists into something bitter. "They ruled it an accident—because of bribes, mostly." His expression falls. "But the papers, when they covered it, they all just went with my father's excuse. They just . . . believed him, didn't ask any other questions. A tragic accident, just like the kind of thing that happens to Dracuvlad. No one called it murder, even though it was."

He barks a painful laugh. "A lot of them were even sympathetic to him, portraying him as this grieving widower, being so nice to him, as though she died in a car crash, not by his hands."

I'm silent a long moment. I don't even know what to say to this. It's too awful.

"You know," Cy says, his voice full with that choked feeling you get before you cry. "It's not the first time I've seen those awful Dracuvlad movies. Or the first time the whole plot of one of his stupid superhero movies has revolved around some billionaire being awful and getting away with it. But this . . ."

He shakes his head. "This feels so *personal*."

"Maybe it is," I murmur.

He looks up at me, frowning. "What do you mean?"

"You left him," I tell Cy. "You robbed him and ran and he hasn't been able to find you. Maybe this is his way of lashing out at you."

Cy hesitates, considering this, then shakes his head. "No. It takes too long to write, film, and produce a movie. This probably went into filming a year ago."

"I see. Were any of his other movies semi-autobiographical?" I consider. "Like the one where the hero was a billionaire who put a mom-and-pop shop out of business, and the villain was the mom-and-pop shop owner suing him?"

"No, that's not autobiographical." Cy shakes his head. "That's just standard manipulation stuff he does. His movies like that are meant to normalize assault; the billionaire hero movies are meant to reinforce the idea that rich people deserve their money and power, and anyone who tries to take it from them, or make them face consequences for abusing that power, is wrong."

Cy makes a face. "That's also why recently he's been making more superhero movies. The genre used to have a lot more stories of normal people with powers saving the world. But he's been flooding the market with movies about superheroes who are billionaires, or kings, or gods. He wants people to associate wealth with heroism."

This is one of the many reasons I don't like the idea of superheroes. So many of these movies are set in Newham, and show amazing masked heroes saving the city—but the only people I've actually seen in masks in this city are robbing it.

And sure, Newham has its vigilante crew, the Chaos

League, which supposedly brings chaos to the villains, but I mean, really? Mostly it just brings more chaos to the regular citizens.

I do understand why people want movies about heroes—how nice would it be if someone swept through Newham and solved all the problems here? Someone incorruptible with the best interests of the regular people?

It's a nice fantasy. But it's not a practical reality. Newham's problems are systemic and far-reaching, and can't be solved by just one person.

They especially can't be solved by a fictional version of Cy's murderous father.

"I wish I could do something about my father," Cy whispers, the neon lights playing over his skin. "Stop him from making more of these movies. Make him face consequences for murdering my mother—for murdering and attacking so many other women too."

He looks down at his hands. "For so many years, I was terrified of him. I knew, I just knew, I was one mistake away from him making sure I had a terrible accident like my mother."

He takes a deep breath. "But I'm not human any longer. I'm strong, I heal fast, I'm powerful. He won't be able to kill me so easily." He bites his lip and looks up at me. "But I haven't done anything to stop him. Nothing. I've just been hiding, running away, like nothing's changed." His expression is pained. "Why can't I manage to do anything?"

Cy doesn't know, but I do. It's obvious.

It's because he's still afraid.

And even though Cy's powerful now, harder to kill, for all that's changed, his fear hasn't.

I can't help but wonder if I'm the same. I tell myself I'm braver now, but am I really? Sure, I'm no longer hiding from the world in a cult, and I can talk to strange Nightmares normally *sometimes*. But I've also made a deal with a dream demon because I'm so afraid of living that I need to make a Faustian bargain to feel safer.

Is the fear so ingrained in my mind, carved right into my soul, that no matter what I do or what I become, I'll never escape its clutches?

Am I doomed to always be afraid?

No. I refuse to believe that.

"Cy, how long have you been a vampire? Three months?" I ask.

"Yeah, about that."

"And how long were you human?" I ask. "Eighteen years?"

"Nineteen," he admits.

"So you were a human, living with your murderous father, for nineteen *years*, and you've been living on your own after running away and becoming a vampire, for three *months*." I shake my head. "Why do you expect that all of a sudden the behaviors you adopted over nineteen years would change in an instant?"

He opens, then closes his mouth.

73

"Look." I lean in. "I'm not saying you shouldn't do anything about him. I think you should. He deserves to be stopped."

I put my hand on his shoulder. "But there's nothing wrong with taking the time to figure out how to do it *right*. Especially against someone as dangerous as your father."

He looks at me with those sad green eyes, and I hold his gaze. Our faces are inches apart.

"Stop blaming yourself for not coming up with a way to stop your father, an incredibly rich, powerful, and established monster, three months after having run away from him.

"Stop beating yourself up for not having everything already figured out."

Our gazes are locked, and suddenly I realize exactly how close my face is to his, and I flush, pulling away.

"Thanks, Ness," he whispers, not seeming to notice my sudden awkwardness—or choosing to ignore it. "I needed to hear that."

I feign casualness. "That's what friends are for."

But I can't help but wonder if it wasn't him I was trying to convince but myself.

I've been running since I was eleven years old. I ran from the memory of what my sister did to our father. I ran from the fear of death that plagued me, right into the arms of a cult.

When I found out that cult was kidnapping people, I ran again. I ran far, and I ran fast, and I haven't done a single thing to stop them. After all, I thought, what could I do to stop a great big organization like them?

But that's just an excuse. The truth is I'm scared to get involved. I'm scared to even *try* to stop them.

Just like I was scared to face the truth of what happened to Ruby. I only confronted it when I had no other options. I thought confronting it would make me brave.

But at the end of the day, I'm still running, just like I always do.

Both of us are trapped in a rut of being the same person. The coward who hides from the fight. The boy who runs from the monsters. Even when we should change, when we have the power to change, we're still stuck in the past.

Even if the Nightmare Phantom makes me indestructible, immortal, untouchable, everything that means safety in this world—will I ever *feel* safe?

I can change my body—but how do I change my *mind*?

8

We arrive at the theater to see the play Cy wanted to go to with me, to find that the building is on fire. The Chaos League had a fight with one of the gangs, and somehow the theater and the three buildings next to it ended up on fire after a rocket launcher exploded when a crocodile gangster swallowed it and then started coughing out missiles.

This is why I hate vigilantes. And gangs. And nonsensical Nightmare physics.

Theater plans canceled, we head toward home.

The streets are still crowded, even this late at night—they're always crowded, this city has too many people in too small an area. It's grown up instead of out, and it rises so high that in the dark, the towering buildings fade into the night sky so their tops are invisible. It makes them look like they go on forever, right up into heaven.

Not that I believe in heaven.

I'm not sure I believe in much of anything anymore, since everything I've ever believed in has turned out to be manipulating me for profit.

Really makes me wonder what kind of scam the people who invented heaven were running.

"So tell me about work," Cy says as we walk. "Was it better than the speakeasy?"

"It was interesting," I admit.

In a hushed voice, I tell him everything that happened today, from the murder I witnessed early in my shift to the Nightmare Phantom's surprise appearance, to the deal we struck.

When I finish, he just stares at me and slowly shakes his head.

"What the hell?" he finally says.

"I know."

"Only you," he says with a deep sigh.

"Only me what?" I ask.

"This kind of thing doesn't happen to normal people," he explains.

"Are you sure?" I ask. "You know one of the people at the speakeasy had a zombie propose to her, and after she rejected him, she had to hire an assassin team to kill him because he decided they'd be together forever if he ate her."

Cy blinks slowly.

I shrug. "These things happen in Newham. Did I ever tell you about the cult of sentient carrots that—"

"I don't need to know." Cy raises one hand in a gesture of peace.

"It's not only me."

"I'm getting that." Cy's humor melts off and his expression

turns serious. "Ness, are you sure this is a good idea?"

"What?" I ask.

"Working with the Nightmare Phantom." He fidgets with his cuff links. "Look, it's not that I don't get how appealing it would be to become whatever you want. If he could change me back to human, I'd be sorely tempted. But . . . is it worth the risk? You're in even more danger working for him."

It's true, the same anxieties have swirled around in my head. When I was speaking with the Nightmare Phantom, this seemed like such a great idea, but now, away from him, the temptation to run away and never return, dodge all risk, is strong.

But if I dodge the risk, I dodge the potential reward.

And dodging this risk doesn't mean I can dodge the next.

I'm quiet for a long moment. "I'm always in danger, Cy."

"But—"

"No," I interrupt. "You don't understand, because you're rich, and strong, and heal fast. But my whole life is dangerous. Walking down the street is dangerous." I gesture across the street, where a mugging is happening. No one is pausing to help the victim or stop the attacker. "Random acts of violence are common here. It just is. And we accept it, because what else can we do? People like me can't change that." I look up at him. "Do you know what the leading cause of death is in Newham?"

He shakes his head.

"Accidental murder," I tell him. "There's some special

term for it, but essentially, it's more common to die being caught in the crossfire of a gang war or stepped on by a Godzilla Nightmare than it is to die from any natural illness." I hold his gaze. "In the last week, I've nearly been shot three times, and nearly eaten twice."

He stares at me, appalled. "Surely it's not that bad?"

"It is, though."

We live in two different worlds. He doesn't even register gunfire because it can't hurt him. He doesn't think about the falling bricks from buildings because he can heal those wounds. He doesn't have to worry about the everyday terror of working a menial customer service job in a world where people get shot regularly. Because he's never worked a day in his life—and if he ever did work, it certainly wouldn't be in the kind of low-level jobs I have.

He hasn't seen the world the way I have. And even though I know he believes me when I tell him about it, he can't truly understand what that's *like*.

Newham is a very different city for each of us. And I'd really like to live in his version instead of mine.

"So what did the Nightmare Phantom ask you to do?" Cy asks.

"There's some exclusive event happening tomorrow night that I'm working. He wants me to"—I clear my throat—"give someone a napkin."

Cy looks as though I've lost my mind. "He wants you to give someone a *napkin*?"

I fish the offending napkin from my pocket. It's black, silk, and of fine quality. It's in a plastic bag that is very definitely sealed.

Cy stares at it. "It . . . really is a napkin."

"Yep." I put it back in my pocket. "But apparently bad things will happen to whoever touches it with their bare skin. Hence the bag."

He stares at me. "It's a murderous napkin."

"Well," I point out, "we don't know it's *murderous*."

Cy gives me a look like I'm being the naive one.

"Oh come on." I roll my eyes. "This is the Nightmare Phantom we're talking about. For all we know anyone who touches the napkin becomes a napkin. That's not murder, just . . . nonconsensual napkinifying."

Cy just shakes his head. "I hate that I understood that sentence."

"I know you do."

"So," he asks, "who are you inflicting the possibly murderous napkin on?"

This was the part I admittedly hadn't liked about this whole thing. I take a deep breath before responding.

"The Mayor."

He stares at me, aghast. "You're going after the Mayor."

"So it seems."

"The Mayor who flies around on a giant pterodactyl and shoots people with machine guns?" Cy's voice rises. "The Mayor who lets her pterodactyl eat reporters? *That* Mayor?"

"Yep."

"Ness." He puts his hands on my shoulders and stares me in the eye. "That's *insane*. That's suicide."

"All I need to do is touch the napkin to her. How hard can that be in a large, crowded party?"

He doesn't look convinced.

To be fair, with my luck, it probably won't be nearly that easy.

But my whole life is dangerous. This is no worse than working in the speakeasy every night—and the reward has the potential to be a whole lot better.

Finally Cy lowers his hands and shakes his head, accepting that he can't change my mind. "Why on earth is he going after the Mayor anyway?"

"No idea." I gesture to one of the many campaign posters spread across the city. "Maybe he's running for Mayor?"

"That's a chilling thought." Cy shudders.

We stroll past a variety of cute stores as we walk from bookshops to a laundromat that looks like all it launders is money. We have to cross the street when we pass a camera shop, since the whole place—including the air around it—is full of silver nitrates, a necessary chemical for developing photographs, and also a very toxic chemical to Cy, a vampire type affected by silver.

We walk past a clothing store, and I slow to admire the pieces in the window. Aesthetically, they're nothing special. Finely made waistcoats and trousers in moderate browns and blacks.

What makes them special is that they're bulletproof.

Bulletproof fashion has been big for a long time in Newham, especially for gang lords. Everyone wants to look stylish while being protected from enemy gunfire. And over the years, bulletproof suits have looked less and less clunky, smoother and more streamlined. They're still heaver than regular clothes, they have a heft to them, but they no longer sacrifice mobility for protection.

I've always wanted a bulletproof suit, but they're absurdly expensive.

Cy's expression softens as I look. "You like them?"

"Of course," I tell him. "Who doesn't like clothing that protects them?"

He laughs. "Fair enough."

He turns and then frowns at something he sees. I follow his gaze and see two men leaning against the side of one of the buildings, gesturing with their hands as they talk.

"Isn't that one of the mayoral candidates?" Cy asks.

It is indeed one of the mayoral candidates, talking to infamous gang lord Giovanni Montessauri, who is looking crisply murderous in his bloodred suit. He's even got a bit of blood spatter on one cheek. Or maybe raspberry juice. But I'm going with blood spatter.

"Looks like," I agree, unbothered.

"Well, isn't it bad?" Cy asks. "For them to be together?"

I snort. "Cy, the gangs fund the mayoral candidates."

He stares at me, stunned. "What?!"

"All the mayoral candidates have backers," I explain. "Gangs or companies, usually. It takes money and power

82

to run for Mayor here. Sometimes independents run—I think there might even be one in this election—but usually they're assassinated pretty fast. You need a powerful backer to protect you." I pause. "And of course, once the gangs or companies have installed their candidate in office, the candidate thanks them by making sure all the laws they want to go away, well, go away. And all the laws they want passed get through."

Cy is stunned. "Oh."

I snort. "Don't look so shocked."

He just shakes his head. "This city is insane."

"You get used to it."

"That's terrifying to think about."

I shrug. Newham is what it is, nothing to be done about it. I can't imagine it any different, and I can't imagine anyone who could actually make it different.

We walk the rest of the way back to Cy's apartment building, his expression pensive.

The park across the street from his building is bustling, despite the late hour, full of families picnicking together in peace, smiling and laughing at some sort of theater troupe that's performing. They've lit up the evening with neons, and at least three different food carts are selling dinner. A pop-up mulled wine stand has a long line, and a group of people my age sip their hot drinks and laugh, leaning against each other for support.

It's strange, to see that kind of peace in Newham. Or maybe I'm just living in all the wrong places, that I find the idea of peaceful happiness rare and strange.

Something tugs in my heart as I watch the smiling people, something sharp and envious. I want what they have. Or rather, I want the illusion they're projecting. Because that's what it has to be. An illusion. No one can really be that happy and safe in Newham.

Can they?

Maybe they can. Maybe this is just another example of the different worlds Cy and I come from. He lives in the kind of place where that happiness isn't an illusion. It's a fact, one protected by guards that beat off the homeless people who try and sleep in the park.

Or maybe it is all just an illusion. A moment in time of happiness before the chaos descends again. Even I've had those.

"Ness," Cy says, pulling my attention away from the park.

Uh-oh. I don't like that tone of voice.

"Yes?"

"Tomorrow"—he takes a deep breath—"I want to come with you."

I blink. "Um?"

"I'm not saying you're not capable, or that you can't handle this on your own," he rushes to reassure me. "You're almost as good at getting out of trouble as you are at getting into it."

I don't know if that's a compliment or an insult.

I'm gonna pretend it's a compliment.

"But let me be your backup," he presses. "Or if you don't want me, call Priya."

"Okay," I say. "You can be my backup."

He hesitates. "Yeah?"

"Sure." I nod agreeably. "If guns start firing, I'll hide behind you. You can be my meat shield."

"Uh . . ." He makes an expression that he clearly wasn't imagining it going quite like that. Probably he imagined himself heroically sweeping in and rescuing me. Personally, I don't think the two images need to be mutually exclusive. He can sweep in to take all the bullets meant for me.

"Sure. I guess." He clears his throat. "So I can come?"

"Of course you can." I roll my eyes. "What kind of idiot would I be to turn down backup? Have you met me? The more people between me and danger, the better."

He snorts. "Right. How could I forget?"

"Clearly, its been too long since we've been in mortal peril together," I tell him with a wink.

He laughs.

I tap one finger to my chin. "Though, I'm not sure you'll even be able to get in to be backup. These parties can get pretty exclusive."

"I'll bribe my way onto the guest list." He raises his eyebrows. "Isn't that what a proper Newhamite would do?"

"It is," I say. "But this might even be too exclusive for you."

"I guess we'll find out."

I smile at him, and he starts for the apartment building.

I cast one last look at the people in the park, smiling and laughing, and looking so relaxed. I've always been so focused on the dangers of Newham, I rarely take time to see the good points. Maybe, if this works, I'll be able to finally enjoy a picnic like that without being afraid.

I can't imagine what life without fear is like—but I know I want it.

And I'm willing to do almost anything to get it.

9

The sun is setting, the last streaks of red patterning the Newham sky like rivulets of blood trailing from the stars before staining the dark silhouettes of skyscrapers.

Cy and I are on our way to something that will either make my nightmares come true, or make the homicidal Mayor of Newham really mad at me.

When I put it that way, I see why Cy is concerned.

I tried calling Priya earlier today, because I tell Priya everything, and also, knowing Priya, she'd want to be involved. She's been so unhappy at work lately, I was sure that something like this would perk her up.

Unfortunately, her sister Adhya answered the phone and informed me that Priya was at a training exercise with Nightmare Defense all day, and was unreachable.

I admit, I was disappointed. But I consoled myself by telling myself that if everything went right, next time I saw Priya, I'd be indestructible, invincible. Maybe I'd breathe fire. I bet she'd like that.

I try and imagine the two of us fighting Nightmares. Her, leaping onto a dragon's back, rocket launcher over her shoulder, head held high, grinning, and me . . .

Me . . .

I try and picture myself, powerful and untouchable, fighting the dragon too. But the image won't come. It's all wonky and twisted, like a funhouse mirror. Every time I try and force it into being, it shifts around me. It's not me on that dragon, it's just two Priyas, except one is short like me. Or the dragon just disappears and it's me and Priya having coffee.

I groan, running my hands through my short hair. I can't even see myself as being brave in my own imagination. How pathetic is that?

Cy asks to stop at Estelle's on the way to the hotel, and I agree. I don't like dragging Cy anywhere hungry, if only because I know my own ability to make decisions gets worse the hungrier I am. And it isn't great to start with. We can't *both* afford to be idiots. One of us has to be the smart one in this friendship, and I know it's not me.

"Are we heading to Estelle's apartment?" I ask, once we're settled in the taxi.

"No, we meet at the speakeasy," Cy tells me quietly. "I don't think she trusts me to know her address."

He looks out the window of the taxi into the dark of Newham, expression pensive. He hates it when people are afraid of him.

"It's not you, you know," I tell him gently. "It's the world. Newham isn't a safe city. Estelle's just taking basic safety precautions."

"I know," Cy says softly. "I just wish . . ."

"You wish you could skip ahead to the part where she trusts you implicitly," I finish for him.

He flushes, and glances at me, then away. "How do you always know what I'm thinking?"

I shrug. "You're not that hard to read. Besides, you're making the sad puppy face, and that always means you're feeling sorry for yourself. Which usually means you're blaming everything on how you're a bloodsucking monster."

He choke-laughs. "I don't blame everything on being a monster." He looks me in the eye. "Some of it I blame on my father being a monster."

I snort, smile pulling at the corner of my mouth. "Sure, sure."

He smiles a little, then leans back in the taxi, his shoulder brushing against mine. "I'm glad you're here, Ness. You always make everything better."

I flush, and clear my throat, looking away, trying to pretend my heart isn't beating much too fast. "You say that now, but after another month of my mooching off you, living in your closet, you'll change your tune."

He smiles slightly, his eyes hooded. His voice is soft and low and much too intimate. "I doubt it."

The blush on my face rises higher.

Thankfully, we arrive before I have to think of a response.

I wait in the taxi while Cy meets Estelle, thinking about the way Cy brushed off me being a mooch. He's so blasé about me staying for free, which is great, I don't want him to feel like I'm overstaying my welcome.

But I also feel like sometimes he's *too* blasé. Like he's not thinking about how awkward this is for me.

Sometimes, I read those penny novels about kings falling in love with maids, but I can't enjoy them. Every time, I can't help but think that the king has so much power over the maid. He can have her executed. He can ruin her family. He can hurt her friends. He can do anything he wants, and she has to smile and profess her love through it all, because if she doesn't, much worse could happen. Because he has so much power, and she so little.

When one person has that much power over another person's life, can you even *have* real love?

I don't know.

But more than anything, I wish I were in a situation where I didn't have to ask questions like that. Where I could trust my own feelings without having to worry about anything else.

Maybe, if this works out, I could be.

When we arrive at the hotel, Cy gets out of the auto first, and holds his hand to help me out, as if I'm wearing a ball gown and not a barkeep uniform, and it's a carriage with a step down and not a low-hanging auto. But it's a sweet gesture, so I take his hand anyway.

Château Newham is one of the swankiest buildings in the city. Massive Roman-style columns stretch all along the entrance, and the steps up are solid marble. It looms above me, not as tall as the buildings that have grown up around it, but imposing nonetheless. Its domed roof is plated in copper that's oxidized to a pastel turquoise over the years. The stone in the walls is full of ancient sea creatures, ammonites and trilobites and even dinosaur bones, vertebrae jutting out and making the surface uneven.

Local legend says that the bones of the people who designed the building are also trapped in the walls, hidden among the fossils.

"I have to go in the servers' entrance," I tell Cy.

He smiles at me. "Of course. I'll see you in the event."

I still have my doubts he'll be able to get in, but I just say, "See you there."

I go around to the side entrance, which is much less glamorous. It's just a polished wooden door on the side of this magnificent building. My new boss, Nigel, is waiting just inside for me, talking with one of the other servers.

"Ness, excellent." He turns to me, shooing the other server away. "The event is starting soon. You're new, so you're going to be our backup barkeep."

"Backup?" I ask.

"You'll be swapping in when our regular one takes breaks," he explains. "The rest of the time, you'll be doing general waitstaff duty." He smiles at me. "It's not hard, you just walk around with plates of hors d'oeuvres, and when they empty, you come back and refill them."

"Sounds good," I say.

If I'm walking around with hors d'oeuvres then I'll have plenty of chances to loose the evil napkin on the Mayor, which suits me fine.

He calls over another server, a petite brown girl with thick curling black hair, to guide me to the bar. Her eyes are honeycombed, like a disco ball, and they're strangely compelling, the way the light reflects off them making them sparkle.

We weave through the kitchen, both of us grabbing a plate of hors d'oeuvres on the way to take up. It's tiny little pieces of bread with reddish sauce and green sprigs on top. It looks incredibly decadent and very expensive.

Once we're in the hall up to the gallery, the girl glances around and, seeing the coast is clear, grins at me. "Wanna sample the rich-people food?"

"Do I ever." My return smile is wicked.

She pops one of the little cracker breads into her mouth and I follow suit.

Given how expensive everything is here, I expect this hors d'oeuvre to be the best thing I've ever eaten, but it just tastes like bread with tomatoes on it. I think it actually might literally be toast with tomato paste. I could make this myself for less than a penny and it would taste just the same.

Maybe I'm in the wrong business. I should start making fancy little tasteless hors d'oeuvres and marking them up a thousand percent.

I swallow my sad bread and say, "Well, that was underwhelming."

"But it's free," the girl says with a wink.

"You make a good point," I admit, and eat another tomato bread.

We stop after another few pieces because we don't want to be too conspicuous, and head up to the event. It's in a different room than the restaurant, a room I haven't been in yet, and I pause when I enter, just taking it in.

Glittering crystal chandeliers hang from ceilings covered in paintings of fat winged babies with weapons—who gives a child a bow and arrow, really? They won't even be able to use it. If you want to arm them, it should be a gun, or at least a knife.

Clearly, the artist wasn't very intelligent.

Tables are scattered around the room, tall and circular, just at the height you could leave your champagne glass on. Waiters dressed in the same hotel uniform as me weave through the crowds, offering drinks and tiny appetizers.

Currently, about thirty guests mill around the space. Cy won't get in—if there were a hundred people, then he could slip in unnoticed with a bribe, but with this few, his presence would be noted.

Especially given who the clientele are.

The room is a gallery of who's who of powerful people in Newham. I recognize Marissa Koval, CEO of Koval Enterprises, the wealthiest company in Newham, talking to Giovanni Montessauri, notoriously vicious gang lord. On the other side of the table, the police commissioner is laughing gregariously at a joke made by rich playboy and darling of the Newham newspapers, Francis Yang.

At the entrance to the venue, a large sign is posted: **PLEASE REFRAIN FROM ASSASSINATING MAYORAL CANDIDATES IN THE VENUE. USE THE WASHROOMS AS THEY ARE EASIER TO CLEAN.**

That's how you know a place is classy. They tell you where to do your murdering.

I weave through the event goers, offering my tomato bread. Some of the people pluck one off the tray, but most don't. I don't blame them. They're not that good.

The more people I pass, the more I realize just how rich you have to be to get in here. A white woman with platinum blond hair wearing nothing but diamonds studded all along her body walks arm in arm with a Black man in a white tuxedo, his beringed fingers containing enough wealth to buy Cy's apartment. A brown woman in a sari of literal spun gold chats with her twin sister, who's wearing a floor-length ball gown of embroidered silk.

I wonder if I should try and pickpocket some jewelry, since I can't steal the clothes off their backs. I'm sure the money I'd get at the pawnshop for that jewelry would go a long way to setting my independence up.

My fingers twitch hopefully, and I'm just plotting who I could sneak a bracelet or ring off, when I see her.

The Mayor.

She's dressed as she always is, in a smart, formfitting black tuxedo that accentuates her slender frame. Her long black hair is pulled up into a high ponytail and her bangs are cut sharply across her forehead. Her dark eyes and pale skin remind me a little of the Nightmare Phantom. The only color on her comes from her lips, painted a vibrant, candy red.

Her pterodactyl is nowhere to be seen, which is probably a good thing, as I don't think she'd have nearly as much fun if it ate one of these rich, powerful people, as she does when it eats reporters.

My heart rate rises, and my hand dips into my pocket.

This is my chance—it's also my last opportunity to turn back.

I don't know what this napkin will do, but I know it won't be nice.

The truth is, I've never really had a moral problem with killing someone. This is Newham, after all—I think at least half the city has a body count. Myself included. Sure, I've never pulled the trigger myself, never got close enough to do the deed with my own two hands—that seems much too dangerous, frankly. If you're that close to someone, they can kill you as easily as you can kill them.

But I chose to free the Nightmare Phantom, I asked him to get rid of Nightmare Defense and save me. Sure, there's an argument it was self-defense, but it doesn't change the fact that those people are dead because of my actions.

I mean, probably a lot of other people are dead because I freed the Nightmare Phantom too, but I'm not counting them in my kill count. I'm not responsible for the Nightmare Phantom's actions. He's an independent entity, and he makes his own choices.

And besides, I probably saved just as many lives when I freed him, since he can no longer change thousands of people at once all over the world as they sleep.

Why, I'm practically a hero.

Well, as close as a city like Newham can get to a hero.

Anyway, it's not the moral implications that make me hesitate, going over my choices again. It's the risk versus reward calculation.

Do I really trust the Nightmare Phantom to keep his word? And is it worth risking myself for?

I look down, and my fingers tighten on the plastic bag.

I can't keep living my life like this, afraid every day that this will be my last. I want the safety the Nightmare Phantom promised. I *need* it.

And in my eyes, setting an evil napkin loose on the Mayor is a small price to pay.

The Mayor is surrounded by people, but I blend in seamlessly, unnoticeably. I move forward and pull out the silky black napkin with a gloved hand.

I pass by murderous gang lord Giovanni Montessauri and his serial killer mayoral candidate, proffering my tray of tomato bread, and they each take a piece.

I'm almost there, only a few steps from the Mayor, the napkin in my hand.

Someone grabs my wrist.

"Ness?"

I spin around at the sound of the familiar voice, my heart sinking in horror and disbelief, because no, he can't be here, there's no way my luck is that bad, and why would he be here, he has no reason to—

Standing in front of me is the Director of the Friends of the Restful Soul.

10

I haven't seen the Director since I bashed him on the head with a drawer. I'm still proud of that moment—I mean, yes, I hit him from behind, and yes, technically it was a sneak attack, but I took him down, which is the important part. I rescued Priya from being shot.

It's probably the only time I've ever rescued anyone, so I've got to take those wins where I can.

He looks much the same as he did a month ago—still a giant green lizard Nightmare, not that I expected that would have changed. He's wearing a long emerald silk robe, and his scales gleam in the light, freshly oiled. His tail comes through the back of his robe in a tasteful gap and curls around his front. His yellow eyes are fixed on me, wide with surprise.

"Ness." His eyes narrow, and his claws tighten around my wrist, freezing me in place. "How intriguing to see you here."

Everyone's paused to stare at us, and it's over, this whole plan is a bust, and the Director is probably going to kidnap me and I need to do *something*, anything—

I slap the napkin against the Director.

Or more specifically, against the nearest bare skin to the napkin—not his wrist, which has immobilized mine, preventing me from twisting around to hit it.

No, I hit his tail.

The napkin gloms onto the Director's skin, sticking instantly. For a moment, it sits there, just . . . existing, and I wonder if whatever it was supposed to do only works on the Mayor, and that I've thrown my only tool away for nothing.

Then the napkin begins to move.

It begins crawling up the Director's tail, seesawing back and forth like some sort of evil silk caterpillar.

The Director stares at it a moment, my wrist still trapped in his grip. He reaches his other hand out and grabs at the napkin, trying to rip it off. It doesn't work. The napkin continues inextricably upward toward his body.

He grabs the tray of hors d'oeuvres from my other hand and swings it at the napkin, clearly hoping to bat it off.

The tray bounces off the napkin so hard it's ripped from the Director's hand, tiny bits of tomato bread spattering the marble tiles. The tray itself flies across the room, right into Marissa Koval, CEO of Koval Enterprises, embedding itself in her stomach.

Blood drips on the floor, and my eyes bulge, wondering exactly how many dangerous people I'm going to piss off today.

Marissa scowls, annoyed but not afraid, and plucks the tray from her stomach, holding her gory prize pinched between two perfectly manicured fingers before tossing it aside. The wound heals over the instant the tray is gone. The dress, of course, does not.

It doesn't surprise me that she's invulnerable. Cy's father paid someone to turn him into a vampire for the immortality. Why couldn't Marissa Koval have done the same? Or paid to become some other invulnerable Nightmare? Or drunk an invulnerability potion brewed by someone who'd been turned into a witch in their nightmare.

It's well known that when you get to the top of the pecking order in Newham, no one is human anymore.

The whole room is still, attention shifting back to the Director as the napkin climbs his tail, slow and sure. I have no idea what will happen when it reaches his body, where it's going, what it's planning. I'm kind of wishing I'd asked the Nightmare Phantom a few more questions.

Finally, the Director realizes this is serious. And that he does, in fact, need both hands.

He lets my wrist go.

I don't wait around to watch what he does next.

The moment he lets me go, I take off for the door, dodging between the other patrons and making for the servants' entrance. I'm getting the hell out of here before I end up in some musty dungeon in the basement of the Friends' building.

Behind me, a cry rises up from the watching people, but I don't look back. I can't be distracted.

Unfortunately, the guards operating the event aren't easily distracted either.

And they're blocking the door.

I swivel, looking for another door, but there's only more guards, I'm surrounded. But I'm small, and I'm fast, and I'm not going to be put off that easily.

I run for the guards, as fast as I can, and they raise their arms, ready to stop me.

I duck.

Sometimes, being short is an advantage. I'm slipping between then, I'm almost through, I'm going to get away, I'm going to—

Something hits me on the head. Hard.

Then my face is in the carpet, and I'm groaning as rough hands haul me to my feet and drag me toward another door.

Looks like my luck finally ran out.

They drag me away, kicking and screaming and, yes, biting—unfortunately, one of the guards is some sort of steel-skinned Nightmare, and I think I chip a tooth on his wrist. The other one is wearing a bulletproof shirt and leather gloves, and my sad little teeth can't gnaw through them. It doesn't stop me trying though.

I'm hauled out of the gala and down the hall, up the stairs, passing door after door spaced wide enough apart they must be meeting rooms, until the space between the doors narrows and I realize I must be in the hotel, where people's rooms are.

A suspicion that's confirmed when I'm dragged into one of the rooms. It's got a large canopy bed, an engraved wooden desk, and an expensive-looking Persian rug. Only the best for the swankiest hotel in the city.

Better enjoy it while I can, I'll never be in a swankier room than this one. The fact that my prison is the nicest place I've ever been probably says something very sad about my life.

My captors unceremoniously dump me on a chair, and after removing my gloves—rude—they bind my wrists and ankles to the chair by straight up bending pieces of metal around them. Hardcore. What do they think, I'm going to gnaw on ropes like a rat and chew my way out?

Well, I did do quite a lot of biting on the way here, so I can see why they might have made that assumption.

The door opens, and I look up from my pathetic wriggling, as though I'm going to get away from my two guards currently tying me to a chair with pieces of *metal*. I'm expecting the Director, coming to gloat about my capture.

It's not.

It's *Cindy*.

Cindy Lim was a disciple in the Friends of the Restful Soul, the same as I was. We never really got along, but that was because I thought she was a religious fanatic and she thought I was involved in a kidnapping ring. We were both wrong, but it's hard to push down the instant defensiveness that rises up when I see her.

"Ness," Cindy says, clearly unimpressed.

Her straight black hair is cut in a fashionable bob, her trousers and waistcoat are immaculately pressed, this time a deep purple over a white oxford shirt. Her face looks a little thinner, the cheekbones a little sharper, but she still looks as perfectly put together as always.

I clear my throat. "Cindy."

Last time I saw her, she was fishing through the Director's filing cabinets. She claimed she was a spy trying to gather information on the Friends for a journalistic exposé. But none of the newspapers had ever heard of her when Priya and I called around later.

All I really know about Cindy is that she has her own motives for being with the Friends. I'm just not entirely sure what they are.

"What are you doing here?" I ask her as the guards continue tying me up.

"Overseeing your capture for the Director, of course," Cindy says as she examines me with pursed lips. "I don't know what possessed you to sneak in here and try to assassinate him, but it was a mistake."

I bite back my first instinct, which is to deny her words. It's not like I can tell the truth.

I was here to assassinate someone *else*.

Yeah, no. That will just make even more problems.

"You're working for the Director?" I stare at her. "I thought you left the Friends?"

"Leave?" She smiles a perfect smile. "Why would I ever do something like that?" She puffs out her chest. "I've been promoted. I'm now the Director's personal assistant."

I stare at her, agog.

"After you and Priya so dreadfully attacked him," Cindy

continues, "I nursed him back to health and have been assisting him ever since. With absolutely *everything*."

Oh. Oh I get it now.

She weaseled herself in deeper. Deep enough, perhaps, to find whatever she was looking for?

And here I thought she'd be happy with the file room. I guess not.

"I see," I say.

The guards finish binding me, and nod respectfully to Cindy as they depart.

After the door closes, I ask, "These rooms soundproof?"

"Of course they are." Cindy rolls her eyes. "This is an expensive hotel. They protect clients' privacy." Her lips curl in displeasure. "I've heard of people being eaten alive in these hotel rooms and no one heard their screams for help."

Well, that's just the cheeriest thing.

But at least it means the guards outside won't hear us.

I wiggle my bonds expectantly. "Okay, so you're going to help me escape, right?"

She stares at me like I'm insane. "No."

I blink. "What? I thought we were on the same side?"

"Hardly." Cindy crosses her arms. "You're on the side of 'Ness at the expense of everyone else,' and I'm on the side of 'playing a long complicated game to take down a massive human trafficking ring.' Sorry, but I've done a lot of work building this identity up. I've only just managed to get clearance for their other branch in Newham—you know, where all the people who disappear go."

Damn, Cindy is good. I bet she even knows what the Friends are doing with their kidnapped people by now. Not that I care.

Okay that's a lie. I definitely care, mostly because if I don't get out of here I'm probably going to share their fate.

"Look, Ness. I'll give it to you straight," Cindy says. "You're not worth compromising my cover for."

Ouch.

Honestly, it's not that I think she's wrong. What's the life of one person when you're a spy who might be able to save hundreds, even thousands, of kidnapping victims, current and future?

But when I happen to be the one person, I stop caring about all the hypothetical other people who *might* be saved *someday*.

I need saving *now*.

"Well," I say, "that may be, but if you don't let me out of here, I'm going to tell the Director you're a spy."

Cindy scoffs, "Typical. Like I said, always on your own side."

"You say that like it's a bad thing."

"It is." Cindy snorts. "And there's no way the Director will believe you over me."

She has a point there. I'm not exactly the most trustworthy person in the Director's eyes.

"But it will sow doubt," I insist.

Cindy just shakes her head.

"Oh come on." I'm sweating, and I bite my lip. "Okay,

fine, don't free me. But I have a friend, he was trying to get into the event tonight. Our age, tallish, white, dark hair, green eyes, lots of eyeliner. Very good-looking, his name's Cy. Could you at least tell him where I am?"

She's not buying it. "Ness—"

"Come on, Cindy, you *owe* me."

"I owe you?" She bursts into laughter. "For what? Nearly breaking my ankle?"

"For the boat explosion!" I burst out. "I nearly died!"

"You *stole* my ticket. You only have yourself to blame."

"But *you* were the target." I lean forward. "They planned the whole damn assassination around *your* mail run!"

Cindy freezes. "What?"

I didn't intend to hook her with this, but I know when to grab a straw. "Oh, didn't you know? You were an assassination target in that explosion. The main one, in fact."

Cindy goes deathly pale.

"You know"—I shrug oh-so-casually—"I might be worried your secret identity is already compromised, if I were you."

"What do you know?" Cindy demands. "Who ordered me assassinated?"

I smile, smug. I've got her. "Wouldn't you like to know."

She grinds her teeth.

"Maybe," I say causally, "if you help me escape, I'll tell you more."

I don't actually know any more than that. But she doesn't need to know that.

Yeah, I am exactly the manipulative little rodent she thinks

106

I am. I don't give a shit as long as it gets me out of this alive.

Cindy hesitates.

She takes a step forward.

And then the door behind her opens, and the moment is lost. We're out of time.

The Director is here.

11

The Director walks into the room—or at least, most of him does.

It takes me a moment to realize that he's missing a piece.

"Director!" Cindy cries, eyes wide, back to playing her devoted assistant role. "Your tail!"

The Director strides the rest of the way into the room, and it's clear that his tail is completely gone. His robe, which is cut up the back in a careful way to allow his tail to poke through, now shows a gaping, round, tail-shaped hole. What's beneath the hole is covered by the addition of a cloth wrapped around the Director's waist, under his robe, so I'm not treated to a bare green butthole. Small mercies.

"Unfortunately"—the Director casts a disgusted look at me—"I had to take some necessary measures to protect myself."

I stare back at him, absolutely incredulous. "You *cut off your own tail?*"

"It'll grow back," the Director snaps.

Right. He *is* a lizard.

But still. I had no idea he was hardcore enough to cut off his own tail. That's just . . . intense.

And probably means he's *really* mad at me right about now. Even more than usual. Which is saying a lot, because I feel like the three years I lived with the Friends of the Restful Soul, his default state was being mad at me for something.

Which was entirely unjustified. I only set the building on fire once. No, twice. But still, that's not a bad record, all things considered.

"Cindy," the Director says, "can you go make the arrangements for transporting Ness to our facility?"

"Of course, sir." Cindy gives him a perfect smile. "Anything else I can get you? Are you in pain? I can pick up some medicine."

"That won't be necessary. Just the transport." He considers. "And one of those frothy coffees from the place on the ground floor."

"Strawberry?"

"You know me too well."

Cindy smiles at him, perfect and polite. "I'll see to it, sir."

She casts me one last, inscrutable glance, and leaves. The door thuds behind her, like the step of a giant monster, an omen of terrible things to come.

Now I'm alone with the Director. The Director who planned to kidnap me for three years, who runs a massive kidnapping ring, who is mad at me and who, ten minutes ago, and I cannot get over this, *cut off his goddamn tail*.

Which is very definitely my fault. And I'm pretty sure he blames me for it.

Well, this evening has already crashed and burned into a spectacular disaster, but things can *always* get worse.

"Ness." The Director steps forward, looking down his long lizard snout at me. "You didn't really think you could assassinate me, did you?"

I clear my throat. "Well, I didn't plan to assassinate you, if I'm being honest."

"Oh? So what was the little napkin-like thing supposed to do?"

I have absolutely no idea.

"Wouldn't you like to know?"

Smooth, Ness. Real smooth.

"Not really." The Director smiles thinly. "It's been neutralized. At the cost of my tail."

Yeah, he's definitely mad about that.

"What I don't understand," the Director muses, "is why you decided to come back and try and assassinate me. I thought when you left, you'd crawl in some hole and I'd never see you again."

That was indeed the plan. Too bad it didn't work out.

"What possibly possessed you to come back and risk yourself to kill me?" the Director asks, pacing. His eyes never leave me. "Did you finally learn what we do with the people who come through our doors?"

No. But that sounds like a great excuse to grab on to. And

also a chance for me to get him to admit what he's doing with the people he kidnaps without me having to be like Cindy and work for months to weasel into his trust.

"I did find out," I lie, and I lean forward, trying to channel that intense righteous justice Cindy is so good at. "And I knew I had to stop you."

Damn, I sound just like her. Maybe I should take up an acting job.

The Director stares at me for a long, disbelieving moment before he says, "You're a terrible liar."

I lean back, offended. "I'm a *great* liar."

"Then what was that?" He shakes his head. "Sloppy."

"Excuse me," I tell him. "I am a first-class liar here."

"You're an idiot," he tells me. "I've known you for years, Ness, and I know that you would never come back and stop me out of some idealized version of justice. If you're going to lie, you've got to make it believable."

Ouch.

Unfortunately, he's not wrong. That would be very out of character for me.

He smiles at me. It's not a nice smile. "Whatever idiocy possessed you to come here and attack me, I'm grateful. Because now we have you back." His smile widens. "And we can proceed as we always planned."

Ohhhh no, I do *not* like the sound of that.

I swallow, and when my voice comes out, it's a little high. "Proceed as planned?"

"Yes." The Director leans in. "Do you want to know what

we really do at the Friends of the Restful Soul, Ness?"

I gulp. I mean, I do, yes. I have been intensely curious about why the Friends were kidnapping people since I discovered it. Not curious enough to *do* anything about it or look into it, which might risk myself. But still, I'd be lying if I said I wasn't curious.

But now, with the Director smiling malevolently in front of me, his cheery grandfatherly demeanor discarded, I'm not sure I want to know.

Sometimes ignorance is bliss.

"Um," I say eloquently.

"Of course you want to know," the Director says, arms spread, smiling with those tiny sharp lizard teeth bared. "And I'm sure you want to know why, if we were planning to kidnap you, we let you live with us so long."

I admit, that part never made sense to me. Why would they bother to keep me around so long if they had nefarious plans? Why not just make me disappear the day I moved in with them? Why did they want me to transfer voluntarily— and why wait so long before even suggesting that I transfer?

No, none of it has ever really made sense to me. I've just chosen to chalk it up to one of life's mysteries that I'm not going to poke at, in case it pokes back at me.

But no secret lasts forever.

The Director puffs his chest out, and I sense an impending villain monologue. At least I'll probably get some answers while he brags about how smart he is.

"Therapy is a powerful tool," the Director begins, which

isn't at all how I thought he'd start this. "People's minds are delicate things. A single event can completely rewrite the way you think of the world."

Like how my sister turning into a giant spider and eating my father alive while I cowered under the sink turned me into a perpetual coward.

"But with therapy, you can reshape the mind. Undo the influence of that event." He glances at me and smiles. "Or change its impact."

"Change it," I repeat slowly, frowning. Something is tickling the back of my mind, a thought that's starting to form, but I can't quite grasp it.

"Yes. With therapy, one can change their fears. Focus them." His eyes glitter. "Cultivate them."

Wait a moment.

Shaping minds. Cultivating fear.

"Do you understand now?" the Director asks, his gaze intense.

I do. But I don't want to. I don't want to hear him say it. I want to press rewind on this whole conversation, want to stop my mind barreling down the path it's on, stop it from reaching the inevitable conclusion.

But it's too late for that.

"We make custom-designed Nightmares."

Custom. Designed. Nightmares.

For a moment, the world disappears. Everything blurs out, like I'm fading out of existence, or like the world is. It's like I'm back in a nightmare, and the Nightmare Phantom is changing the setting around me. Everything feels fake. Unreal.

The Friends specialize in therapy. Therapy, at its core, is essentially a way to manipulate someone's mind. Obviously, most people who go to therapy are looking for help to work through issues in their lives. Trauma, stress, fears, anxiety, depression, whatever it may be. It's a tool to help people pull apart the blocks of their own mind and rebuild broken pieces into something more healthy and stable.

But the same tactics that are used to help people work through their fears can also be used to double down on those fears. The same tool kit that can help build up your confidence can be used to tear it down.

Therapy can be a powerful tool for reshaping your mind.

But your therapist is doing the shaping.

That's why trust is so important—you have to trust the person messing with your mind has your best interests at heart. I always did trust that the Friends knew what they were doing.

I suppose I wasn't wrong—they did know what they were doing. It's just that they had profit in their heart instead of their patients' well-being.

Because if you can tailor someone's fears . . .

And then lock them away to have a nightmare . . .

You can determine what they become.

"No," I whisper, as though my not wanting this to be true will make any difference.

When I came to the Friends, I had a debilitating fear of spiders, so terrible I could barely cope in my day-to-day life. Everyone I saw reminded me of Ruby, every scuttle they did made me think of her crunching on my father's bones.

Therapy helped me work through that fear.

But now, looking back on it, it's clear to me that my other fears became amped up at the same time—like my fear of Nightmares. I worked one fear out of my life, only to replace it with another—one that the Friends wanted me to have.

They were going to turn me into a Nightmare.

They were going to turn me into the thing I feared most.

Nausea rises up, fast, my closed-off throat burning, and I need to get away from here, I can't breathe, I'm going to throw up, I need out, I need—

"I see you finally understand," the Director says.

I wanted the truth, and now that I have it, I don't want it. I wish I could scrub this knowledge from my mind, go back to ignorance. Ignorance truly is bliss.

"What were you going to make me?" I ask, my voice small, so small, barely a croak.

The Director smiles. "You mean what *am* I going to make you." He laughs. "Well, I'll save that surprise for later."

He checks the clock, smiles, and straightens his coat. "But for now, I have some investors to talk to."

And he slips out of the room, leaving me alone.

12

The room is unpleasantly quiet after the Director leaves.

I'd known it would be bad. No one kidnaps people for *good* reasons, obviously. I thought I was prepared for anything, that I'd accepted the Friends were evil, that I was ready for whatever the truth was.

I was wrong. I wasn't ready for anything at all.

It's not just that they were turning people into Nightmares—it's the horror of deliberately manipulating someone's worst fear and then turning them into it.

It's the horror of becoming my own worst Nightmare.

The thing is, I don't even know what that would *be*. I've been terrified of all Nightmares for so long, I don't think there's any specific one that's worse than another. Maybe it was Ruby's giant spider form they planned to turn me into. I don't know.

I take a deep breath, and then another, because no matter what, they can't do that to me now. The Nightmare Phantom is out of dreams. Even if they kidnap me and drug me into sleep, I won't change.

They can't change me.

Only the Nightmare Phantom can—and I doubt he's at all interested in what the Friends want.

I let out a long breath, feeling not calm, but calm*er*.

Even if they throw me in a cage, even if I can't get out of this, at least they can't do that. They can't make me into my worst nightmare. They can't change me.

Or my body, at least.

Who knows what they can do with my mind?

No, don't think about that. Think about escape. Think about getting the hell out of here. Panic attacks and existential crises are for later, when I'm curled up against Cy, safe in his apartment and emptying my heart out.

Right now, I need to get the hell out of here.

I let out a long breath. All right. Here goes nothing.

I start jumping in my chair.

I'm bound to the wood chair, but it's an old chair, and I know that it won't stand up to my abuse long. The carpenter's glue between the joints is meant to withstand someone sitting in it, not actively trying to smash it to bits by pretending it's a pogo stick.

Each smash of the chair on the floor makes my muscles tighten more, and my eyes flick nervously to the door, waiting for someone to come and stop me. But the door doesn't open. I guess Cindy was right about the soundproofing.

Finally, with a terrible splintering sound, the chair comes apart.

The legs collapse, snapping right off and sending me

smashing to the floor, face-first, of course. The carpet scrapes my cheek, and a bruise starts forming on one shoulder.

I lie there, breathing heavily, just giving myself a moment to rest.

Then I roll over and try to wiggle out of my restraints.

It doesn't work.

On the plus side, with the chair splintered this way, I can move myself into a normal, uncontorted position. But because those asshole guards bent metal around my wrists to the wooden chair legs, the pieces of wood are still strapped to me. It won't stop me moving, but it's annoying.

I try tugging at one of the chair legs attached to my wrist, trying to tug it out so that I can just slide the metal off, but it's too tight.

Well. Fine. I guess I'll just go around with pieces of wood strapped to my ankles and wrists.

I stand awkwardly, because the pieces of wood are longer than my legs, and then kick the wood against the wall, trying to snap it enough to walk easily, which is only somewhat successful.

I stop to think for a moment. Normally, when trying to slip out of something too tight, I'd put water on my hands, make them slippery and squeeze out, but I'm pretty sure the wood will absorb the water and bloat, making it harder to get out.

Looking around, I finally head to the fireplace, hook one end of my metal restraints under a poker, and lean, pushing my whole body into levering this metal.

Finally, it bends. Just enough for me to wiggle the remaining pieces of chair out and free myself, one limb at a time.

Okay. Step one, done.

I look at the door. I have no idea if there are guards on the outside. It's also probably locked, which means picking the lock, and then facing the guards. I certainly can't take the guards in a fight, and outrunning them didn't work so well last time.

I look at the window, considering.

I peer out at the city far too many stories below me. Right, I can't jump that, and there's no convenient trash to land on either, just the roof of a motorcar. Ouch. No fire escape either, which is definitely illegal, but the hotel is definitely wealthy enough to bribe their way out of that.

There's plenty of open windows along the side of the building. If I could just get to one of them, maybe I could crawl into the room and escape through the door. But that's a pretty big if.

I bite my lip, and then turn back to the door. Which of these options is better? The window, where a mistake plunges me to my death?

Or the door, where if I fail I get to be tied up and try again?

Yeah, I'm gonna try the door.

I creep to the door and test the knob, carefully, so carefully—

Locked.

Okay, that's fine, I've picked locks before. I look for the lock here, and then pause, staring. There's no lock. Instead, someone has melted a large piece of metal over where the keyhole is, effectively meaning it can only be unlocked from the outside.

I guess the window it is.

I look around the hotel room, at the bedsheets and blankets—they'd probably rip—to the chairs, which don't have anything to balance on, and aren't long enough anyway.

I look back to the bedsheets.

Finally, I go over and rip the sheets off the bed. One top sheet, one bottom sheet, and one blanket. Alone, they're each weak, but if I braid them together . . .

Braiding them doesn't take long, and when I give the finished product an experimental tug, it feels strong. The only disadvantage is that it's not very long—maybe four feet.

It will have to be enough.

I go back to the window and tie the makeshift rope to the radiator just below the window, and then hurl it over the edge. It goes halfway down the wall to the window below.

A window that isn't even open.

Charming.

I test my braided sheets again, and they hold my weight as I slowly ease myself down the side of the building, hand over hand, muscles straining. I just need to get low enough to reach the window, and then I'm going to kick it open, and this will definitely work out and I won't fall to my death.

I finally get to the end of the rope, and my legs reach just far enough to touch the window. With no other way to get in, I start doing the only thing I can.

I kick the window.

It doesn't break, of course, so I keep at it, pounding my boot into the window over and over until finally, the glass cracks. Then, with one more almighty kick, it shatters.

Glass shards rain about my boots, and I grimace, looking at the jagged hole I'm going to have to swing myself through to get inside the room.

I'm just putting my feet through the hole, readying myself to let go of the rope—oh god—and launch myself into the room, when I'm interrupted.

"Ness, what are you *doing*?!"

Cy is looking down at me from the window of the room I just escaped from.

I look back up at him, dangling out the window, and clear my throat. "I'm escaping. What are *you* doing?"

"Rescuing you," he says, staring at me in bewilderment. "Being your backup. Like I said I would."

"How did you get into the room?"

"I broke the door," he says.

"And the guards?"

"What guards?"

Ugh. Of course. I should have tried using the bedpost as a battering ram. But how was I supposed to know I didn't even rate guards?

I clear my throat. "Well, I suppose we can leave your way."

"Oh no." He raises an eyebrow. "I want to see what you were planning to do next."

"Shut up," I mutter as I haul myself back up to the window where Cy waits, leaving the broken window behind.

"Let's just get out of here."

Cy grasps my forearm and helps pull me back into the room. I teeter over the windowsill and promptly fall on my face on the carpet. I get up quickly, dusting myself off, pretending nothing happened.

"How did you find me?" I ask.

"Some girl told me where you were. I assumed you were friends but when I mentioned it she said 'absolutely not.' So, ah, your enemy told me where you were."

Well. Looks like Cindy did come through.

"She also gave me a phone number and told me to tell you to call her or else."

"Yeah, that sounds right," I agree.

"What happened?" He gestures at all this.

"Let's get out of here and I'll update you."

We hurry down the stairs, keeping to the servants' stairwells to avoid being seen by security or any of the people attending my disastrous event. At one point we have to go down the main hall, and Cy grabs my arm and yanks me into a bathroom as a shadow comes around the corner.

We hide there, our breaths mixing, close in the tight space, and I wonder who Cy saw. Outside the bathroom, I hear the faint click of claws on the carpet.

The Director.

I hold my breath as he walks by, and we wait, hearts pounding, until Cy finally signals the coast is clear.

We slip out of the bathroom.

In the hall are a small group of people I don't know, and

they notice us leaving and start nudging each other and smirking. I blush, realizing what it must look like, a rich boy and a girl in a server's uniform, both of us all messy, coming out of a bathroom together. I take an awkward shuffle step away from Cy, as though that will make our disheveled state look any less like what it does.

Cy notices the glances too, and he laughs. "I'm sorry about your reputation, Ness."

"Worry about your own," I mutter.

"Oh, I ruined it a long time ago," he says, laughing, which is probably true. I did meet him by interrupting a tryst he was having, after all.

A wealthy middle-aged man all in gold, from his hair to his skin to his suit to his jewelry, walks by and smirks at Cy. "Having fun?"

"We were just talking," I interrupt.

"Well, it certainly looked like you talked . . . vigorously."

The man laughs and continues on.

I think my whole face is flaming, and I'm reminded of the first time I met Cy, when he one-hit KO'd me with a single dirty joke. Pull a gun on me and I'll stare you down, but whip out a dick joke and I'm mortally wounded.

Oh god. Did I just make a dick joke in my own head? Betrayed by my own brain.

We take the elevator after that, hoping that no one is waiting for us in the main lobby. Just as the doors are closing in front of us, Cy startles. I have one moment to look through the crack in the elevator doors and see a blond man in his twenties I don't recognize before the doors close and we're speeding down toward the lobby.

"Cy." I touch his arm. "What is it?"

"It's—" He hesitates, then shakes his head. "Nothing. It's nothing."

I want to press, but the elevator doors open, and we're back in the lobby, with its polished marble floors and glittering chandeliers, and nonsensical baby-archer art. It's a beautiful sight, and the most beautiful part is the large, open doors less than thirty feet from us.

Almost free. I'm so close I can taste it.

We step out of the elevator and head for the doors. Twenty feet. Ten feet.

"Hey! You there!"

Oh no.

I don't even know if they're yelling at me, and I'm sure not going to wait around to find out.

Cy grabs my hand. "Time to run!"

And even though Cy is superstrong and fast and all that— running is still my specialty, and I don't hesitate to launch myself across the lobby and out into the dark streets of Newham.

13

A couple of blocks away from the hotel, Cy flags us down a cab, and we hustle into it.

Pressed against the vinyl seat as we speed through the Newham night, I finally let myself relax, slumping against Cy like deadweight, completely unable to hold my own body up as the adrenaline drains from me.

Cy's voice is gentle. "Want to tell me what went wrong?"

I groan, but I do, starting with how I never even got close to the Mayor before the Director appeared, how I accidentally on purpose used the napkin on him, and then going to the part where the Director revealed what the Friends of the Restful Soul have been doing all these years.

By the time I finish, Cy is shaking his head. "Not even I could have predicted just how badly this would go. And I thought it would go pretty bad."

I grimace. "Tell me about it."

My head sinks into my hands, and Cy gently rubs my back, trying to comfort me.

"Did you know that custom-designed Nightmares were a thing?" I can't look him in the eyes. "You grew up with the kind of people who . . ." I can't even say it. "Did you know?"

He hesitates long enough before responding that it's answer enough.

"I suspected that it might be an industry," he finally says. "But I didn't know the Friends were involved. I swear I'd have told you."

I nod. I believe him. I don't think he would have kept the truth about the Friends from me.

"It's going to be all right," Cy assures me. "You got away from them. You're safe now."

I choke-laugh. "Am I?"

"Well," he says, "you can't know anything for *sure*. We could be crushed by a skydiving giant at any time. This is Newham, after all."

I snort-laugh.

It's good, making light of things. Making fun of all the scary things in the world makes them less scary. It makes me feel like I've taken away a bit of their power over me, makes me feel more in control. It makes life bearable.

Maybe Cy is finally getting it.

"I just . . ." I swallow. "I was so happy there, you know? I knew they were evil. I knew it was a lie. But you know, there's a part of me that missed them, if you can believe it. Missed the illusion of safety I had there."

Cy is quiet for a long moment, before gently saying, "It was an illusion, though."

"I know."

And I do. But it still hurts. And it still doesn't stop the longing for what I thought I had. For the simple, safe life I believed I was leading.

Unlike my life now, which is painfully complicated.

The taxi drops us off at Cy's apartment building. It's so late it's almost early, and the sky is starting to lighten at the edges, which means we need to go inside before Cy burns.

I lean against Cy in the elevator, my body barely holding up from all the abuse I've put it through tonight—what was I even thinking climbing out a window, my arms don't have the muscles for that—and then practically crawl down the hall back into the apartment, where I shed my sweaty waistcoat and kick off my shoes. Cy brings me some water and I gulp it eagerly.

"Go rest," he tells me, his eyes soft. "You look dead on your feet. We can deal with everything once you've had a good sleep."

I don't even have the energy to reply, I just nod and curl up in my closet.

Usually, lying in my closet calms me. It's small and contained, no one here except me. My own little haven. And I'm exhausted enough that I should just fall right asleep, and any other night I would.

But tonight, I just stare up at the faint light coming through the slats and think of how much this little room reminds me of my room with the Friends.

For years, I lived alone in that tiny, isolated room, cut off from the world, and I thought it was happiness. I never had friends until Priya came along—I was afraid to get close to people, afraid they'd turn into a Nightmare just like my sister and kill me.

Being alone, isolated, apart from everyone else, was a form of safety.

But now, as I shudder, alone and scared, in my tiny little closet, I wonder if I really felt that way, or if the Friends manipulated me to feel that way. How can I know which thoughts are from them twisting my fears and which thoughts are genuinely my own?

I'm sure that some of my fears are justified—I'm just not sure which ones anymore.

How can I trust any of my instincts? Instincts are built by your mind. If everyone tells you something is bad, when you see it, obviously you're afraid. But what if everyone is lying or wrong or manipulating me like the Friends did? My instincts are *awful*. I trusted the people abusing me. The first time I saw Cy, I was terrified of him, even though he'd never done anything to me, and now he's one of my closest friends.

How much of my mind is just plain *wrong*?

I stare at the closet walls closing in around me, and suddenly, they seem too small, everything is too small and it's too much like my home with the Friends and I can't do it, I can't be in here.

I can't be alone right now.

I slip out of my closet, awkwardly shuffling into the living room, past the couch Cy has offered me a million times to sleep on that I've refused because . . . why? A small closet was better?

I don't even know anymore.

I creep over to Cy's room. He's lying in bed, fully clothed except for his shoes, which rest at the edge of the bed. He's writing something on a notepad, frowning slightly. He looks up when I come in.

"Hey," he says, looking at me expectantly.

"I . . ." I look away. I feel too awkward. He knows I've never been able to sleep when other people are in the room, and now, here I am unable to be alone.

"Trouble sleeping?" he asks.

I nod.

"Wanna sleep with me?"

A flush rises up my cheeks, going right to my forehead.

"I— You—" I'm sputtering awkwardly, blushing terribly, I can't even get words out. Curse this weakness of mine.

He laughs. "I'm sorry, I shouldn't tease. You just look so adorable when you're flustered."

This isn't helping my stammering, blushing situation.

"I'll stop." He holds up a hand to his heart. "I promise, no flirting, no suggestive comments. Just napping."

"Mmmhmm." I eye him skeptically, but I crawl into bed with him anyway. Cy usually means what he says, and while he can be a bit of a tease, he's always been good at respecting what makes me uncomfortable.

129

I snuggle under the covers and lie against him, curling up like a child in her parents' bed hunting for warmth and reassurance.

"Do you want to talk about it?" he asks, his hand stroking my hair in a soothing pattern.

I lean into his touch, savoring the closeness, the comfort he's giving me, the feeling of connection, of not being alone, of being cared about.

"I—" I shiver. "I don't know what to think anymore. Or what to believe. How can I trust my own mind, knowing how badly it's been tampered with?"

I always thought the truth would help me. The truth will set you free, isn't that what they always say?

I've always wondered why I'm so afraid. So many people in Newham go through so much worse than me, and they come out the other end fine—or at least, functional.

But now I have my answer. I know why my mind is such a mess of fear.

And I have no idea how to fix it.

Cy's expression is solemn as he tips my face up to look at him.

"Ness," he says. "I know a lot about mental manipulation. I grew up with a man who made it his entire career to convince the world he was a hero through his movies, instead of a villain. Do you want to know the trick to seeing through it?"

"Yes. Hell, yes."

"The key," he says, tapping the side of my head gently with one finger, "is knowing it's *there*."

I blink.

"If you know what's happening, you can start learning to recognize thought patterns that don't seem right. And once you recognize them, you can ignore them."

"But how do I recognize them?" I whisper. "I can't tell anymore."

"But you will. You've already started," he says. "Why did you crawl in my bed tonight?"

For once, he doesn't make it sound dirty.

"Because the closet reminded me of the Friends, and how I wasn't sure if I really wanted to be isolated or if they made me think that," I admit.

"So you've already started asking questions," he says.

"Yes." I look away. "But I don't know the answer."

"I think you do," he says. "Tell me, right here, right now, do you wish you were back in the closet, alone?"

"No." The answer is fast and easy.

"Exactly." He smiles at me. "And I'm not saying there won't be times you genuinely want alone time. I know what you introverts are like." He winks at me. "But before tonight, you would have crawled into that closet to be alone, even if what you actually wanted was company, wouldn't you?"

I think about that seriously. "I don't know. Maybe."

"Now that you know what was done, you'll be able to really examine your thoughts," he says. "When you have an instinct, just ask yourself if that's what you really believe. Don't doubt yourself—just double-check."

"But how do I know what to double-check?" I ask. "And what if I still can't tell?"

"Then ask for help," he says simply. "Ask me. Ask Priya. Ask the people you do trust. We're here for you. We'll tell you what we think. And you don't have to think the same way as us—I know there are things that are true for you and not for me and vice versa—but you can ask other people and compare. You can dissect the things you're not sure about and try and form new opinions."

I bow my head, and my voice comes out raspy with nerves. "And what if some of my fears are about *you*?"

"Then you should *definitely* tell me. I don't want you secretly worrying I'm going to eat you while you sleep." He pauses, eyebrows drawing together in concern. "That's not your fear, right? Because I really thought we covered that and you know I'm definitely not going to eat you in your sleep."

I choke-laugh. "No, that's not my fear."

"Well, good." He smiles at me. "But seriously, Ness, if you're ever afraid, if you're ever concerned, *talk* to me. I can't help you if you don't tell me."

I nod, choking with feeling, and rest my forehead on his chest, just breathing. He strokes my back, and I close my eyes.

"It's going to be okay, Ness," he tells me soothingly.

I shudder out a breath, and even if it's a lie, I let myself believe it for now, because some lies you have to believe to stay sane.

The Friends encouraged me to be afraid. They made my fear of Nightmares into something so irrational I couldn't even sleep in the same room as another person.

So, in defiance of them, to prove to myself that I am more than what they made me, that I control my mind, not them, I snuggle against Cy, wrapping my arms around him, and close my eyes.

I'm going to take my life back.

Bit by bit, piece by piece, I'm going to undo everything they've done to my head. And I'm going to live my life on my terms, not theirs.

Tucked against Cy's warm body, soothed by his gentle words of reassurance and my own resolve, for the first time since I was a child, I willingly fall asleep in the same room as someone else.

14

I wake up in Cy's bed, with my face pressed against his shoulder, half spooning him.

For a moment, disorientation hits, and my brain goes an awful lot of weird places—especially weird given that we're both still clothed, but thanks for the images, brain, I'm not going to be able to get rid of those anytime soon.

Blushing because for once I'm the one with inappropriate thoughts, I gently extract myself from the still sleeping Cy to go to the bathroom and wash the smell of sweat and fear off my body.

I soak in the shower, catching the occasional glimpse of myself in the steel mirror—Cy doesn't have a regular mirror with silver backing because he wouldn't show up in it. So steel mirrors, because he can't do his hair without seeing himself.

I don't know why his silver allergy means that he melts when touching silver and can't be reflected in silver-backed mirrors, or show up in photographs developed in silver nitrate, but Nightmares rarely make scientific sense. Their logic makes no sense to anyone but the dreamer. And maybe the Nightmare Phantom.

Speaking of the Nightmare Phantom . . .

What the hell am I going to do?

I've been so preoccupied with the Director and the Friends that I haven't even *thought* of the part of last night when I bungled the task the Nightmare Phantom assigned me comedically badly.

We're supposed to meet up later today to discuss how the event went. I have two options: I can go and tell him what happened, and hope he's not mad and gives me another chance. I'm not really a fan of this option, because it relies on him being understanding and sympathetic to how I screwed up, and in my experience, people are rarely sympathetic when I bungle things in disastrous fashions.

Or option two: I don't show up to our scheduled meeting. I instead lie low, pretend I never met the Nightmare Phantom, and avoid him forever.

This is a much more appealing option. I'm a Newham girl, and I know how to cut my losses and run when things go wrong. Sure, I've invested time and energy and all that shit in this plan—but it went wrong, and digging in deeper in the hopes that the Nightmare Phantom still wants to bargain and will do what I want just seems naive.

All right, well, that's settled.

Unless, of course, this makes the Nightmare Phantom mad.

He can turn people into literally anything. Why couldn't he turn someone into a dowsing rod to find me and turn me into a cockroach?

Hmm. He definitely could. But would he bother?

I don't know.

I run my hands over my head, fingers clawing down my face. Why are decisions so *hard*?

I think of Cy's words last night and take a deep breath. He said when I was in doubt, I should ask a friend their opinion to help clarify my own. I can do that. That sounds like a great way to shift responsibility for decision-making onto someone else.

I get out of the shower, dress, and slip out of the bathroom. Cy is still asleep. His arm is draped over the empty space where I was sleeping, and his face is soft and relaxed, the worries smoothed from his expression, like a sleeping angel.

I look away, flushing. Way to go, me, staring at him like some creeper while he's asleep.

I decide not to wake him. He deserves some rest.

Instead, I call Priya.

Priya has known me longer than anyone else. She's my best friend, and I trust her completely, more than anyone or anything in the world. She's brave, and smart, and won't coddle me or sugarcoat the truth. If anyone will have a good idea of how to get me out of the mess I'm in, it'll be her.

We set up a meet over the phone, and on the way, I stop by a local pawnshop and empty my pockets.

My stash isn't that great. One pearl bracelet, an engraved mahogany coaster, a fountain pen, and an antique watch of some sort, all of it plucked off wrists and out of pockets of last night's guests, before everything went wrong.

At a fancy party like that? Well, it would have been a crime *not* to rob them.

I get a nice little chunk of money, which I promptly squirrel away my bank account. My savings isn't great, but I'm proud of how much is in there, considering a month ago I had absolutely nothing.

I meet Priya at her favorite café just before noon. It's bustling, crowded with office workers and students all trying to get their caffeine fix. A sign at the counter notifies people that the coffee is not spiked with any "additives," something most coffee shops had to put up after that one chain of coffee stores was found to be spiking their drinks with cocaine to addict customers to their brand and drive out the competition.

That brand is still in business—they bribed the police commissioner, but now they advertise their cocaine coffee openly. If anything, their business has only grown.

Priya flops dramatically into the seat across from me. "I'm so glad you called."

"Oh? Why?"

Priya groans. "I'm so *bored*."

I'm guessing the Nightmare Defense training exercises didn't go well.

"So I'm a distraction?" I say, amused.

"Well"—Priya shrugs—"knowing you, you've got your-self into some awful mess again and need help."

I wince. Right on the money.

"I knew it!" Priya leans forward, grinning. "Spill every-thing. Who are we fighting?"

I stare at her. Maybe I should stop feeling bad about involv-ing Priya in my messes. Given her enthusiasm every time, I'm starting to realize maybe she likes being my friend *because* of all the excuses she has for action and adventure.

I'm not sure what I think about that.

I decide I'm not going to think about it either.

I tell her about the Friends, what I discovered. I tell her about the Nightmare Phantom, and the deal we had, and how dramatically I bombed my one and only task, followed by a long spiel about what the Director told me, and a side mention of Cindy and whatever she's up to.

Priya listens through it all, leaning forward, eyes glued on me. When I finish, she leans back and downs the dregs of her coffee like a shot.

"Ness," Priya says, her voice full of righteous indignation. "Why didn't you call me yesterday?"

"I did!" I insist. "Your sister said you had training!"

"Training." Priya snorts. "I'd have skipped that waste of time for this any day."

"For what?" I ask dryly. "Waiting in the lobby with Cy to rescue me?"

She laughs. "You underestimate me—I'd have broken into that party in five minutes flat."

"I don't think that would have gone so well," I tell her, but I'm smiling at the thought of Priya banging down the doors to dramatically rescue me.

"Well, we'll never find out now, will we?"

I grin, then hesitate. "You're not mad? About me working with the Nightmare Phantom?"

"Why would I be mad about that?" Her voice is quizzical.

"Well, I mean, your mom . . ." I trail off.

Priya sighs and places her cup on the table, her voice going serious. "I know that maybe to an outsider, it looks like I've got some unresolved mom issues or whatever, and I fight Nightmares because my mom disappeared, presumably because she became one. It looks like I resent them, or blame them or whatever and I'm taking out my rage on them. But I don't. That's not it at all."

Priya runs a hand through her hair. "I don't think I've ever told you the story of the first Nightmare I killed, did I?"

Now that I think about it, she hasn't. It seems like the kind of thing that should have come up at some point.

"No," I finally say.

She nods, and leans back in her chair.

"I was twelve when the next-door neighbor turned into a Nightmare," she begins. "I'd never liked the man. We could hear him beating his wife sometimes through the wall. I hated it. I hated how powerless I felt to help her. I hated how useless the police were at stopping him."

Classic Newham. The police never do anything unless you bribe them.

"But one night he turned into a Nightmare." Priya's voice is low, her expression tight. "One with giant razors for hands. One so strong that he threw his wife right through the wall between our apartments."

I wince. "Did she . . . survive that?"

"She did," Priya says. "But she was badly hurt. He barged through the wall after her, claws out, full of rage, ready to finish the job. Everyone around me was screaming, and I just"—Priya's eyes are lost in the past—"I had this moment of perfect clarity. This man, this monster, he needed to be stopped, or he'd do this, again and again.

"No one else was going to stop him—so I decided I would."

Priya's expression is hard and unamused. "I grabbed the first jar I saw in the spice cupboard, opened it, and threw it in his face. It was freshly ground chili powder."

Oh that would have *burned*.

"He was screaming in pain, and he reached up to rub his eyes—and gouged them." She shrugs. "Long razor claws. For a moment, he'd forgotten he'd become a Nightmare."

"Ouch." I wince in imagined pain.

"Yep." Her expression goes a little more fierce here. "And while he was screaming that he was going to murder me for doing that, I picked up our frying pan, and I swung it like a baseball bat. I got him on the back of his head—and the force of the swing sent his head forward, right into his own claws, which were still in front of his face. The claws went all the way through his head and, well . . ."

140

"One dead Nightmare," I finish.

"Exactly." Priya's eyes are lost in memory. "I remember standing there, covered in blood, just breathing. My heart was going a mile a minute. It was like I could feel every cell in my body, and all of them were vibrating." She meets my eyes. "It was my first time facing death—and I'd never felt so *alive*."

The air seems to hum with pressure, and I wait silently for her to continue.

"His wife," Priya says, "was crying while she thanked me for saving her life. She'd been too frightened to leave him, and she'd been certain he'd finally kill her."

Priya's voice lowers, like even all these years later she can't quite believe it. "I'd never felt as alive as I did in that moment, never felt as charged, as powerful—I'd fought a monster, and I'd *won*. And I'd saved someone's life doing it." She grins. "There's no rush in the world like it."

She holds my gaze. "*That's* why I fight Nightmares."

Listening to her story, I finally realize why Priya never told me about this before. Our first encounters with death by Nightmare are so similar, it's like looking in a mirror. But where I hid, fled the fear and terror, and let other people die, Priya faced the monster, stood toe-to-toe with it, and conquered it.

She probably thought it would make me feel bad about my own reaction. But Priya and I are very different people, and while I often wish I were more like her, I know that I could never have done what she did. Especially not as a child.

"Anyway"—Priya spreads her hands and steers the conversation back on track—"the reason I told you the story is so that you'd know—I don't really have an issue with Nightmares themselves, or even the Nightmare Phantom. I'm not in Nightmare Defense out of hatred or a grudge."

She pauses a beat. "But still, I probably would have recommended you *not* work with the Nightmare Phantom." Priya's tone is dry. "He's not exactly the most trustworthy person around."

"Well, he kept his word last time," I say, then slump in my seat. "Not that it matters, since I screwed up the one simple thing he asked me to do."

"That was very typical of you," Priya agrees.

I glare. "I don't mess *everything* up."

"The other disciples didn't call you Ness the Mess for nothing," Priya points out.

I grimace. "Did they really call me that?"

"Among other things."

Great. What a wonderful moniker. It sounds like a children's book villain.

"Speaking of the Friends." Priya smiles at me, wide and angry. "Let's talk about how we're gonna kill those assholes."

I give her a pointed look. "Not even you can take on an entire cult."

"I don't need to," Priya points out. "Half of the people in it have no idea it's evil, which means it's not really a whole cult we need to stop, so much as a few important people. Like the Director. And whoever is helping him run his kidnapping ring."

She has a point there.

"Cindy said they have another facility," I tell her. "One where they take the kidnapped people."

"You have an address?"

"Nope."

"Very unhelpful."

"I know," I admit. Then I hesitate. "I'm just wondering if . . . you know. We *need* to do anything. Can I just wait it out? Hide until they fall apart?"

"Why would they fall apart?"

"Well, the Nightmare Phantom is out," I say. "The Friends can't create their custom Nightmares. Because there are no new Nightmares."

Priya's eyes widen in understanding. "Which means that the Friends can't fulfill any of their orders."

"Exactly." I nod. "The Friends' whole cottage industry of customized Nightmares will collapse."

The Friends' business model is based on the Nightmare Phantom being trapped in dreams. And he's not anymore.

"Once people realize that the Friends can't deliver on all their orders," I say, "what do you think will happen?"

Priya smirks. "The Friends will be eaten alive by their customers."

Probably quite literally in some cases.

143

It's a cold comfort, but it *is* a comfort. I did manage to take down the Friends after all—just not intentionally, and not in a way they'll ever know. But as long as they're destroyed, does it matter?

"I'm shocked you haven't decided to speed that along," Priya says with a grin.

"How?"

She laughs. "By going to every single customer you can find and telling them that the Friends can't deliver because Nightmares don't happen anymore."

I actually had thought of doing that. I'd reconsidered very quickly.

"Last time I tried something like that, not only did it not work, I ended up making myself a kidnapping target for Nightmare Defense. I'd rather not have a repeat."

"I forgot about that," Priya says. "How rare of you not to repeat your mistakes."

I make a rude gesture at her in response.

Priya laughs and leans back in her chair. Her expression turns thoughtful. "I still have questions, though."

"About?"

"The Friends." Priya frowns. "If they're custom-making Nightmares . . . why are they also buying Nightmares?"

I blink. "What?"

"When Nightmare Defense caught you, Charlie Chambers told you the Friends were his biggest customers, didn't he?"

"Yeah, he did," I agree, pulling up the memory.

"So if they're making their own Nightmares"—Priya raises a palm in a half shrug—"why are they buying *more*?"

I blink. "I—have no idea."

Priya's right. For all the horror I've discovered, I might have only just scratched the surface of what the Friends are up to.

"You think they're making money another way?" I hesitate. "You don't think the Nightmare Phantom's release will crush them?"

"I don't know," Priya says. "It might, simply because their clients are powerful and won't like being lied to. But I suppose it depends what exactly they've got going on besides that."

She's right.

Which means it's entirely possible that the Friends won't go down unless we make them. But I can't do that—I'm a nobody. I can't take down the Friends. Not even with Priya's help.

I pause at the thought, remembering what Cy told me last night.

Examine my thoughts. Why do I think this? I've thought it without questioning it for ages. And now that I am—yes, they're powerful, but Priya *does* have a rocket launcher.

Have the Friends conditioned me never to fight back? Or have I done that myself?

"Ness?" Priya asks. "What's wrong?"

I rest my elbows on my knees. "It's what the Friends did to

me. Messing with my head. I've been having trouble figuring out if my thoughts are my own anymore."

"In what way?" Priya asks.

"Well, I'm—I'm always afraid." I swallow. "But some fear in this city is justified. I guess I've been trying to figure out what's justified and what's . . . not."

Priya considers this. "Some examples?"

"Well, when you said we could fight the Friends, I just kind of thought . . . what's the point? They're too powerful to win against."

"Well, that's definitely nonsense," Priya says.

"Why? They have money, people, power . . ."

"Eh, you're thinking of playing by *their* rules though," Priya tells me. "You're imagining trying to get at them through a fair fight, which we would lose. Or through the legal process, which we'd also lose. But that's not the only way to take the bad guys down."

Priya leans back. "I have a high-powered rifle, and I'm a good shot. The Director wouldn't stand a chance."

"That's a very murder-y option."

Priya doesn't smile. "When the non-murdery systems are protecting the abusers at your expense, then sometimes more drastic solutions are necessary."

I don't disagree. It's not like I haven't resorted to drastic measures in the past to survive. Releasing the Nightmare Phantom to slaughter Nightmare Defense, for example.

"What other thoughts have been giving you trouble?" Priya asks. "What else aren't you sure is real?"

"Everything," I admit. "This has me questioning absolutely everything. I never thought the Friends would be planning to turn me into a Nightmare. I *trusted* them. I never saw any of the red flags." I look up at her, pleading. "How do I know I'm not repeating the same terrible patterns?"

Priya's expression softens. "Oh, Ness."

"Maybe I'm a bad judge of character." I look at her, my eyes imploring, begging her to understand. "How do I know that my next employer won't try and sell my kidneys? Or that my landlord won't sell a spare set of keys to my apartment to a flesh-eating Nightmare?"

"Well, I think you're getting ahead of yourself." Priya's smile quirks up. "I don't see you affording rent anytime soon."

"So I'm trapped at Cy's place," I whisper. "And what happens if things go wrong there? How long have I known Cy, really? The Friends were grooming me for years. What if Cy's the same, he's just grooming me to be a live-in blood bank?"

Priya's expression is deeply skeptical. "You don't really believe that, do you?"

"No, I don't," I admit. "But I've been wrong about so many people. How do I know I'm not wrong about him? Or even you, for that matter?"

"I'm not going to betray you. And neither is Cy," Priya says, her voice calm and steady. "Which you must know on some level, since you've been living in his closet, and you're talking to me about it. You haven't run out onto the street to live in a tree yet."

"Newham doesn't have trees."

"You know what I mean."

I shrug again, a limp, empty motion. "Everyone knows being homeless is even more dangerous."

Priya closes her eyes and takes a long breath.

"Look, I won't say that your fears are completely without merit," Priya acknowledges. "It's true that Cy holds a lot of power over your life right now because he's your home. And while he doesn't strike me as the type to abuse it, you are right in that he *could*. So no, you're not wrong to be concerned about the power dynamic."

My shoulders ease a little. It's not *all* in my head. At least this fear has *something* rooted in reality.

"But," she says, holding up a hand, "just because he *can* doesn't mean he *will*." She leans forward. "In an ideal world, everyone would be on equal footing all the time. We don't live in that world. Pretty much every relationship has its ups and downs, with someone having more or less than the other person. That's just life. People lose their jobs, or get injured, or any number of other things and their partners or family or friends have to support them while they get back on their feet."

Priya crosses her arms. "If someone in your life is an abusive piece of shit, their true colors will come out the moment you're at your weakest and most vulnerable."

I stare at her flatly. "You mean like I am all the damn time?"

"Exactly." Priya winks at me. "I think you've long since seen Cy's true colors."

She's right. I know she is. And I'm glad she is—I don't even want to think of how it would destroy me if Cy turned out to be evil.

"I just wish," I finally whisper, "I could stand on my own two feet. I wish I had money and stability. I hate that I keep having to lean on Cy. And on you. I wish I could be independent."

Priya shakes her head. "Ness. You're thinking about this all backward. You live in a society. There's no such thing as independence."

I frown. "What do you mean?"

"Think about it," Priya says. "On a basic level, you're always relying on other people. You're relying on people to truck food into the city, relying on stores to sell you that food."

I shake my head. "Yes, but that's different."

"Is it? Let's take housing, then." Priya raises one hand. "When you rent a place, your landlord trusts you'll pay, and you trust he won't evict you. But that trust gets broken all the time." Her tone lowers into sarcasm. "The landlord doesn't fix building problems, and then what are the tenants supposed to do? Pay to live in mold?"

"That's why I wish I could own my own place."

Priya shakes her head. "Even if you could afford it—which I doubt in this city—it's not free, you know. There's apartment taxes and city taxes. And if you own an apartment, you're relying on the building administration to do maintenance so you have running water. Your property value can plummet because your neighbor loosed a murderous Nightmare in the pipes. If you own the place, you can't just *move*. You have money tangled up in it."

I blink slowly.

"My point is, Ness, there's no such thing as complete independence. You'll always have to work with others, whether that's landlords or building management or neighbors, and there's always opportunities to get screwed. Always. Being rich doesn't mean you can't get fucked, it doesn't mean you somehow get to stop needing to rely on other people." Priya raises a hand. "It's just that the reliance looks different— you're hiring plumbers with your own money and trusting they won't scam you, rather than fighting a landlord to try and get them to pay for plumbers. Either way, you still need a plumber."

"I . . . I suppose so," I admit.

"No matter what you do, you have to work with other people." Priya shakes her head. "A lot of people talk about independence like it's living alone, having a job, and supporting yourself, with no one else there. But that's not independence—it's *isolation*.

"And the problem with isolation," Priya points out, "is that when something goes wrong, you have no one to lean on."

Priya looks me in the eye. "You can't live without people

to help you. You're thinking of safety nets as just money, cold cash in the bank," Priya says. "But there's more than one kind of safety net. And it's okay to lean on friends when things are bad. It's okay to ask me for help while you get back on your feet. Because I know that if something happened to me, you'd be right there for me to lean on too. That's what friends are, and it doesn't make you feel as powerful as money, but it's much more reliable when things get bad."

I bow my head. "Is it more reliable?"

"It is," Priya says. "Think about it. If you were in some random apartment, and you took a week off work to job hunt, you'd never have made rent. Most Newham landlords would have thrown you out. But Cy would never."

I stare at my hands. She's not wrong.

My dream of independence has always felt a little like a fantasy, but it's something I've clung to since I had to leave the Friends. The idea of my own perfect little room, my own little cubbyhole with no one there, nothing to bother me. Alone. Safe.

Isolated.

Even when I left, even when I was trying to escape them, their mind manipulation still steered the path I chose. I left one cage and immediately started searching to build another one.

But what do I *really* want?

I'm not sure.

I think it'll take time for me to unpack everything in my

mind and figure out which thoughts are mine and which aren't. I've locked myself into this one idea of what it means to be safe and happy, and it'll take work to unravel those bonds. But at least today, I feel like I've undone a few of the knots.

"Thanks, Pri," I whisper.

She claps me on the back. "That's what friends are for!" She pauses, seeming to realize what she said. "Real friends. Not the cult."

I snort-laugh, making my sore throat ache. "I figured."

"Now." Priya leans forward. "Let's start planning how we're going to fuck up the Friends."

I smile. I'm finally ready to hear Priya's plan. And maybe, I'm finally ready to face my problems. Maybe.

"I'm afraid that won't be happening."

I freeze at the sound of the familiar voice.

No.

No, he can't be here. It's not possible.

We both turn to the front of the shop, where the Director stands, smiling at us.

15

I stare at the Director, my brain not processing.

How is he here?

I accept that I had bad luck last night, that he was attending the same event I was working at—but I refuse to believe that the next day, he just randomly walks into the same café Priya and I are meeting at.

There's a point where it's not bad luck, it's something else, and this is that point.

Around us, a group of people who obviously came with the Director are quietly positioning themselves throughout the coffee shop. I don't recognize any of them, and given I lived with the Friends for three years, I really should. If they are disciples, that is—which, sure, they're with the Director, but for all I know he hired mercenaries for his evil dealings. These people walk like mercenaries, and they certainly have enough weapons.

They ask people to leave, and within moments, the café has been vacated by all customers, as well as the barista and the terrified owner, who seems to be checking his insurance policy to make sure he won't be penalized for running away if the shop blows up.

Classic Newham behavior.

Newhamites can smell trouble, and none of them want to be involved in it.

My eyes flick to the exits, but there's too many mercenaries between me and the door. We're sitting by the window, and going through it is definitely the fastest escape route, but that supposes I can break the window, which seems unlikely, since, despite me constantly promising myself I'm going to work out, I never do, so my arms are thin as chicken legs.

The Director pulls up a chair and sits in between us, smiling with his tiny sharp lizard teeth bared. It's strange to see him sitting in a regular chair—all the time I've known him, he needed a special chair with a hole in the right place to accommodate his tail.

But of course, he doesn't have a tail anymore.

Which is my fault, and he's probably kind of mad, if I had to guess. I mean, his robes look pretty dumb now, with a blatant hole right in the butt and no tail coming out. It just makes him look like a pervert, and I know he's the type to be real mad about that.

"Why are you here?" Priya asks, her arms crossed, seemingly completely unbothered that we're surrounded by armed mercenaries and facing a cult leader who holds grudges against both of us.

"For Ness, of course. We have some unfinished business." He smiles at me with needle-sharp teeth.

"Sorry, I've got an important appointment later today," I tell him breezily, trying to imitate Priya's confidence and only being somewhat successful. "But I'll pencil you in for another day. Next century, perhaps?"

"You always thought you were so funny." The Director shakes his head. "It's sad, really."

"Hey, I *am* funny. I'm hilarious." I huff. "There's no cause for insults."

Both Priya and the Director grimace, and in the same way. Ouch.

Well, *I* think I'm funny, and my opinion matters most, given that it's my humor.

"How did you find us?" Priya asks, turning to the Director, her voice hard.

"How do you think?" He snorts, raising one clawed hand in a gesture of *duh*. "Come now, Priya. Your sister's address was your emergency contact information. After a night like last night, I knew Ness would call you. She's incapable of facing anything without hiding behind you. All I had to do was follow."

I'd be offended by his remark if I hadn't done exactly that.

Priya's hand twitches at her side, and her eyes narrow. She's clearly mad—about them following her, knowing her family's address, and being used to lead them to me. Priya hates when people use her. She hates it even more when them using her puts her friends and family in danger.

"So, what, you're here to get vengeance on Ness?" She sneers.

"Don't be absurd." The Director waves this away. "I'm not so small-minded."

I'm not sure I believe that, but I'm not going to press. If he doesn't want to get vengeance for his lost tail, I'm hardly going to tell him that he should.

"Then why *are* you here?" I ask.

"Well, I'd always planned to come find you, Ness." He smiles at me, yellow eyes gleaming in the light. "I still have big plans for what you're going to become. You were almost ready before you decided to leave us last month."

I stare at him blankly as the words sink in.

He was always going to come and find me.

When I left the Friends, I really thought that was it. I've always been someone replaceable, someone who causes more problems than they solve. Even when the Director told me that they'd been grooming me to become a Nightmare, somehow it hadn't really clicked how much investment that was. They'd been manipulating my mind for more than three years. That's a lot of time and patience.

You don't invest that kind of time and energy without big plans.

Plans I definitely don't want to be a part of.

"I'd have come to you earlier," the Director continues, "but we've been having some problems turning people into Nightmares recently. So we've been more concerned with fixing that before we reacquired you."

A nice, smug little thread of satisfaction slides through me. I caused that. I freed the Nightmare Phantom, I'm the reason his business is in shambles.

For once, my ability to unintentionally destroy things works in my favor.

"So what's the point of kidnapping me now?" I ask, voice a little high, trying to play it cool and wave off how ominous his threat of kidnapping is. "Surely nothing has changed. I still can't become a Nightmare."

"Not yet, you can't. But that will change soon." He smiles. "And truthfully, I didn't come here today just for myself. I tracked you down for a business associate of mine."

The awkward smile freezes on my face.

Oh that *cannot* be good.

The door to the café clangs open, and boots click on the floor.

God, why do these people always have such dramatic timing? Like, do they plan this shit in advance? Script it for maximum effect?

Honestly, villains in Newham are vain enough that it wouldn't shock me.

I turn to see which dramatic-timing-obsessed villain had the Director track me down.

It's the Mayor.

She's smiling, her red lips stretched, her smooth black hair pulled into a high ponytail, not a single strand out of place despite the fact that on the other side of the door, I can hear her pterodactyl screaming, which means she probably *flew* here. Whatever hair gel she's using, I hope she's selling it. She could make a lot of money off that.

The Director rises from his seat and waves his hand toward me. "As requested, the server from last night."

Ah shit. This is *not* good.

I'd figured that while last night went awful, and I screwed up things for the Nightmare Phantom, and made the Director mad, at least I hadn't managed to get close enough to the Mayor that people knew she was the real target. One less villain enemy.

But I'm not that lucky.

"Much appreciated." The Mayor's voice is smooth and cool, and her eyes on me are like ice.

There's a reason *Newham Magazine* did a glossy photo shoot feature with the Mayor for their Villains of Newham edition and not, say, Giovanni Montessauri or Marissa Koval. All the scandals she's been involved in are running through my head to an off-key, too fast carnival theme, from her use of kidnapped slave labor to how she burned a competitor's children alive one by one until he came out of hiding, to how she crushed my favorite ice cream shop because she didn't like their pistachio ice cream.

And now she's here to see me.

I clear my throat nervously. I need to think of a lie to get out of this. Maybe two lies. Or ten.

Maybe I should run—sure, the only way out is through the window, but honestly, I bet with enough terror motivation I could get through that glass. I'm determined.

Priya's hand is shifting closer to the weapons on her

belt—she knows the same stories about the Mayor that I do. She can tell things are going sideways fast.

The Director walks away, pausing as he passes the Mayor. "Once you're done questioning the girl, I need her back."

"I'll make sure she's not *too* badly damaged." The Mayor laughs.

Wow. That's so comforting. I feel really reassured that I will survive this conversation intact.

The Mayor strolls up to us, and I half rise from my seat slowly, not out of respect but because I want to be in a better position to run for my life.

"So." The Mayor eyes me. She doesn't seem impressed by what she sees. "Tell me what you know about the Nightmare Phantom."

I freeze. How does she know? I never mentioned the Nightmare Phantom's involvement to anyone but Cy and Priya.

"I have no idea what you're talking about," I tell her.

"Don't play obtuse, I haven't the patience for it," she snaps. "That little napkin assassin last night has his fingerprints all over it." Her teeth are bared in a hungry, angry smile. "He's too much of a coward to face me, so he sent someone else to do his dirty work."

I never thought I'd hear the Nightmare Phantom referred to as a coward. It's weird, because he's so powerful, so unstoppable, he's reshaped the entire world over the past century. He's bulletproof and untouched by fear or empathy. I never thought he was afraid of anything.

But—she has a point. Why *didn't* he face the Mayor himself? Why did he get me to do this instead of just doing it himself?

Could it really be because he's afraid of her?

No, I decide. That doesn't seem like him. He probably had me do it because he thought it was funny. He has a sick sense of humor.

Yeah, that sounds more reasonable. Probably.

Because if even the Nightmare Phantom is afraid of the Mayor, then I'm *really* screwed right now.

"So I want you to tell me"—the Mayor looms over me, still smiling in a way that looks like she wants to eat me—"where he is."

I gulp.

"Why?" I manage to croak as I lean away from her face, which is just far too close to mine. "Why do you want to know?"

She laughs then, head thrown back, ponytail swinging. "Isn't it obvious?"

I shake my head. Maybe it is, but I'm not smart enough to get it.

"I'm going to send him back where he belongs." Her teeth are stained with lipstick, and it looks like blood.

"You don't mean—"

"Oh, but I do. I've trapped him in dreams before." Her voice is low and full of anticipation. "I'm going to do it again."

16

The Mayor trapped the Nightmare Phantom in dreams.

I'd known he'd been trapped in dreams against his will, but I'd never given any thought to who had done it. Or whether they'd still be alive.

Age doesn't mean what it used to—Nightmares have changed the rules. Vampires are immortal and ageless unless killed, people become ghosts and phantoms and all sorts of things time can't touch. And, of course, what does age mean when you end up turned into a sea dragon or a cockroach? Do you keep your own age? Do you get the lifespan of the creature you've become? Something else entirely?

I have no idea what the rules are for the Nightmare Phantom himself either. He caused the Nightmares, but what caused *him*? For all I know the Mayor is another creature like him—whatever he is.

And while I'm curious what she is, that's not the pressing question right now.

"Why?" I ask, stunned. "Why do you want to put him *back*?"

The world was a *terrible* place with the Nightmare Phantom trapped in dreams. He reshaped the whole planet into something chaotic and full of disaster. I can't even imagine how the people in the before times lived, not having to worry about sea serpents eating cargo ships and rampaging dinosaurs thundering through their cities every day. Whole countries collapsed into chaos, hell, one island nation in the Pacific literally sank under the weight of someone's nightmare.

Even if the Mayor didn't know the consequences of trapping him in dreams the first time she did it, she has to now.

Why would she put him *back*?

The Mayor laughs. "He's already sent one assassin after me, and you wonder why I want to be rid of him?"

"Well, no, I get why you want to be rid of him." He's dangerous, unpredictable, and, to reiterate, *destroyed the world*. Getting rid of him makes complete sense to me. "But I don't understand why you don't just kill him?"

The Mayor raises an eyebrow. "How do you know he *can* be killed?"

That's an excellent point, I must admit.

"But he's escaped from dreams before," I say slowly. "He could again."

"And I'll just keep putting him back."

I frown, trying to understand. "But there are other ways to contain him. Better, more secure ways."

Especially for someone with her money and resources.

"Is this about money?" I hedge.

"Money?"

"You're losing money now that he's out of dreams, from the Friends' custom Nightmare business?"

She laughs. "I don't give a shit about their business." She leans forward, her eyes narrow, her voice low and threatening. "You really want to know why I want to put him back?"

I freeze from terror at the menace in her voice, but she doesn't seem to care I don't respond to her.

"Because I want to see him *suffer*."

I flinch.

Oh. I get it now. This isn't about containing him. It's not about fixing the world, or putting it back, or anything other than the fact that she wants to torture the Nightmare Phantom.

And she doesn't give a shit who else has to suffer.

I mean, I'm not surprised that it's some selfish reason about vengeance. That's pretty par for the course with people like this. And the Nightmare Phantom isn't exactly an endearing person—I'm pretty sure there's a lot of people in this city who'd torture him if they had the opportunity. He's caused a lot of pain and heartbreak over the years.

That said, I admit I feel a little bad for the Nightmare Phantom, because whatever he did to the Mayor, surely a century of madness, trapped in an unstable dream world, losing his sense of self, is enough.

From the Mayor's tone of voice, she sure doesn't think so. And I can't help but wonder what he could have done to make her hate him *this* much.

It must have been *awful*.

"What did he do to you?" I ask softly.

The Mayor shakes her head in disappointment. "How boring. What makes you think he did anything to me? Perhaps I just don't like him."

She laughs, and I have no idea if she's serious or not.

"I think we're getting a little off topic." The Mayor strolls over to Priya, still smiling. "I need to know where the Nightmare Phantom is. And you're going to tell me." She pulls a gun from her side holster and points it at Priya's knee. "Or I'll start shooting body parts off your friend."

Oh shit.

Priya stiffens, her body tensing into readiness, but her eyes are on the gun, calculating angles, clearly trying to figure out the best strategy for escape. It doesn't help that we're surrounded by the mercenaries the Director brought.

I look to the window again, hoping for an escape idea, and nearly jump out of my skin at the sight.

A giant pterodactyl stares at me.

I stumble back when I see it. Its eye is right up to the glass, flickering over the scene inside, and it opens its long beak and screeches, exposing its teeth.

"Oh, ignore her," the Mayor says dismissively.

"Kinda hard when it's right there," I choke out.

"Don't be absurd. You have a window between you." The Mayor has clearly finished with this concern. "Now, tell me where the Nightmare Phantom is before I start blowing body parts off."

"And if I do, you'll let her go unharmed?" I confirm.

The Mayor smiles, wide and toothy. "Of course."

I stare at her, mind flipping through options.

The obvious thing to do, of course, is tell the Mayor where I planned to meet the Nightmare Phantom and when. I don't give a shit about the Nightmare Phantom, and I give quite a lot of shits about Priya.

The problem is, I have no way to know that the Mayor won't just kill Priya anyway when she has the information she wants.

It's not like I can trust the woman who notoriously murders her own staffers when they're no longer useful. Who has her pet pterodactyl eat reporters when she doesn't like their questions. Who, in front of me, once shot up a street of innocent bystanders while trying to kill one of her competitors.

If I tell her what she wants to know, she's absolutely going to shoot Priya anyway.

My eyes meet Priya's, and I see the same understanding there. She knows the Mayor's reputation as well as I do, and we both know that doing what the Mayor wants is just going to get us dead faster.

Priya's eyes flick down, and I follow her gaze. Her hand is resting on the arm of her chair.

Three fingers on the chair.

Oh shit, she's not—

Two fingers on the chair.

Okay, she's totally going to—

One finger on the chair.

God, I hope she has a plan because I sure don't—

No fingers on the chair.

We explode into action.

Priya is a trained fighter, and she knows how to disarm someone, so that's what she does. She knocks the gun out of the Mayor's hand with one hand and goes for the pistol at her own belt with the other, all while managing to kick the table into one of the mercenaries reaching for their own gun.

Then she shoots the Mayor.

I expect that to be it, but the bullet bounces right off the Mayor's skin like it's made of steel, ricocheting and going through the window in a perfect, neat hole.

The Mayor is bulletproof—just like the Nightmare Phantom.

No time to dwell on that, though. We're outnumbered and outgunned, and need to get the hell out of here. I pick up my chair and smash it against the window, right over where the bullet hole has weakened the glass.

In my head, this ends with glass raining down around me and an easy way to escape.

In reality, the chair bounces off and smacks me right in the face.

I reel back from the painful attack I've inflicted on my own face, yelping in pain. One of the mercenaries is advancing on me, and I swing the chair around threateningly, as if my chair can stand up to his gun. Beside me, Priya is fighting three—no, four—people and holding her own, and I'm bleeding from my nose because of my own incompetence.

Back in school, I used to get a lot of math problems that went something like this:

A mercenary stands directly in front of Ness. On one side, her best friend is fighting four people, on the other is, a wall, and behind her is a window she can't break with an angry dinosaur on the other side. She has approximately ten seconds to figure out what to do before she ends up shot. What should she do to stay alive?

Unfortunately, I failed math.

Then I dropped out.

Maybe if I'd stayed in school, they'd have taught me how to solve this problem. Too late now though.

Something smacks against the window.

I glance, and see the pterodactyl outside, pressing its eye against the glass, watching with interest. Its iridescent scales gleam in the light.

An idea blooms.

Maybe *I* don't have to break the glass.

The mercenary comes for me, and I swing my chair with all my might, whacking it into his side and throwing him against the window where the pterodactyl watches, its eyes flicking around the chaos.

It opens its mouth, banging it on the glass where the mercenary hit, clearly wanting to eat him but foiled by the glass.

The dinosaur screeches in rage that it can't reach its food.

Then it smashes its head against the glass again.

And again.

The mercenary, clearly sensing what's about to happen, is on his feet and running from the window. Good call. No job is worth getting eaten for.

With an almighty crash, the window of the café shatters, and the pterodactyl sticks its head in, screeching bloody murder. It swings its long beak around, hunting for prey.

Priya hurls one of the mercenaries at it.

The pterodactyl snaps at its victim, grabbing it in its massive beak and then pulling its head out of the shop so that it can tip its head back and gulp the man down like a worm.

Leaving a very large hole in the glass.

I grab Priya's hand and yank her toward the window. We're running, jumping through the hole, and then we're crunching on glass, out on the pavement. I turn, ready to race down the street and away.

Priya yanks me the other way.

Toward the pterodactyl.

"Wait, Priya—"

"Come on!" she yells, clambering up the side of the pterodactyl, which is still distracted with gulping down its meal. "Let's get out of here!"

I look back at the enraged face of the Mayor as she steps out the window, her gun raised.

I climb onto the pterodactyl.

Priya yanks the reins up just as I wrap my arms around her waist, and the pterodactyl screeches and whips its massive wings out, beating the air. Anything not nailed down goes flying through the air from the sheer force of the wind its beating wings create.

Then we're up up up in the air.

And we're soaring away through the Newham skies, leaving the enraged Mayor and Director behind.

17

When I was a child, my teacher, Miss Truong, told me that there's nothing more exciting than trying something new.

She was referring to eating the cafeteria meatballs—which I maintain were sentient and plotting murder—but it was a policy she practiced in her classroom too. To her, all new knowledge was a chance for us to discover something special about ourselves or the world.

She once made us go to the top of the school and drop eggs off in various protective casings, allegedly a lesson on gravity and the transference of force.

Mostly, it taught me that things that fall go splat.

I'm thinking of her now, and how I never thought I'd be feeling sympathy for the eggs—because I'm pretty sure I'm about to splat on the pavement much more dramatically than they ever did.

I cling to Priya in abject terror, my arms wrapped around her waist like a vise. I clench my thighs around the back of the pterodactyl beneath me, but its scales are slippery and sleek, and as it soars through the air, I slide from side to side, just a little, enough to send my heart racing and to make me very certain that I am absolutely going to slide right off.

And falling would be very fatal.

We're fourteen or fifteen stories in the air, the only thing keeping us afloat the thin membrane of the pterodactyl's massive, outstretched wings. Tall skyscrapers flank us on either side, some of them rising even higher than we fly, some of their roofs visible from our height. On one roof, a ransom exchange is happening, and the people all pause and look up as we fly by, guns raised in case the pterodactyl wants a snack, then lowered as we pass and they go back to exchanging their hostage for money. We soar past windows, where bored people ignore the dinosaur flying by or, if they do notice, shut their windows so its beak can't get in.

Below us, the ground is *tiny*. Miniature autos speed down the roads, and ant-size people crowd the sidewalks. The tall buildings on all sides make looking down almost like looking through a tube, like I'm watching the world through a strange alien microscope.

Also, it makes me nauseous.

I press my face into Priya's back, trying not to vomit as the wind whips past me. The air up here smells different than on the ground. On street level, it smells like a mix of auto exhaust, whatever restaurant is nearest, along with a hint of sewer. Beneath the street, in the subways, it smells more strongly of urine, but less of exhaust and food. But up here, high in the air, it smells . . . not fresh, I can still smell smog, though it's coming from the factories rather than the cars, but there's a crispness to the air that is lacking on the ground.

I don't like it. It means that even with my face smashed into Priya's back so I can't see how high we are, I can still smell it. Still feel it on my skin.

Very rude that up here, I truly can't stick my head in the sand like I usually do.

We turn suddenly, and the pterodactyl banks, throwing me to the side, and I'm certain this is it, this is the moment I'm going to slide off its back and fall fourteen stories and splat like an egg on the Newham pavement, oh god, this is it, this is—

"Will you *please* stop screaming," Priya says in an exasperated voice. "I'm trying to steer this thing."

I clamp my mouth shut. We're through the turn and I am, in fact, not dead or at all splatted.

"Relax and enjoy the ride," Priya says, and I can hear the smile in her voice. "I got this. We're gonna be fine."

"We're not fine!" I squeak. "We're fifteen stories too high to be fine!"

Priya ignores my concerns. "Do you see the collar on this thing?"

"My eyes are closed in terror. I see nothing!"

"Ness." Priya makes an exasperated sound. "We're *fine*."

"We are *not*."

"Seriously, look at this thing."

I gather my courage, and brace myself, opening my eyes and peering around Priya's shoulder to look at the collar.

Oh. Oh, well, that certainly explains a lot.

The collar is wide, maybe a foot high, and thick, several inches of what looks like a solid steel frame. Which makes sense, given how strong this pterodactyl is, and that it probably wants to get rid of the collar. Metal chains used as reins are attached at the sides. None of that is what's unusual though.

The center of the collar is hollow, filled with clear glass tubes bursting with a bubbling green liquid. Spikes jut from the collar inward, piecing the flesh of the pterodactyl's neck in multiple places. Green fluid oozes around the open wounds.

"It's some sort of . . . drug-dispensing collar?" I say, frowning.

"I think so," Priya says, her voice serious.

Once upon a time, this pterodactyl was a person who had a nightmare, and became a flying dinosaur. The Nightmare Phantom has repeatedly claimed he can't change minds, and, on that at least, I believe him. Which means that this giant dinosaur *should* have a human mind.

The Mayor has never treated it like a human, but, well, the Mayor has never treated anyone as human. I've always been leery of the pterodactyl because it eats people. And yes, I'm pretty sure at least half the people in the city, if they turned into a pterodactyl, would eat at least a few people. Heck, if I turned into a pterodactyl, first thing I'd do would probably be eat that snake of a Director.

But still. Anything that's dangerous, anything that's terrifying, anything that's Nightmare-ish has always given me trouble. So I've never really thought much about the ptero-dactyl's circumstances.

Now I'm forced to face that no, the pterodactyl likely doesn't have some weird kink where it likes eating people, destroying things, and being ridden like a monstrous mount.

It's just drugged out of its goddamn mind.

"I'm gonna take that collar off," Priya says decisively.

"What?!"

"No one deserves to be abused like this," Priya says, slid-ing forward. "Especially not when I'm right here and can help."

I love that Priya is a good person who wants to help people.

I don't love that we're fifteen stories in the air with no seat belts.

"Not while we're flying!" I yelp. "Land us first!"

"How?"

I stare at her in horror. "You don't know how to land?"

"Of course not!" Priya raises a hand in exasperation. A hand that should, in fact, be on the reins. "Where would I have learned how to land a drugged flying dinosaur?"

"Then why did you drag us onto it?!"

"It seemed like a good idea at the time!"

Why, oh why did I follow Priya's lead? Why didn't I just run into the sewers like the cowardly rodent I am? Sure, it smells bad and there's man-eating alligator nests down there, but the city is right above and there's many places for a good coward to run.

Up here, there's no escape except the splat.

Priya nods to herself, eyes focused on the spectacular vista of Newham in front of us. "We're going to have to jump off."

"We're *what*?!" My voice rises high. "The wind must be twisting your words because I swear you just said we were going to *jump*."

"We are," Priya says amicably, leaning forward, toward the neck. "I just want to get this collar off first . . ."

"Not while we're in the air!"

But no one ever listens to me, and so, midflight, far too high in the air, Priya reaches up and tries to remove the collar. The collar, which has *actual spikes* that pierce the neck of the pterodactyl. The spikes that, when the collar is jiggled, slice into the dinosaur's flesh in a way that looks extremely agonizing—especially since the existing wounds look raw, swollen, and infected.

The pterodactyl screeches in pain.

And dives.

I scream, sliding across too smooth scales, my arms still wrapped around Priya's waist. We're both shooting forward, gravity taking control as we plummet.

I'm tipping backward, or maybe the pterodactyl is simply dropping out beneath me, because while I can still faintly feel the pterodactyl's back beneath me, I'm no longer pressed tightly against it, there's a thin layer of air between us, and it's getting thicker. I'm pulling away. My eyes are squeezed tightly shut, even though I know I need to open them, what if there's something I can grab, but I'm too scared to move, to do anything except cling tightly to my best friend's waist and hope we don't die.

The pterodactyl twists, and suddenly I'm nowhere near its back.

I'm falling.

We're falling.

I'm in the air, there's no dinosaur beneath me, only empty space, and I've still got my arms wrapped around Priya's waist in a death hold, but it won't do anything now because we're falling, oh shit, we're *falling*—

I jerk to a stop.

Priya is still clutching on to the dinosaur's collar, and I'm holding on to her, so now we're both dangling fifteen stories up from the neck of a pterodactyl, which is of course exactly where I want to be right now.

And, of course, the spikes in the collar are digging into the pterodactyl because we're both hanging from it.

"Oh god, oh fuck, oh shit." I'm just repeating a mantra of terror as I cling to Priya for dear life.

"That could have gone better," Priya admits, unconcerned by our imminent death.

I just scream wordlessly, pressing my face into my upper arm to muffle the sound.

The weight of two people hanging off the spiked collar is making the pterodactyl insane with pain. It whips its head around, shrieking to the sky, and we both swing back and forth with it, me screaming in terror, Priya yelling at it to stop, as if it's going to listen.

The pterodactyl finally twists its head down and starts snapping at us, its sharp beak way too close for comfort. I can feel the heat of its breath, smell the blood and rot of its last meal on the air. Its teeth are so close I could reach out and touch them, if I were suicidal.

Luckily for us, since we're dangling below its neck, the angle makes it almost impossible for that beak to get close enough to snap us up. That sure doesn't stop it from contorting itself through the air in increasingly elaborate twirls, trying to find a way to eat us.

We swing back and forth, an unhinged mass of chaos over the skies of Newham.

"Okay, are you ready?" Priya shouts at me.

"Ready for what?" I shriek, terrified.

"To let go."

My eyes widen and I yell, "What? NO!"

But it's already too late.

Priya has found the mechanism for the collar and unlocked it.

For a moment, we hang in the air.

Then we fall.

18

I hit the ground much sooner than I thought I would.

Probably because it's not the ground I'm hitting, but the roof of an apartment building.

I hit it with my shoulder and then roll, the rough surface of the concrete scraping my cheek, ripping my shirt, and staining my waistcoat, until finally I stop moving, lying on my back, staring up at the gray-blue sky.

I'm alive.

I can't quite believe it, and I take a hesitant breath, which, ow, what the *fuck*, that hurts. I've bruised something in my chest, and my shoulder aches, throbbing in pain from the force, and I think my knee is twisted. I'm battered all over, but at least I didn't land on my head. I can't afford to lose any more brain cells, I need the few I have.

A moment later, the collar clanks onto the rooftop about two inches from my face, nearly destroying those precious brain cells for good, and I jerk away from it, which sends another wave of pain through me.

Green fluid leaks out from the cracked glass tubes and drips off the spikes, making a toxic puddle. It's so bright it looks like it would dye my skin and hair, poison my brain until I was insane, and then kill me from cancer in a year. I know you can't judge a chemical by its color, but I absolutely am.

I edge away from it. I don't know what's in there and I sure don't want to find out.

The pterodactyl shrieks.

My head snaps up, and my body tenses, ready to run, muscle pain be damned.

Above us the pterodactyl is screaming, its mouth wide open, serrated teeth visible. It circles in the air above us, shaking its massive head as though it can still feel us hanging on it.

I surreptitiously scan the roof for places to hide, but it's flat except for a locked roof door access. Okay. So no running. If I stay very still maybe it won't notice me.

So I lie as frozen as a statue and hope that it's full from that mercenary it ate.

For once, I get lucky, and the dinosaur dips, turning away and soaring off over the jagged maw of the Newham cityscape. Its black outline is stark as it flies toward the afternoon sun, a pterodactyl-shaped silhouette against the sky.

I heave out a long breath of relief and lie flat on my back, eyes closed. I'm alive. I don't know how I'm alive, but I am. Maybe I can just lie here for a few hours, pretend I'm a rock. Nothing interesting happens to rocks. That would be nice. I should have been born a rock.

Yes, I know rocks aren't born. No, I don't care to change my metaphor.

"You alive?" Priya asks, her voice heading toward me from the other side of the roof.

"No," I tell her, unmoving.

"Oh good," she says amicably, plopping down to sit beside me. "I wasn't sure that would work."

"Please tell me you at least knew there was a building beneath us," I beg.

"Of course."

I open one eye to give her a skeptical look.

She rolls her eyes. "Look, what with all the flailing that dinosaur was doing, it was hard to tell what was beneath us, so I made a guesstimate."

I groan, covering my face with my hands. I don't want to think about how badly wrong this could have gone.

"It worked, didn't it?"

I sigh, but I have to admit, "It did work."

Priya grins, her face a little scraped, from either the fight or the fall, I'm not sure. "Damn, that was *fun*."

I make a pathetic sound of pain.

"That's the most alive I've felt in ages!" Priya continues, ignoring my squeak of protest. Her eyes are practically glowing with delight. "I've *missed* this."

I'm quiet for a moment, before I ask, "Is Nightmare Defense really that bad?"

Priya's expression falls, and she looks away. "No—no of

course not. It's just . . ."

But she doesn't finish the sentence, and I cautiously point out, "You don't have to stay, you know. You could do something else."

Priya shakes her head vigorously. "Nightmare Defense has been my dream since I was a kid. I'm not going to abandon it when I just got in!"

"Dreams can change," I tell her, thinking of how my own dreams have changed in just the past month. "Sometimes we get what we want, only to realize it wasn't what we thought it would be." I soften my voice. "It's okay to give up on one dream and make a new one."

"I know." Priya bows her head. "But I can't imagine myself doing anything other than this."

"This is Newham, there's lots of jobs—"

"But not jobs like I want," Priya interrupts. "It would be easier if I just wanted to fight, you know? Then I could join some shitty evil organization." She grimaces. "But I don't want to join a gang and beat up people who couldn't pay protection fees. Or work as a bodyguard for some mad scientist's lab, helping them kidnap people for experiments."

Priya runs a hand through her hair. "I don't mind working for terrible people—I doubt there's an employer in the city without skeletons in their closet." She holds my gaze. "But I'd like to have a job where I get to *fight* the bad guys. Not be their minion."

She spreads her hands. "Where else in Newham could I find a job like that?"

She's not wrong. Newham is a hard place to be a good person. And Nightmare Defense, for all its flaws, was one of the few places where she *could* make a difference. No one can say that killing Nightmares like the man-eating harbor kraken wasn't a good thing.

"Priya." My voice is gentle. "You're forgetting this is Newham—there's a new supervillain every day. Not all the monsters worth fighting are Nightmares."

"I suppose," she admits. "But who would pay me for it?"

I raise my eyebrows. "I'm sure the kind of people we're talking about have a lot of enemies. You just need to look for them."

She nods slowly. "Maybe."

Her eyes follow the pterodactyl flying off into the distance, a wistful smile on her face, as though she's already missing our terrifying flight on its back.

I'm sure not.

"I bet nothing in this city is as fast as that pterodactyl," Priya comments idly.

"Maybe," I say, my voice turning more serious. "But even if the Mayor and Director can't fly as fast as we did, they *could* have followed the reports coming from this part of the city of a pterodactyl with two idiots hanging off it, and then caught a taxi here."

"Hmm, good point, we shouldn't stay long."

Neither of us moves.

"We should decide next steps first," I say, not because I

believe it, but because everything hurts and I don't want to move.

"Okay," Priya says agreeably. She leans her elbows on her raised knees, staring out over the cityscape.

I'm sure it's a nice view, but I'm happy staring at the cloud above me that looks kind of like a French fry. I don't have the energy to even sit up.

"So who should we deal with first?" Priya asks. "The Mayor, or the Director?"

I don't particularly want to deal with either of them.

"What if I just . . ."

"Hide?" Priya sighs. "Ness, they're actively trying to kidnap you. They followed me to get to you. We can't do nothing about that."

I hate that she's right. "I know."

Priya looks at me expectantly. "So, do you have a plan?"

"Convince them not to kidnap me?" I hedge.

Priya just stares at me.

"I know, that's not going to happen. But if I could make them think I was already a Nightmare . . . but no. They've been kidnapping people who'd already been Nightmared too, so that wouldn't help."

"It wouldn't," Priya agrees.

"I could run," I say, and grimace. "Or hide. Just lie low for a while, not go out."

"And what if they know where you live?" Priya asks. "If they've been following me to get to you, how do you know they haven't tracked you back to Cy's place before?"

I consider this seriously. "But then why wouldn't they have come for me right after I fled the hotel? Why wait until I met with you?"

Priya concedes this point. "True."

"But you're right," I say. "If they want to find me, they will. They have resources and patience. I'm sure they could bribe the telephone company for records of who called you, and trace me that way. Heck, they could post a wanted ad in the paper with a big cash reward and the doorman could turn me in."

I pinch the bridge of my nose. "It's probably not a good idea to assume they can't find me. There's a lot of ways to track someone down, and I haven't exactly been trying to hide."

"So staying inside won't help," Priya says.

I feel like Priya's trying to lead me toward a conclusion she's long since reached, but I don't want to go there, I don't want to be told that the only way to get out of this mess is to actually do something about the Friends.

I'm just one person. One small, deeply unlucky, scared person.

I don't want to face an entire evil organization.

Even with Cy and Priya beside me, it's just so . . . big. So daunting.

And I know, I know, I've been trained to think this. Trained to see myself as small, trained to see the Friends as something big and overwhelming. I know that I've still got some mental fuckery going on in my head from my time with the Friends and taking them on probably isn't as impossible as I've been led to believe.

But it *will* be dangerous, and it would be very easy to fail.

And today has already been full of failures.

Even knowing everything they've done to me, even knowing what they plan, I don't really want to confront the Friends. I can be vengeful and petty, but that's for the small things. For the big things, the things that really hurt, that burrow deep into your soul and carve pieces out—for those, I'm not vengeful. Vengeance means engaging with the thing that causes pain, and I'd rather just bury it deep and never look at it again, run away and let time scab over the wound, rather than carving it open again and again every time you think about it while getting your vengeance.

Vengeance, to me, is about holding so tightly on to pain that it can never heal. And I don't like pain. Or hurting. Or confrontation. Or dealing with my life.

I just want to hide and pretend it doesn't exist.

But I can't do that this time. I can't hide, or run, or any of that. I mean, I could, but I'm pretty sure the Friends would find me. I don't think it's a realistic option. Not with their resources.

If they want me, they'll find me.

"Okay, okay. I get it," I concede. "We have to do something about the Friends."

"I knew you'd get there eventually." Priya grins. "So, what are you thinking?"

I have two ideas. If one of them works, I won't have to do anything about the Friends. But if it fails, and I actually have to do something, then I'll need information.

"I have an idea," I tell her. "But we need to know where their evil lair is. The place where the kidnapped people go."

Priya considers. "You know, we know someone who knows where the building is."

I instantly know who she's referring to.

"Cindy isn't going to help us," I say dryly. "Especially after she finds out I lied to her about knowing anything about the assassination attempt on her just to convince her to help me escape."

Priya rests her chin on her hand. "That was interesting, wasn't it?"

"What?"

"Well, Nightmare Defense structured a whole assassination around her," Priya says.

"So Charlie Chambers said."

She frowns deeply. "There were diplomats and gang lords and heiresses and mayoral candidates on board."

"Yeah."

"But *she* was the main target?" Priya's eyebrows rise. "Who the hell can command *that* much importance?"

I open my mouth, then close it.

She's right.

Who the hell in this city is that important?

And why would someone like that be living with the Friends?

"Maybe she's not spying," I murmur. "Maybe she's *hiding*."

Priya nods slowly. "That could fit."

"Hiding from who or what though?" I murmur.

"And why hide in the Friends, of all places?" Priya muses.

"I always figured that was personal," I say. "I mean, if she really wanted to investigate and take down an evil empire in Newham, there's better options. She could have gone for, I don't know, Koval Enterprises, or the Mayor, or one of the gangs, or even the police department."

"The Friends is pretty middle-of-the-road sort of evil, all things considered." Priya's voice is thoughtful. "For Newham, I'd honestly put it on the tame side."

Still evil enough to be trying to kidnap me though.

"Exactly," I say. "I bet they kidnapped a family member or something."

"Could be."

I think about this, and then finally say, "I don't think we have enough with this to blackmail her into helping us though."

"No," Priya agrees. "And if we tried, I give it a solid fifty percent chance she'd betray us to the Director."

"Really? Only fifty?"

Priya reconsiders. "All right, more like eighty."

"Sounds better."

Priya is silent a long moment. "This means we have to follow the Director and hope he leads us there, doesn't it?"

"Probably," I admit. "Unless you have a better plan?"

"Not really." Priya grimaces. "And it still doesn't solve the problem with the Mayor."

"I'm going to let the Nightmare Phantom handle that," I tell her.

"He doesn't seem to be handling it," Priya says dryly. "Looks like he off-loaded that to you."

I sigh. She's not wrong.

"We just got in between a pair of monsters having some sort of vendetta," I insist. "We need to get out of the way, and let them take care of each other."

Priya frowns. "How do we do that?"

"I'm supposed to meet the Nightmare Phantom later today," I tell Priya. "After last night went so wrong I was thinking of ghosting him and never reappearing, but now . . ." I run my hands through my short hair. "I don't know. Maybe I can convince him to do something."

"Sounds dangerous," Priya points out, expression worried. "You have no idea how he'll respond to you messing up last night."

"I know," I admit. "But he doesn't *seem* like the type to get mad over an accident."

"Do you know him well enough to know what type he is?" Priya asks.

"Ehh." I hold a hand up and wave it back and forth in a "so-so" motion. Priya has a point. "Probably better than most anyone else in the city."

"That's not saying much."

"I know." I rub the bridge of my nose. "So, what? You think I shouldn't go?"

Priya considers this carefully, then admits, "Honestly, I have no idea. If he actually is mad at you, he could probably find you."

"Yeah, I'm pretty sure he could turn whoever's near into a magical item to locate people if he wanted."

"So running is . . ."

"Not going to work," I agree.

Priya makes an annoyed sound. "Well, if you're going to go see him, I'm coming with."

I shake my head. "No, I don't want to add another element to the equation. I don't know how he'd react to that. Besides"—I raise an eyebrow—"didn't we agree someone has to follow the Director around to find out where the Friends' evil lair is?"

"Wait, you want *me* to do that?"

"Who else?" I ask. "I'll be busy with the Nightmare Phantom."

Priya mutters something uncharitable under her breath, then says, "Tailing him will be hard. He'll recognize me."

"So become unrecognizable," I say. "A wig, a hat, and some less stylish clothes and you could be anyone."

Priya gives me a look. "He's not that dumb."

She's probably right. "Or you could pay some of the paperboys to tail him for you."

She sighs, but it's the sigh that means I've won.

"Great." I grin at her. "I'll take care of one problem, you take care of the other, and we'll use Cy's place as our headquarters. Call him when you find anything."

Priya nods. "Fine then."

Good. Settled. Plans made.

Whether the plans will work, of course, will be another story. One I'm really not looking forward to.

I deeply regret taking the Nightmare Phantom up on his offer right now. Even though, realistically, even if I hadn't, most of this would have happened anyway. The Director still would have been at the banquet I was working at. He still would have tried to kidnap me eventually.

I guess I wouldn't have the Mayor on my back. That's something.

Priya interrupts my thoughts. "You realize what all this means though, right?"

"Which part?"

"The part where the Mayor plans to put the Nightmare Phantom back in dreams," Priya says.

Right. That.

I'd been trying not to think about it, if I'm being honest. But sticking my head in the sand, no matter how temporarily satisfying, has never once worked out in the long run for me.

"If she succeeds, the Friends' business goes back to normal." The words are heavy in my throat. "And if they kidnap me—which they will—they'll mess with my mind and drug me to sleep and turn me into . . . something."

Something I definitely don't want to be.

"Yeah," Priya says, and she's quiet.

I stare at the sky, bright and smoggy blue above me. I made a deal with the Nightmare Phantom because I hoped that I could get what was promised to me—safety, power, security. The ability to live my life without fear.

I don't know if I'll get that. I've absolutely ruined the plan, completely failed at my end. And even if somehow we make a new deal and I actually succeed in doing my part, and he honors the agreement, I don't know if him making me invulnerable would actually fix the fear that eats at my mind every day.

The more I question my own fears, my own thoughts, the more I realize my fear is a product of the Friends' manipulation—and the only way to fix it is by fixing my mind, not changing my body.

Though invulnerability still sounds nice. I can't imagine any scenario where I *don't* want that kind of ability.

But even if I don't get that ability, even if the Nightmare Phantom refuses to honor his side of the agreement—and given how badly I bombed my one task, that's a strong possibility—it will be okay. Just having him out here, in the real world? That's a win for me in and of itself.

Not just because there's fewer people turning into Nightmares in their sleep. But because as long as he's out, that means the Friends are in a world of trouble. Their entire business model runs on him being caged.

I've always thought of myself as powerless. What can someone like me, a nobody, do against an organization like the Friends?

But now, I have my answer.

I can make sure the Nightmare Phantom *wins*. I can make sure he stays out. I can make sure that the Friends don't have their key ingredient, and then I can watch as they crumble from pressure, as all the powerful people they've furnished with monsters sic those monsters against them.

I don't have to fight the Friends head-on. I don't have to be powerful, or indestructible, or rich to prevent them from destroying more lives, to completely annihilate them.

I just need to be strategic.

I exhale slowly, resolve settling into me. It doesn't matter if the Nightmare Phantom doesn't want to make me invulnerable. It doesn't matter that I don't give a shit about the Nightmare Phantom himself, or his vendetta with the Mayor.

I need to help him stay in this world.

The Friends made me afraid. I can't change that. I can't undo what's done.

But I can choose to face my fears. I can choose to try and take down the people who hurt me, and I can try and reshape my mind into someone who's less afraid. I can be brave, and in being brave, I can start the process of undoing all the mental manipulation that was done to me.

The first step is to face my fear.

And destroy it.

19

The Nightmare Phantom and I are supposed to meet in Victoria Park, the largest park in Newham, midafternoon.

It wasn't always the largest park, but most of the others have either been torn down to make way for construction or destroyed by Nightmares—one became a toxic waste dump after a radioactive slime Nightmare crawled through it—so now only Victoria Park is left.

It's a nice park, I guess, with big leafy trees that are currently patterned red and orange, and a carpet of leaves blanketing the pathways throughout. I've never really been a nature person, I prefer the careful order and containment of the city.

Also, I might have a few bad memories of this park. I haven't been back here since a traveling carnival set up in the open space when I was fourteen, and my aunt and I came to see it. The carnival turned out to be evil, and we ended up fleeing, chased by a homicidal clown through a tunnel full of horrifically mutilated guests who'd been fused with various attractions in grotesque nightmares of a different sort.

Ah, such charming memories.

The Nightmare Phantom is waiting for me right where he said he would be, in front of the turtle pond. He's got a loaf of bread and is ripping tiny pieces off and tossing them into the pond for the turtles to squabble over.

I pause before approaching, my expression softening at the scene. Maybe the Nightmare Phantom isn't so bad.

Then I see the sign next to the turtle pond. The one that warns that anyone who touches the water will be turned into a turtle.

The pond has an awful lot of turtles.

Some poor sap was turned into a turtle pond in their nightmare, and now they're forever doomed to turn strangers into turtles to swim in it. I wonder if they're still awake and aware in there, just looking out over the world, immobile and unable to speak, only to make people into turtles.

The Nightmare Phantom has had some real fucked-up ideas over the years.

He looks up at me, his ethereal white hair catching the sunlight and glittering like crystal. He rises, dusting the bread crumbs off his hands.

"Ness," he says. "I wasn't sure you were coming."

"I'm not *that* late."

All things considered, it's amazing I made it here close to on time at all. Priya and I had a devil of a time getting off that roof, mostly since after we broke down the roof door, we found the interior of the building filled with carnivorous plants that attempted to grab us and drag us down into the dark, moldy interior of the building and eat us.

We closed the roof access door and used the fire escape instead.

The Nightmare Phantom smiles, his teeth sharp and pointed. "No, I wasn't sure you'd show up because you failed last night."

I wince. "You know about that already."

"The Mayor has been quite active today. It wasn't hard to surmise."

I slump onto the bench next to the turtle pond, a healthy few feet between us.

"Yeah," I admit. "I messed up big-time."

The Nightmare Phantom sits down, and I tense, assuming he's going to slide closer to me, but he doesn't, leaving the comfortable amount of space I've set between us as is.

"So what went wrong?" he asks, his voice curious, not judgmental.

I considered before I came here what I should tell him. I could lie, try and make myself look better—but there's really no lie that makes me look good, and anyway, I always find keeping track of lies hard, so I'd rather not give him any more reasons to be mad at me.

So I tell him about how the Director interrupted me before I could get anywhere near the Mayor.

"Hmm." He shrugs. "Well, I wasn't expecting much."

I blink. "You weren't?"

"Oh no, I highly doubted this would work," he says breezily. "I just wanted to give her a good scare. Let her know I was back, and I was coming for her." His smile is mean. "It's always more fun when your enemies know you're coming, but don't know when you'll strike."

Looks like the Mayor isn't the only one who wants to torture her enemy. What a great duo. I wish I could lock them in a room to fight each other without getting me or the rest of the city involved.

But that will never happen. Newham is the sandbox of psychopaths and monsters, and somehow, it's people like me who always end up caught in the middle.

"You could have told me that before I went in," I say dryly.

"Nonsense—I'd have been even happier if you succeeded." He raises a finger and speaks as though imparting an important lesson. "Torturing your enemies is fun and all, but I could torture her just as well if you'd succeeded."

Charming.

"Well," I say, then pause. "Given your goals, I think I performed perfectly last night."

And I tell him about the Mayor showing up at the café where Priya and I were. And how the Mayor very definitely knew the Nightmare Phantom was responsible, and was planning on putting him back in dreams.

His expression cools a little as he listens to me, his black eyes glittering with malice.

"She won't get me," he hisses. "She might have tricked me last time, but not this time."

His hands are fisted on his lap, and his jaw is clenched, and for the first time, I realize it:

The Nightmare Phantom is *scared*.

He's the one who decimated the world, who can turn people into monsters or cockroaches or evil turtle ponds with only a touch, the bulletproof, unstoppable menace who terrorized the world in dreams for a century.

And he's afraid.

No, no that can't be. Sure, if he loses he'll go back to dreams and he doesn't want that, but . . . but people like the Nightmare Phantom don't get scared. They're the things other people are scared *of*.

He looks up at me, noticing my gaze. "Something wrong?"

"I—no. Of course not."

He snorts disbelievingly.

"I was just wondering." I choose my words carefully. "If you're . . . anxious about the Mayor. About the possibility that she'll win."

His lips quirk. "The word you're trying so hard to avoid is 'scared,' isn't it?"

I wince. "Are you?"

"Of course I am," he says with a laugh. "I'd be a fool not to be."

I stare at him blankly. He admitted it?

"You? Scared?" I gesture at him. "But you're—you're *you*. You're the Nightmare Phantom. You're what other people are scared *of*."

He smiles at that. "All true."

"How can you be scared when you're so powerful?" I ask.

He laughs, head tipped back, and the light catches his otherworldly silvery white hair. "No matter how powerful you are, you are always afraid of something."

I blink. "What?"

"Power doesn't make fear go away. It just changes the shape it takes." He stares at me with those endless black eyes. "When you're weak, you fear the strong taking from you. But when you're strong, you fear the weak rising up against you."

He raises a hand in a half shrug. "Power and fear are independent things. Just because I'm not afraid of the same things you are, doesn't mean I'm not afraid of *something*."

I shake my head. "Bullets literally bounce off you."

"They do," he agrees. "I'm completely invulnerable—but that doesn't mean that I can't be sealed in a cement coffin and thrown to the bottom of the ocean, does it?"

I blink, then really think about that. The horror of that, being trapped in the dark, sunk alone in the depths for the rest of eternity. Trying to move but being unable to, trying to die but being trapped. Slowly, inexorably going insane.

Honestly, I think I'd rather be shot.

"I know fear better than anyone." He smiles slowly, a knowing expression. "I know every fear people have, even the ones they don't consciously realize they have. And the truth about fear?" He leans toward me, voice lowered. "Is that everyone is afraid."

He leans back, his expression amused. "Fear is universal."

I want to deny it, to tell him he's wrong. That I know

people who aren't afraid, like Priya.

But that's not true. Priya *is* afraid—she's just not afraid of death or pain. She's afraid of something happening to those she loves. She's afraid that her dreams are collapsing in on her and she'll never live the life she wants.

Priya's fears are very different from mine. But they're still there.

"Fear is in the mind, not the body," the Nightmare Phantom says. "To fear is to be alive."

I curl my hands into fists. On some level, I already knew that—everyone is afraid, at least some of the time. The existence of so many Nightmares is proof of that.

But somehow, I feel like my fears have always been *worse*. They consume me, often to the point of irrationality. Like my fear of Nightmares—I ran from people who did nothing to me, had no intention of doing anything to me. I still do sometimes. It's not logical, not rational, just an instinctive fear response. I can't even live a normal life because my constant terror ruins everything.

Other people don't seem to have that. They seem to function fine, even when they're afraid. They don't run screaming when they see someone with too many tentacles. Even when they're scared, they don't behave like the world is ending, they do smart things like pick up weapons or call for help. They're still in control, even when they're afraid. It's like the fear is a part of them, but it wholesale consumes me.

That's why I've always felt like my fear is somehow worse. But now, I have to pause and wonder—is it worse? Or have I just never been given the tools to deal with it? Did the trauma of my sister murdering my father, the mind manipulation of the Friends, my terrible practice of hiding from all my problems—did that strip me of my ability to cope?

Maybe facing your fear is like a callus. If you never face it, your skin breaks and bleeds if you poke it. But if you poke it often, it calluses over and doesn't bleed.

Or maybe we're all bad at facing our fears, and I've simply been so consumed by my own problems, I just never really notice other people's. Despite the way I put my friends on pedestals, none of them have been facing their fears either. Cy has been avoiding his father's new film, and his father, even though he wishes he could stop his crimes. Priya has been sticking with Nightmare Defense even though she's unhappy, afraid to quit something she's dreamed about for so long.

Maybe I'm not the only one running from my fears.

"How do other people handle fear?" I ask the Nightmare Phantom, staring at the ground. "Because I've been doing a shit job of it."

"Have you?" He seems surprised. "I think you've been doing quite well actually."

I look up at him, baffled. "What makes you think that?"

"Well, you've certainly improved since our first meeting," the Nightmare Phantom says, his head tilted, almost birdlike in its angle. "Three Nightmares have walked by while we've sat on this bench, and you haven't cared. The first time I met you, you'd have been running at the sight of them."

That's true.

"I'm still afraid of them though. I can just control that fear better," I point out.

He raises an eyebrow. "If you always look ahead, and never look behind, you'll never realize how far you've come."

I open my mouth, then quietly close it. He's right. I've been so focused on how I'm still not the person I wish I were, I haven't really looked at the person I used to be.

Am I happy with the progress I've made?

Yeah, I realize. I am. I *have* come a ways, and I'm proud of it. Maybe I'm not where I want to be, but I'm on my way there.

I let out a long breath. I can't believe I'm taking life advice from the Nightmare Phantom. Things must be really dire.

"Do you ever look behind?" I ask.

He laughs. "It's harder for me."

"Why?"

"I don't remember much of the behind," he says. "Living in dreams made it hard to hold on to myself. My identity eroded away, day by day, my memories sanded down until only a vague impression remained." His black abyss eyes shift to me. "And then people's nightmares filled in the rest."

Well, that's just disturbing as all hell.

"So my past? Aside from the few pieces I managed to cling to, it's gone," he says conversationally, his tone far too light for something so terrible. "You know, I don't even remember what I looked like."

Which explains why there's been so many different descriptions of him over the years, his appearance shifting and morphing based on the dreamer. Not even he knew—so it changed based on the dream.

"Oh" is all I can manage to say. What can you even say to something that horrifying? To have completely washed away your mind with a constant deluge of other people's hallucinations?

That's a very different kind of terrifying.

He grins, sharp teeth red in the light of the smoggy sun. "Just so."

I try and imagine who he would have been before, but I can't even picture it. I think of what he must have been like as a child, sly and clever, pulling pranks, but the image won't hold. There's only him now, with his inky black eyes and sharp smile, and the joy he finds in making other people into their fears.

I wonder what the person he was before he was trapped in nightmares would think of him now. Would he be horrified by what he'd become? Or was the creature who went into nightmares much worse?

I don't know. Probably, I'll never know. The world has changed him, broken pieces off him, just like it has everyone else. We're all made up of the pieces of ourselves we've managed to reassemble.

I'm not the same girl who laughed with her sister over birdhouses, who dreamed of following her sister everywhere. I'm the person stitched together after her sister's brutal death, glued with the blood of our murdered father.

It's not that either me or the Nightmare Phantom isn't

ourself—we are. Most of the pieces are us, but now they're slightly off, or in some cases in a different place than they used to be, and held together by outside experiences.

"What is the Mayor?" I ask. "That she can send you into dreams?"

"She's human." He laughs. "Or she was."

"Then how did she get this power?"

His lips curl up, but it's not a smile. "Because I gave it to her."

20

I stare at him, stunned.

I'm not sure what I expected—maybe that the Mayor was the same kind of creature as him, that all of this was some overdramatic family feud between bulletproof monsters, like one sees in the penny novels. Or that she'd discovered some sort of weapon or arcane spell or—I don't know.

I just know I wasn't expecting this.

"You . . . *gave* her the power to trap you in dreams?" I clarify, not quite certain I've heard right.

"Well." His lips twist in a crooked smile. "It wasn't *meant* to be that. That was an . . . unintentional side effect."

Unintentional side effect. That's a nice way of saying that he gave her a power that destroyed his life and decimated the entire world order.

"What power *did* you give her, then?" I ask. What could have a side effect of sending people into dreams?

"I changed her so that she could send the things that frighten her away." He shrugs, seemingly unconcerned. "I didn't really specify *where*."

I lick my lips and say, choosing my words as delicately as possible, "You didn't think, when you changed her to be able to send things she was afraid of away, that you would be included in that?"

"No, I didn't." His smile quirks, and he raises his eyebrows as he looks at me. "I didn't think she was afraid of me."

I stare at him a long time as my mind slowly turns over what he's said, and what that actually means. What kind of person he'd assume wasn't afraid of him.

"You were friends," I say.

I don't say "lovers," though I'm definitely thinking it. But people tend to get testy when you accuse them of being in bed with their mortal enemy, and anyway, I would hope if you're lovers you're also friends, so really, the broad terms work better.

"Yes, we were . . . friends," he says, neither confirming nor denying my personal theory. He tips his head back to look at the smoggy sky. "Or at least, I thought we were."

I'm surprised to find an emotion tugging in my chest—pity.

I don't think I've ever empathized with the Nightmare Phantom as much as I do right now. Both of us have been betrayed by people we've trusted—him by the Mayor, and me by the Director. No matter what the Nightmare Phantom's done, or whether or not the Mayor was justified in betraying him, there's nothing as exquisitely heartbreaking as being stabbed in the back by people you trust.

"It was a gift," he says, lips twisting into a warped smile. "The change."

"A gift?" I repeat skeptically.

The Nightmare Phantom has always been up front about how he believes he's doing people a favor when he changes them; he claims he makes people strong enough to face their fears. I just thought it was utter bullshit, since he also admitted he loves to change people just because he gets joy from imagining the sheer chaos they'll cause.

There's nothing that prevents both of those things from being true, though. He can change people for multiple reasons.

But if I were his "friend" and he surprised me by turning me into something to "help me" without asking, I'd be . . . well, perhaps not "I will torture you for centuries"–level enraged, but honestly, it would depend on what the change was.

"Did she . . . ask for this gift?" I prod.

"Yes."

Oh. All right, not one of his unwanted surprise gifts then.

But wait—if she asked for it, does that mean she was planning to get rid of him all along? That she picked what he should change her into specifically to hurt him with it?

That's both incredibly clever and incredibly messed up.

Which is, when I think about it, how one would describe much of the Mayor of Newham's tenure.

"Why?" I ask. "Why did she send you away?"

He shakes his head. "I don't know."

I raise an eyebrow, skeptical. "Really?"

"Really," he says, quirking his mouth. "I know what you're thinking. That I did something worth sending me away for. Perhaps I did." He waves it away. "But I don't remember. It's all gone. All I have left is the moment of betrayal. The rest has been sanded away over the years."

I grimace. I don't know whether I believe him. This no memory thing is *awfully* convenient—but then again, he could just as easily have lied and said he didn't do anything.

I definitely wouldn't have believed that though.

A nicer person than me would probably reserve judgment, but honestly, I've seen enough consequences of the Nightmare Phantom and his boredom and twisted idea of fun over the years that I am not inclined to give him the benefit of the doubt when it comes to wronging people.

He definitely fucked shit up and then faced the consequences.

"So why did she say she wanted to be changed?" I ask.

"Oh." He blinks, and gives me a look like I've asked the most obvious question in the world. "The war."

"War?" I echo.

We don't really learn much about the world before Nightmares. Or, well, we might actually, but it's not like I was a particularly good student. And that was when I cared about the subject—which I definitely didn't when it came to history.

My knowledge of history is there was a world before Nightmares, and a world after. That's it.

"You think my Nightmares are bad," he says. "But have

you ever crouched in a bomb shelter as missiles, hundreds of them, rain from the sky with devastating power? Or had your windpipe melted by breathing in mustard gas?"

"No."

I try to imagine it, but I just can't. We have random Nightmare attacks that destroy the city, buildings toppling as monsters storm through them, liquid lava decimating parks. But hundreds of explosives falling from the sky . . . I suppose that would cause more destruction than a few giant Nightmares on the loose.

"For someone who claims he can't remember his past, you seem to remember a lot about what living in this war was like," I comment dryly.

"Of course I do," he says agreeably. "It featured in people's nightmares for decades after it ended."

Oh. Well, yes, actually that does make sense.

"My personal life"—he grins—"unsurprisingly did not."

"I can't imagine why," I deadpan.

He laughs, his grin stretched wide.

I surprise myself by smiling a little with him. What is the world coming to? Sitting here having a laugh with the embodiment of what was my worst fear for most of my life. Maybe he's right—I am braver. Or maybe just less afraid. Maybe both.

"There's still one thing I don't understand," I say. "You said the Mayor's ability was to put the things she feared somewhere else. That's how she put you in dreams. But when

I met you in the dream world, you had a whole list of instructions for getting out. That didn't come from nowhere."

"Ah." He smiles too wide. "You didn't think you were the first dreamer I'd bargained with, did you?"

I hadn't thought about it, to be honest.

"I've made deals with dozens of people over the years. Sometimes they couldn't fulfill their side because the power I gave them didn't work the way I'd hoped. Sometimes they woke and backed out of the deal. Only one honored her side." He considers. "Well, she tried, anyway."

"Tried?"

"Yes, I'd made her into a bargain witch," he explains. "For the price of your eye, you could be made to live forever. That kind of thing. It was based on a fairy tale that terrified her as a child."

He raises a black-nailed hand in a half shrug. "But it was an ability with limits. The exchanges needed to be things that she felt were equivalent. So she created a bargain for me, that since I'd been put in the cage by a human, I had to have a human help me get out."

His gaze shifts to me, and he smiles knowingly. "You saw that bargain for yourself."

I shake my head. "That's . . . complicated."

"But it worked!" He grins at me, delight dancing in his face, a sort of chaotic gleam. "I'm out!" His expression becomes serious for a moment, something angry and vicious in it. "And I'm *not* going back."

I shiver at the tone of his voice, but I can't say I blame him. I wouldn't want to be trapped in dreams either.

"So what will you do about the Mayor?" I ask, because, at the end of the day, as interesting as all of this has been, that's why I came here.

To make sure he's going to get rid of the Mayor before she hunts me down again.

His smile widens, his sharp teeth somehow seeming longer and sharper.

"Would you like to see?" he asks, turning his inky black eyes on me. "I have quite the event planned."

"Ah, no thank you." I smile awkwardly. "As long as you have plans to get rid of her, that's all good with me."

I'm already stuck between two homicidal psychopaths at war with each other. I don't need to actually *be* there for their confrontation. In fact, I'd rather not be within a seven-mile radius of their confrontation.

"I insist," the Nightmare Phantom says, still smiling, but his words are iron. "Come see the show!"

Fear makes my heart beat fast and hard, and I debate saying no again, just running off. But if the Nightmare Phantom wants me there, he'll find a way to make sure I'm there. And I doubt I'll like the way he escorts me if I run now.

"Of course." I smile, a little wobbly, my fear tucked inside. "Let's go see the show."

21

The last mayoral debate of the season is occurring this after-noon. Not that there's many candidates to debate anymore.

But it's the one place the Mayor is certain to be. Everyone knows that—including the Nightmare Phantom.

And, I suppose, any of her other enemies that are still alive.

The debate is being held in Newham Central Square. It's directly in front of the infamous clock tower and across the street from the Mayoral Palace. The plaza is wide and cobbled in a style that is blatantly meant to look like Italy, complete with a carved marble statue of naked people splash-ing in stone water.

Looming over the plaza, the clock tower rises up in the background. The building itself is not actually that tall, it's long and opulent, one of the oldest surviving buildings in the city. Naturally, it houses some corrupt government office, whoever can bribe the most at any given time. But the clock tower on the end of it is the part that's famous, and it rises high above the rest of the building, and high above even many of the surrounding buildings. It must have been spectacular when it was first built, the tallest point in the city. Now, taller, more modern buildings have grown up around it. But the clock tower still has an ageless charm.

For an exorbitant fee, you can climb to the top, and I've heard the view is spectacular.

I've never gone up. Partly because of the cost, and partly because it's the one thing in Newham my sister always wanted to see, and every time I think of going up, it feels like a betrayal, because Ruby's not here to come with me.

I wonder sometimes what she'd think of all this. In many ways, she died saving me, and I never even knew it. It feels like a betrayal of her memory to be as much of a screwup as I am. Ruby wouldn't have been a screwup. She'd never have ended up in my situation.

But she's gone, and only me and my messes are left.

A podium has been set up in front of the clock tower, on the far side of the plaza, and massive cameras are being wheeled around by several people, setting up for the coming broadcast. Reporters, sound technicians, and security all buzz around the setup, their movements fast and frenzied. These televised debates are always a big hit—everyone likes to see murder and carnage from the safety of a distance.

It always amazes me, how much of a spectacle all this is. It reminds me of a beauty pageant, all the contestants strutting across the stage, basking in the spotlight, people voting on the shallow surface things they can see.

Not that there's much else to vote on. Newham politicians' policies are all essentially the same, something along the lines of "I'm here to make myself rich at the expense of you, the people."

That's why I always vote for the joke candidate.

Cy, of course, went carefully through every single candidate's platform and picked the one he liked most. I didn't have the heart to tell him the candidate was already dead.

The Nightmare Phantom has led me into an apartment building on the side of the square. We're in a two-bedroom suite on the fifth floor, with a large window that has a gorgeous view overlooking the square. The apartment is reasonably well appointed, but nowhere near the lush opulence one sees in the wealthier parts of town—rich people tend to stay away from areas of the city where fighting regularly occurs, and Newham Square is one of those places. Still, this is far from the squatters' dens you find near the factories. It's somewhere in the middle. The furniture is all older but well taken care of, and the rooms are tidy and pleasant. The owner, however, is nowhere to be found.

I don't ask what happened to him.

The Nightmare Phantom pulls up a recliner in front of the window, and another for me.

"Sit," he says, taking his own advice and relaxing into the chair. "The show's about to start."

I sit, tentatively, just on the edge of the chair, ready to run at any moment. Whatever he's got planned, it's likely going to be messy—and I doubt it'll be contained to the square.

And unlike the Nightmare Phantom, I'm not indestructible.

I try and think positively. If the Nightmare Phantom can

take out the Mayor, that's one major enemy off my list. I don't know if he'll still make me invulnerable, but even if he *doesn't*, the Friends won't have any reason to kidnap me anymore, since they won't be able to make me into a Nightmare. If things go well today, I can finally be free of all my problems in one fell swoop.

Well, my current problems.

The Mayor arrives in style, as she always does, lounging on the roof of a motorcar that plows through the crowd of camera people, hitting at least two who can't get out of the way fast enough. She raises one hand, waving to everyone, mouth stretched in a smile. Beside her, a machine gun is artfully spread across the roof, as though lounging with her, but her hand rests casually on the handle, and I'm sure that she could have that up and firing in less than a second if she needed to.

A part of me expected her to fly in on her now signature pterodactyl, even knowing that Priya and I stole it and set it free. Her image is that strongly associated with it these days. Which, now that I think about it, losing that piece of her image probably made the Mayor even more mad at us.

Oops.

"Have any of my opponents shown up?" the Mayor asks the crowd as she hops off the auto and mounts the stage.

Silence.

"None of them?" she eggs, laughing. "Are they cowards, too scared to show their faces to me?"

214

I think of myself and the Nightmare Phantom, sitting here, hidden away and observing. I glance at the Nightmare Phantom, who seems unperturbed by her catcalls.

"You're wondering why I don't go down there myself," the Nightmare Phantom says casually.

"Ah, I mean, I wasn't—"

"Normally, I would, of course," he says, still watching the event. "But unfortunately, her power works by sight."

"Sight?" I echo.

"Anything she sees that she's afraid of, she can send away."

"But." I hesitate. "Does she know what you look like now?"

He considers this carefully, and then says simply, "I don't know. I'm not sure how much I've diverged from my original appearance." He smiles, his teeth sharp. "But she'd figure it out quite quickly if I was down there turning people into monsters, wouldn't she?"

He has a point.

Or maybe he's just making an excuse to justify hiding away. After all, I make excuses to hide away from things I'm afraid of too. And I also convince other people to solve my problems for me.

I'm doing it right now.

Maybe the Nightmare Phantom and I are more similar than I care to admit.

A gunshot thunders through the square.

I whip my head back toward the stage, my eyes wide. But

215

nothing has changed, the Mayor is still standing boldly on the stage, the crowd around her.

Maybe the bullet bounced off the Mayor like Priya's shot and I didn't even notice. Rare good luck it didn't ricochet into anyone in the crowd though.

Then I see the napkin.

It's black, just like the one the Nightmare Phantom gave me, and it *did* land on its target, the Mayor—it just landed on her stomach, the black silk of the napkin itself barely visible against the black of her tuxedo.

She strips off her jacket, flinging napkin and jacket into the crowd. People move out of the way quickly, even though they clearly don't understand what the napkin is. But any good Newhamite knows that when one person doesn't want something, it's probably a good idea not to get too close. There's a reason we have the saying "one man's trash is another man's murderer."

Though that saying might have actually come from someone turning into a garbage bin Nightmare and devouring people who hurled trash into him. I feel like I read that in the paper once.

Despite the camera people and technicians scrambling to get away from the tuxedo jacket, it's too crowded to move anywhere quickly, and one unfortunate man gets hit by the napkin.

The napkin gloms onto his neck, and he screams, reedy and terrified.

Unlike with the Director, this napkin doesn't have far to

crawl. It seesaws like a caterpillar, sliding up the man's neck and over his face. The man claws at it with increasing desperation, trying to rip it off as it covers his whole face, muffling his screams.

Then it crawls into his mouth.

He falls to his knees, choking, gagging, trying to pull it out of his throat even as his eyes roll in panic. But the napkin can't be stopped, and it vanishes inside him—

Only to pop out again.

Through his eye sockets.

His eyeballs pop out like horrible marbles, rolling across the cobblestones, before tumbling into a sewer grate. The napkin bursts from the empty eye sockets, like a terrifying black flower, blooming in the gore.

It continues blooming, getting larger and larger, even as the man shrinks and shrivels, desiccating like a mummy, like the napkin is absorbing his life to grow, until the napkin is so large that the man can't be seen at all anymore, his body wrapped in a tight cocoon of black silk.

Once the man is entirely wrapped, the napkin falls still, and both body and the napkin wrapped around it lie peacefully in the middle of the square, unmoving.

I turn away in disgust.

The Nightmare Phantom leans forward eagerly, grinning ear to ear. "Here we go."

The Mayor sneers at the crowd, her eyes roving the assembled people, who mostly are still focused on the horrifying cocooned man.

"Nice try," she yells, her grin fierce and angry. "But you'll have to do better than that!"

The Nightmare Phantom leans back and smiles. "Oh, I will."

From the streets around the square, people pour in. They're all dressed in a uniform of white jackets and waistcoats, with a single bloodred lapel. Uniform color coding like that means only one thing—a gang. And with the white suits and red lapels, I know exactly which gang.

The Montessauri gang.

Somehow, the Nightmare Phantom has convinced the Montessauri gang to take on the Mayor. And every single one of them is armed with a massive weapon that rests on their shoulder, that looks almost like a rocket launcher, but not quite. The muzzle is a little too narrow, the metal too matte and strangely textured, not like the standard Koval rocket launcher at all.

Yes, I can recognize a rocket launcher on sight. I suspect most Newhamites can.

The thing that really confirms that they're not rocket launchers of the regular kind is that they're not shooting bullets or explosives.

They're shooting napkins.

My eyes widen as a black cloud of silk arcs over the square. That's a *lot* of napkins.

"Are all the napkins people?" I ask the Nightmare Phantom.

"Hmm?" He tips his head. "No, of course not. That would have been far too tedious."

Oh, all right then.

"All the rocket launchers are."

Ah. Yes. Of course. Silly me.

The Mayor doesn't seem to be having any trouble dodging the napkins. She's jumped into the panicked crowd of people trying to flee, and grabbed someone to use as a human shield. When that person is too covered with napkins, she discards them and grabs another unfortunate victim.

Of course, many of the napkins miss their target and are decimating the bystanders anyway.

I don't think most of the camera crew, technicians, and security that are working today will survive this.

"Wouldn't it have been easier," I hedge, looking at the carnage below, "to just . . . not let the Mayor know you were coming? Hit her with a napkin thing from behind, then wait until she was cocooned to drop her to the bottom of the ocean?"

The Nightmare Phantom turns to me. "Well, I suppose that would have been *easier*." He grins, teeth sharp and wide. "But nowhere near as *fun*."

Right. I forgot who I'm talking with. Of course he had to choose the most chaotic, deadly route. Because his warped idea of fun supersedes all else.

This is Newham, and practicality is always thrown out the window for showmanship.

The ground begins to tremble.

My head jerks up, but it stops.

Then it trembles again.

Stops.

Then again.

I stiffen. I know this pattern. I know what this means.

I turn to the Nightmare Phantom in horror, but he's leaning forward, a manic, delighted grin on his face, anticipation writ across his whole body.

And the Tyrannosaurus rex steps into the plaza.

It's at least ten stories tall, much bigger than a real T. rex would have been. It's scaled, rather than feathered, again, a divergence from reality. Its scales are a vivid green that remind me of the Director, and its massive head swings back and forth as it paces forward, huge clawed feet crushing the tiles beneath it and leaving crumbled brick footprints behind.

It roars, mouth open wide, all those deadly teeth on display.

"How," I whisper quietly, leaning away from the window, my hands fearful fists on my knees, "is that going to help?"

"Oh, I doubt it will," the Nightmare Phantom says. "But when I told Giovanni Montessauri I wanted him to kill the Mayor with my weapons, he said he'd only do it if I gave him a pet just as interesting as hers."

Of course he did. Naturally. The villains are constantly attempting to outdo each other.

And now that I'm looking, I can see Giovanni Montessauri, a tiny red-suited dot riding just behind the T. rex's head, laughing as he yells orders at it, reveling in the chaos he's causing.

I don't know why I expected anything different.

Right now, one of the most powerful sociopathic gang lords in the city is wielding magical weapons and riding a T. rex down the street trying to kill the Mayor, an indestructible psychopath, because the most feared creature in the world and she are in some hate spiral of "who can ruin the other one's life the most?"

And somehow, I'm in the middle.

Why do I keep ending up caught in this shit?

The square is a sea of chaos. Black cocoons dot the square, each one a victim of this insane war, and even more bodies are being squashed by the T. rex trampling the crowd. The Mayor has also been retaliating against the gang with her machine gun, so dead gang members litter the square in almost as many numbers as napkin cocoons.

The Mayor hefts her machine gun, a vicious grin on her face as she eyes the T. rex.

Then she runs for it.

Her gun is firing as she circles its legs, embedding them with hundreds of bullets. The giant dinosaur screeches in agony. Even if the bullets are small compared to the T. rex, they're destructive in such huge quantities.

Giovanni Montessauri, perched on the T. rex shoulders, fires down with his napkin launcher at the Mayor, but she's too quick, and the napkin launcher doesn't fire as fast as the machine gun.

Both the Mayor and Giovanni Montessauri are laughing.

So is the Nightmare Phantom.

Psychopaths, all three of them. How they can all be laughing like this is a grand old fun time is beyond me.

The T. rex sways from all the bullet holes in its legs, and then falls to its knees, with so much force that it feels like an earthquake, the ground shaking so hard that buildings tremble, and I grab on to the windowsill in terror, wondering if the whole building is going to come down on me.

The plaza shudders under the weight—

And cracks.

The T. rex jerks as the ground splits, and it falls downward, the weight of it too much for the earth to handle as it falls right into the subway station directly below the plaza.

I guess I won't be taking the subway home.

The Mayor grins, dropping her machine gun and scooping up a fallen napkin launcher. She hoists it onto her shoulder, takes aim, and fires.

Right into the T. rex's face.

Napkin after napkin pummels it, and it roars its rage, tiny arms scrabbling uselessly in front of it, as the napkins swarm into its mouth. Dozens of them now, all of them choking their way into its sinus system and down its throat, life-sucking pieces of silk like parasitic plants.

I look away before I have to see the result, but I can still hear.

The sound when they burst from its eyes can only be described as *juicy*.

With a final whimpering roar, the T. rex is taken off the playing field. When I look back, all that's left is a huge crater in the square, and a giant black silk-wrapped body.

Giovanni Montessauri is nowhere to be seen. I don't know if he ran off, or if he was encased in the black silk napkins too.

The Mayor stands in the center of the destroyed square, surrounded by rubble, corpses, and gore. She whoops into the air, head tipped back.

"Is that all you've got?" She laughs.

The Nightmare Phantom's eyes narrow.

"I know you're here!" she yells. "You'd never miss a chance to watch this. Don't you want to come out and join the chaos?"

I can tell the Nightmare Phantom does, his body straining forward. But he doesn't move.

I don't blame him. Going out right now would be suicide.

"If you won't come out," the Mayor says, expression twisting into a grin full of malicious anticipation, "I'll *make* you come out."

She strolls back to the car she drove in on. The driver is dead, lying half in, half out of the car with a bullet wound in his head. She reaches past him and pulls something large out of the back seat.

An actual rocket launcher.

She hoists it onto her shoulder and twirls around for the empty plaza to see.

Oh *shit*.

Then she starts firing.

Her first strike is to the apartment building to the left of the one we're in. The blast is massive, a single burst of explosive flame, shattering all the windows, and then, like a child's set of building blocks, the entire building collapses in on itself, crumbling into a cloud of dust and broken pieces. Flames and smoke still bloom from the rubble, but the building itself is now nothing more than a pancake-shaped pile of debris on the ground.

It happened in seconds.

I stare at it for a heartbeat, unable to believe it.

And then I'm on my feet and running.

"Sorry," I call to the Nightmare Phantom as I race for the door. "But unlike you, I'm not invulnerable."

Too late.

The floor trembles beneath me, quivering like the first drift of snow before an avalanche, and I understand, with a certainty deep in my bones, I don't have time to go down the stairs and out. I have seconds before the bomb goes off and this whole thing comes down in a fiery inferno.

I dive for the window.

The ceiling cracks, it's coming down, and I can feel the heat of the fireball coming up through the stairwells and halls, barreling toward this room. I can almost hear it.

I leap for the window, even though we're five stories high, even though that's a death drop, even though I can't possibly survive it.

But it's better than being crushed alive in a building and then cooked by the heat.

Before I have a chance to question what I'm doing, I've grabbed the Nightmare Phantom's arm, dragging him into the open air with me.

Later, I'll wonder what the hell I was thinking. If I was thinking of rescuing him, even though he didn't need rescuing, what with him being indestructible. Or if I was remembering that he was indestructible and thinking of using him as a buffer between me and the ground, a subconscious desire to survive by using whatever was nearest to me.

The truth is, I'm still not sure. It was an instinct, and whatever thought process was behind it was too fast for me to comprehend.

But I yanked him out the window with me.

And we fell.

The ground hit him first, because I had the presence of mind to twist us in the air so he was on the bottom and I was pressed against him. He crashed into the ground with the kind of force that would have killed me. Lying on top of him when we landed, all it did was knock the wind out of me.

Dragging him with me *definitely* saved my life.

But not his.

Two people leaping out a window in an empty square draws exactly the notice that the Nightmare Phantom had been hoping to avoid.

The Mayor strolls forward. Her boot heels click on the broken pavement, and I look up blearily to find her looking down at me and the Nightmare Phantom.

The Nightmare Phantom looks right back up at her,

eyebrows raised, silky, thin white hair tangled with dirt and debris, but his expression unruffled.

The Mayor smiles, teeth perfect and even and white, her face up close even more flawless. She looks real good for someone over a century old.

"I like the monochrome look," she tells the Nightmare Phantom casually. "It suits you. Brown eyes were always too boring for someone like you."

"I'm so glad you approve," he replies dryly. "I picked it just for you."

She snorts, then says, smile as smug as a cat that's caught a mouse, "It's been fun. It's always fun when I win."

She laughs.

For a moment, a horrible moment, the world around me is still, as though waiting. The Nightmare Phantom opens his mouth, but whatever he was going to say, I'll never find out.

Like dust in the wind, he dissolves into sparkles.

The air where he once lay glitters and sways, warping like water, before settling back into normalcy, leaving only an empty space, no sign that anyone was ever there. As though he never existed, as if he really were a phantom, nothing more than a ghost or a dream.

The Nightmare Phantom has lost.

He's back in his cage of dreams.

22

I lie on the broken pavement, my throat choked from the dust of the collapsed buildings around me.

The Nightmare Phantom lost.

The Mayor looks down at me, her smile victorious, as she leans back to laugh.

"He really thought he had a hope in hell of beating me. Me!" She grins down at me. "His ego was always his worst enemy."

I don't say anything, just stare up at her with huge eyes and hope she's in such a good mood she forgets how I stole her pet pterodactyl and freed it. Or if she does remember, that she decides I'm not worth killing.

But honestly, a good mood might make her want to kill me more.

She looks down at me like I'm some sort of bug beneath her feet, as though she's wondering if I'm worth the effort of squishing.

Behind her, a loud groan echoes through the empty square, followed by a slow crunch as the podium finally collapses into the massive cavern left in the square, broken pieces of wood tumbling into what was once the subway station.

The Mayor turns at the sound, and I don't miss my chance.

I bolt to my feet and *run*.

The Mayor may be able to send people all sorts of places with her sight, but the Nightmare Phantom was pretty clear she could only do that to people she feared, and she sure isn't afraid of *me*. And without her pterodactyl, she can't outrun me.

The real question is if she can unholster her gun and shoot me before I get out of her sight line.

Sweat beads the back of my neck as I stumble over crushed pavement blocks, shattered in the imprint of the T. rex's footprint. I scrabble over pieces of rubble, ignoring all the bruises and scrapes on me in an effort to get away as fast as possible. Scrapes heal. Death, not so much.

A gunshot fires behind me.

But I'm around the corner in time. A chunk of the side of the building I just turned past comes flying off from the force of the bullet hitting it, and I try very hard not to think about how if I'd been a few seconds slower, that would have been my head.

Too late. The image is already in my brain, and it's never coming out.

Fear makes me fast, and I run, weaving through the streets of Newham, so fast that in another life, I might have been a professional sprinter. On my home ground, the winding, confusing streets of Newham, few humans can catch me.

But the Mayor isn't human, not really.

So I do evasive maneuvers, darting into one of the subway entrances and using the underground tunnels to twist around so I'm going in a different direction. One of the paths is blocked by the destruction the T. rex caused, and the whole thing is probably unstable right now too, but I move quickly, trying not to think about how structurally sound it is and whether it will all crash down on me.

It's quite a while and many blocks later that I finally slow, letting my pace return to something resembling normal, assured that the Mayor isn't going to pop up out of nowhere and murder me.

I lean against a wall and take stock. I'm not that badly hurt, just a little sore pretty much everywhere from my various escapades. I'll survive.

For now.

But probably not for long. The Friends will be coming for me soon, now that the Nightmare Phantom has been trapped in dreams again.

A part of me still can't believe it.

The Nightmare Phantom *lost*.

I don't know why it's so hard for me to accept. I knew it was possible, he'd *told* me it was possible. I'd known he'd been trapped before, so of course he could be trapped again.

I just hadn't thought it would happen.

In my mind, the Nightmare Phantom is something akin

to a force of nature. Sure, he has a body and a face now, but for most of my life he was nothing more than an amorphous concept, something I feared, something intangible and unstoppable that devastated the world.

But he's not. He is a person. A particularly psychopathic person, in a long-standing Newham tradition, but a person nonetheless.

And people can lose.

By the time I make my way back to Cy's apartment, it's nearly sundown.

I'm exhausted beyond words when I stumble through the door, and I promptly kick my shoes off and slump onto the couch.

Cy looks up at me, eyebrows raised. He's got several old newspapers in his hands, which he'd obviously been clearing out to put in the recycling. The paper facing me is a special on the Koval family, complete with dozens of pictures of the missing Koval heir with her family, or laughing with friends, or posing in boardrooms. She's tall, with waist-length golden hair and a sneaky grin, as though enjoying flouting style norms. Which is fine—rich people don't have to worry about all that long hair getting in their way when they're running for their lives.

"Ness," Cy says, putting the papers down. "You look *terrible*."

"You flatterer."

His eyes crease in concern. "I thought you were just going to meet Priya for lunch? That's what your note said."

I groan, flopping back into the seat. "Oh, boy, do I have a story to tell you."

It takes me a while to go over everything that's happened. Cy eventually has to sit down, and he stares at me with mounting horror as I go over disaster after disaster, until finally, throat dry and aching from exhaustion, I reach the end of the story of "Ness's Terrible Day Out," also titled "A Treatise on Why Ness Should Never Leave the Apartment."

When I'm done, Cy presses one hand to the bridge of his nose. "You need a full-time bodyguard."

"Probably," I admit.

His shoulders slump. "I'm sorry I wasn't there to help."

"How could you have been there?" I ask. "It was the middle of the day, sunlight everywhere."

He winces. "I know. But if I wasn't—"

"If you weren't a vampire you'd be no help at all," I interrupt him. "You'd be all human and breakable and probably have been shot."

He snort-laughs at that.

"So what are you going to do now?" he asks.

"I'll move on to my backup plan," I say. "I was hoping the Nightmare Phantom would destroy the Mayor, and then, since he wasn't going back to dreams, we could turn the Friends' customers on them. But since that's not happening"—I grimace—"I guess I have to actually deal with it myself."

And everyone knows how well *that* usually goes.

"Do you have a plan?" Cy asks.

"Priya is following the Director now," I tell him. "We're hoping to get the location of their evil lair. Once we have that . . ."

"Yes?"

"I mean, I figured Priya could practice with her rocket launcher."

Cy gives me a dry look. "And what does Priya think of blowing up a building that's probably full of innocent people?"

I squirm. "I haven't mentioned that part to her."

"And do you think she'd be okay with that?"

"She'd probably want to save the prisoners first," I grudgingly admit.

"And you don't?"

"Sure I do," I agree. "But that sounds more dangerous than just blowing the place up."

"Blowing up a building is the safer option."

"Yep."

"I don't even want to think about everything wrong with what you just said." Cy flops beside me.

"Then don't."

He gives me a look.

"Well, we'll see when Priya finds the building," he says carefully. "We can go investigate it and make a decision then."

"We?" I hesitate as I say the words.

He gives me a flat look and says firmly, "Obviously, I'm coming."

My heart does something then, a tightening in my chest, and I don't know if it's gratefulness, that he'd join in on a fight he has no stake in just to help me, or guilt, that I'm dragging everyone I care about into my mess.

"Cy," I whisper, looking away, guilt winning out. "You don't have to come. It's dangerous, for you too. They kidnap Nightmares as well, remember? This isn't your fight."

"Ness," he says patiently, "any fight of yours is a fight of mine."

Now my heart is really doing that twisty, painful thing. Oh god, maybe I'm having a heart attack? Or acid reflux?

"But—"

"Ness." He pulls back and holds my gaze. "Listen, okay?"

I nod, surprised by his intensity.

He takes a deep breath.

"I . . . haven't told you much about how my mother died, have I?"

I shake my head, confused by the seemingly unconnected topic shift. Why are we talking about his mother? Do I remind him of his mother? I don't think I like that. I don't want him to think of me like his mother, I want— I don't know what I want. But not that.

"All you've really said is that your father killed her, and claimed it was an accident."

"Yes," he says. "But have I told you that my mother knew my father was going to kill her years before it happened?"

"No," I whisper.

His shoulders are tense. "My father had hurt her before.

233

He'd hit her. He'd bitten her. He'd done much worse."

My voice is gentle. "Why didn't she run away?"

"It was too late by then," he says sadly. "He'd set a trap for her, laid the bars for a cage, and she never noticed until the door had been locked behind her."

He closes his eyes. "She used to tell me that when she was a girl, she always dreamed of marrying a handsome, rich prince who would whisk her away to a castle where she'd live like a queen. And so, when she fell for my father, it was like a dream come true."

His voice is quiet. "But some dreams are actually nightmares in disguise."

I shudder slightly at that.

"My mother was an actress before she met my father." Cy's voice goes soft. "She dropped out of high school, got a job waiting tables and was trying to get discovered. She had several small roles, and even one breakout role. And then she met my father.

"She was nineteen when they met. He was rich, and handsome, and he promised her the moon. After she moved in with him, he told her that the bit parts she was taking weren't worth her effort, they barely paid anything, and he'd support her in everything. When he married her, he told her she'd never have to work a day in her life again."

He raises his head to finally meet my eyes. "And she didn't."

I shiver at the ominousness of his tone.

"She had me. She stayed home and cared for me. She was

beautiful arm candy when my father needed it." He takes a deep breath. "By the time he started hurting her, by the time she realized it was only going to get worse, she hadn't held a job in years."

Cy picks at his gold cuff link. I remain quiet, waiting.

"She knew he was going to kill her. But she had nothing. No savings. No money that he didn't give her. No career to fall back on, no family left to lean on. And if she'd run, he *would* have found her." His voice shakes a little here. "Too late she realized she was trapped. The beautiful mansion was full of wealth all around her, but none of it was hers."

The only sound is the occasional *plink* of water droplets slipping from the rain pattering against the window. Cy is staring at his hands, his eyes turned away from me. His eyeliner is blurring a little on the bottom, as though trying to help him contain the tears he feels in his heart, even if they're not making their way down his face.

I put my hand on his and whisper, "I'm sorry."

Weaker, more ineffective words have never been said.

But this, this is why I refuse to let myself rely completely on Cy. Why I won't give up on having my own job, my own money, my own life. Right now, I'm almost as reliant on Cy as his mother was on his father. And I'd like to make sure that my sanctuary doesn't become a gilded cage.

Like it did with the Friends.

"I'm telling you this," he says, "because the night she died, I was there. I was with her."

I sit, silent.

"When my father came into the room," Cy says slowly, "my mom could tell he was in a bad mood. She knew how to read him. And she told me to leave."

His voice catches. "She'd told me to leave before, when he was in a foul mood. I'd seen the bruises and bite marks the next day. I knew what it meant when she asked me to leave. And even though I wanted to stay, wanted to stop him, I left, because I was small, and weak, and afraid."

He looks me straight in the eye. "I'm not small or weak anymore. And I don't want to be afraid."

His eyes are an electric green, and they're so focused I have to look away.

"Ness." He leans in. "Leaving that room is one of the greatest regrets of my life. Even though there was likely nothing I could have done, I left my mother to face a monster alone."

His voice is firm. "I'm not doing that again. I'm going to help you defeat your enemies." He grins. "Just like I'm sure when the time comes, you'll help me defeat mine."

And he's right. I will help him defeat his father. I want that monster dead and ashes for everything he's done to Cy and the world. And I would be just as mad at Cy as he is with me if he tried to stop me from helping him.

I don't know why I'm so hesitant to take help from friends when I would do the same for them. Maybe I don't feel I'm worth it—and thoughts like that sound an awful lot like the Friends whispering their poison to me, rather than actual fact.

The phone rings, interrupting us.

Cy rises to answer it, and listens to the person on the other end. After a moment, he hangs up.

"That was Priya," he tells me. "She's found the Friends' secret building."

23

The sun is down and the nightlife of Newham is opening sleepy eyes. Lights glitter among the dark spires of buildings, the rising spikes and valleys like a jagged mouthful of teeth, the neon signs gleaming like saliva on its hungry fangs.

The city is a living thing, and if you're not careful, it will swallow you whole.

Cy and I weave our way through dark streets, heading to meet Priya. She's directed us to one of the seedier areas of Newham, where clubs line the corners and neon lights spell words that I would have got my mouth washed out with soap for saying at the Friends.

Peeling posters for various shows are pasted on streetlamps and walls, some of them for risqué dance shows, others for sexy spoofs, including a very explicit-looking one that seems to be mocking the Dracuvlad vampire movie franchise. I look away, blushing.

I press close against Cy to hide my own awkwardness as we weave through the crowds that will only build as the evening gets later. Loud club music swirls around us, and inebriated people swirl with it. Along the street lurk several suspicious dark trucks, like the kind pictured in the papers whenever someone gets kidnapped off the street.

I wonder who they'll make disappear tonight.

Cy hooks his arm around my shoulder, almost like we're lovers, as we slip through the crowds. His body is warm, and he seems unworried. Probably because he's been here before—Cy actually *likes* parties and clubbing and all the things that seem to come after. I, on the other hand, dislike people, am uncomfortable around innuendo, and have no interest in wasting money to engage in either. So this isn't an area I know well.

Priya is waiting for us outside one of the clubs. She's leaning against the wall, wearing a long trench coat to conceal what I can only imagine is an obscene amount of weapons. She's sucking on a coffee pop, caffeinated lollipops for adults that have been gaining popularity lately. The white stem of it sticks out from her mouth, so at first glance I almost think she's smoking.

She sees us and grins.

"Hey," she says, and it's only as she approaches that I realize she has a rocket launcher slung across her back. "Took you guys long enough."

"Sorry," I say. "We had to stop and pick something up on the way."

Cy swings the weapon he'd been toting over one shoulder off for Priya to see.

Her eyes widen in surprised delight. "What is it? I've never

239

seen anything like it."

"I'm calling it a napkin launcher," I tell her.

I give Priya a rundown on what happened with the Nightmare Phantom, from what he revealed to me in our meeting to his disastrous confrontation with the Mayor. Mostly, Priya seems interested in how the napkin launcher works.

Before meeting Priya, Cy and I swung by the Central Square to pick one up from the site of today's disaster. It had been surprisingly hard to find one, given how many of the Montessauri gang soldiers had died. The bodies were still there, no one had come to clean them up. But of course the weapons were almost all gone—I shouldn't have been surprised. Free weapons lying on the ground? No one in Newham could resist that.

We did manage to find one, after Cy lifted a giant cement block of rubble off it. On careful examination, we're reasonably sure it's still loaded. Though it's kind of hard to tell. There's no slot to insert ammo. Does the gun produce its own napkins? Does it come preloaded with a certain number and when they're used up, the machine is useless? I have no idea.

I guess we'll find out.

Priya examines the weapon as I talk, and when I finally finish, she says, "When this mess is over, can I have this?"

I snort. "Sure. Go wild."

"Awesome." She grins, stroking it gently, and I already can see it will have a special place in her weapons collection.

"Given your interesting weapon choice," Priya says, "I assume you have a plan."

"Yeah." I grimace. "I know I told you to bring the rocket launcher, but we might not use it. Cy made a good point on the walk over here that if they have a bunch of chemicals or explosives, we'd level the whole block if we aren't careful. Like that time when the Chaos League tried to take out the Puzzler's experiment lab and we lost all of Fifty-Sixth Street."

I don't think the chances are high that they'd have explosives just lying around, but I'm not willing to take the risk. With the way my luck is going, I'd definitely end up blown up.

"Fair enough." She grins. "So what's the plan?"

"The building," I say. "What kind of door locks does it have? Code? Key?"

"Key," Priya says. "I saw the Director use it."

"Great." I nod to myself. "Okay. So I was thinking we'd start by sneaking up on the Director and napkinning him. Then, we steal his key while he's being napkinned, and we break into the building and see if we can ruin everything the Friends are doing so no one can take over where the Director left off." I consider. "And I guess free prisoners or whatever if there are any."

Priya looks thoughtful. "That could work."

"I think so," I say. "But this time, we have to hit the Director on a body part he *can't* chop off."

All three of us are silent for a moment.

I imagine we're all thinking about how hardcore it was for the Director to chop off his own tail. Like, who *does* that? At least, I'm thinking about that. For all I know Priya's thinking

241

about what we'll get for dinner after this.

"It's a plan," Priya says, grinning widely. "I can't wait to finally give the Director what's coming to him. This is gonna be *fun*."

I hear the echo of the Nightmare Phantom in her words, when I asked him why he turned people into monsters.

Because it's fun.

I haven't thought of it before, but in some ways the two of them are similar, thriving on chaos. The difference is, Priya is a good person who hunts monsters and destroys evil cults. She leverages the things she loves doing to make the world a better place.

The Nightmare Phantom just destroys everything and everyone indiscriminately.

Priya leads us down the street, away from the crowds of the club district, into quiet, narrow alleys. I see now why she chose a more crowded area as a meeting point. There's nothing more dangerous than an empty street in Newham—it's such a populous city that you know if an area is empty, there's a reason for it. Either everyone fled or they're dead, and neither option is good.

Finally, Priya stops us at a corner. She peers around, and murmurs, "The entrance is just down there."

I look down at the inconspicuous alley, so much like every other Newham alley. This one is a dead end, only one way in and out. A smooth metal door glows against the side of an old brick building.

"So, what?" Cy asks, frowning. "We wait for the Director to leave and hit him? What if he's not alone? What if he already left while we were meeting Priya?"

These are good points, to which I have absolutely no answer.

Priya shrugs. "We can still break in."

"Sounds good to me," he says, and then strides confidently into the alley and to the door.

Priya rushes after him, and I follow. I don't want to be left alone in such a sketchy area, even though I hate going into alleys with no exit. They make me feel trapped.

Cy has reached the door, and he twists the knob. It doesn't turn at first, and then he applies more force.

He rips the doorknob right off the door.

Priya raises an eyebrow. "Useful."

Cy grins. "I'm more than just a pretty face."

"So I see."

The door, now broken, swings open a crack. Priya raises her gun and stands to one side of the door, Cy to the other. I cower in the background.

Look, they're the ones with training. If something goes wrong, they'll be able to handle it. What can I do if something goes wrong except get shot?

Cy pushes the door fully open, then freezes, eyes widening at whatever he sees.

I know in that instant that this is going to end badly.

"Back!" he yells. "Run!"

I don't need to be told twice.

I swing toward the entrance to the alley, racing for freedom, but I only get a few steps before I screech to an abrupt halt.

The Director stands at the entrance of the alley. Dozens of mercenaries flank him, all with their guns trained on us. Beside us, in the building we just broke into, more mercenaries pour out the door. Behind us, the alley wall rises ten feet high, blocking our escape.

We're surrounded.

"Ness." The Director smiles. "Thanks so much for coming by."

Shit.

We've walked right into a trap.

24

I should have predicted this.

I'm not really sure *how*. I mean, maybe if I imagine someone narrating my life with the goal of screwing with me as much as possible, I could have guessed this would be a trap. Maybe I should live my life with that expectation from now on.

Mercenaries to the front, to the side, and walls everywhere else. I step backward, and nearly bump into Cy, whose eyes are darting around the same way mine are, looking for an exit. I don't think he'll find one though, not if I can't.

The Director smiles, and takes a step forward, arms outstretched like the benevolent spiritual leader he pretends to be.

"Ness, I see you've brought friends with you this time." The Director nods politely toward us all. "Priya."

"Director." Priya's voice is cool.

"And who is this young man?" The Director eyes Cy with undisguised curiosity. "You look familiar."

Cy raises an eyebrow, his expression full of polite disdain

as he says in his haughtiest, wealthiest accent, "I'm afraid we haven't had the misfortune of meeting before."

The Director is unfazed by Cy's disrespect. His yellow eyes narrow, and he taps a claw against his snout, looking even more convinced that he knows Cy.

"What's your name?" the Director asks.

Cy looks down his nose at the Director. "I don't see why that's any of your business."

"Hmmm." The Director eyes Cy curiously. I can't help but think of the fancy party I saw the Director attending, the one with the Mayor and Marissa Koval. Those are some pretty important, rich people. If the Director is running in the same circles as them, it's entirely possible he's met Cy's father before. Maybe they're even friends. Do they joke about the people who they murder together? That's a weirdly uncomfortable thought.

"No matter," the Director says. "You'll all be coming with me. Lower your weapons. You're outnumbered."

Priya hefts the rocket launcher on her back. "But not outgunned."

The Director stares at her, his arms crossed, clearly unimpressed. "So, what? You'll bring the building down on yourself?"

"I thought you'd be a little more concerned for the safety of your evil lair," Priya comments ominously, her hands tight on the rocket launcher.

"My evil lair?" The Director snorts. "Really. If I had an evil lair, it certainly wouldn't be here. This building is empty inside. It used to house some homeless people, and then that cult of sentient carrots ate them all."

Cy looks ill. "Sentient carrot cult?"

"I tried to tell you," I whisper to him. "But you didn't want to hear about them."

"I still don't."

"The building was convenient," the Director says. "When I realized you were attempting to follow me, I set this up fairly quickly."

Priya looks crushed. "How did you know I was following you?"

"You're not the only one who pays paperboys to do things for them." The Director smiles with tiny sharp teeth. "And I pay more."

Of course he does. I don't even want to know what he hires the paperboys to do—probably the same thing Priya did. Maybe they're the ones who followed Priya to our meeting earlier today. Since the Director wasn't going to stalk us personally.

"Now," the Director says, "be rational, put down your weapons, and come with me."

Cy hesitates, but we both know that there's nothing the napkin launcher could do that would turn the tide here. Even if Cy got off a few shots, there's so many mercenaries. And they probably wouldn't stop just because the Director got napkinified.

Priya scowls, and her fingers tighten on her rocket launcher.

Oh no.

"Like hell I'm going without a fight," Priya snarls.

And then she fires her rocket launcher.

She fires it at the end of the alley, toward the Director. One of the mercenaries steps in front of him, hands out, and deflects the missile. Obviously, some sort of indestructible Nightmare of Steel.

I imagine, in normal circumstances, if he were deflecting a bullet, this human shield strategy would work well.

Unfortunately, he's not deflecting a bullet. He's deflecting a missile. And he deflects it right into the side of the empty building.

Which explodes.

Cy grabs me unceremoniously and spins me around, protecting me from the blast with his body. But even with him blocking the flying debris, it doesn't stop the force of the explosion from sending us both crashing to the ground. Gravel and cement shred my skin, and the weight of Cy's body crushes me into the shattered pavement. The heat is scorching, burning the air in the narrow alley, and for a moment, my mind flashes back to the boat where Cy and I met, the explosion that brought us together.

But this time, there's no cool water to land on.

And that building looks like it's about to come down on top of us.

I can barely see through the dust and smoke, but I can hear well enough. Priya is yelling, and the smack of fists on bodies echoes in my ringing ears. I groan, trying to get up, to help, but everything is spinning around me, and I think one of my eardrums might have popped. Cy is too heavy to move, even if I wasn't so dizzy.

A gunshot fires, then another, and Priya cries out, a sound of impotent rage.

A voice yells, "We've got her. Get the others."

Cy grabs me and unceremoniously hurls me over one shoulder. I grunt as the air shoots out of me and the world spins again, much too fast, and for a moment, I think I'm going to be sick all down Cy's back.

Through the mist, the mercenaries appear, racing toward us even as the building above us groans and tips in a decidedly unstable way. That's real commitment to the job.

Cy starts climbing the brick wall at the end of the alley.

Right, he's superstrong. This was never a dead end for him.

"Wait," I yell at him. Or try to yell, it comes out more like a choked cough. "We have to go back and rescue Priya!"

"I can't carry you both over the wall at the same time!" Cy yells back, both of us shouting to be heard over ringing ears and groaning pieces of concrete preparing to collapse.

"But you'll go back for her!"

He doesn't answer me, just keeps climbing. I swing over his shoulder like the limp deadweight I am.

As we crest the wall, the smoke clears enough for me to see Priya, unconscious, strung between two of the mercenaries. She's being dragged out of the alley toward where we last saw the Director.

No. No, Priya can't be captured. She's Priya. Indestructible, unstoppable, untouchable.

She can't have lost.

Then Cy hops down on the other side of the wall and my view is cut off.

"We have to go back!" I choke out as Cy runs, me still slung over his shoulder, bouncing like a nauseous sack of potatoes.

"Ness, we're outnumbered and outgunned!" Cy insists, turning a corner and running full vampire speed down the street, clearly trying to put distance between us and the mess we've left behind.

"No!" I squirm in Cy's arms, trying to get him to put me down. "We have to help her!"

Cy puts me down, because I'm kicking his stomach, and then takes my hand and tugs me toward another street, away from Priya.

"Ness," he says, voice intense. "You're no good to Priya if you get captured too."

He's right.

I know he's right. But I can't just leave her, I can't just abandon Priya, even if it's to make a better plan to rescue her. It's anathema to everything inside me, to leave my best friend behind. It's my fault she's even in this mess, I can't let her suffer the consequences of it.

The building behind us finally gives up the ghost and collapses. It crumples in seconds, blink and you'd miss it fast. One moment it's there, and the next there's nothing left but a crashing like thunder, a boom that seems to shake the world. In seconds, all that's left is dust, the ghost of an outline where a building used to be.

I gulp. I hope the Friends at least dragged Priya away before it collapsed.

Boot steps thud through the alley and voices rise as a wave of mercenaries turn the corner, pointing at us and yelling.

Finally, I stop hesitating and do what Cy was trying to get me to do all along.

I run.

We weave through alleys, trying to shake our pursuers, or at least get to a more populated area where we can hide. But every turn we take, there's more mercenaries waiting, forcing us to backtrack or take more creative paths through buildings or over walls. There must be a hundred mercenaries split into dozens of teams searching for us. They're like rats infesting the whole area.

My breath is coming in pants, my lungs burning and sweat gleaming off my forehead when we burst onto a major road. Cars whip by, and Cy tries to flag down a taxi, but it ignores us.

A black truck slows to a stop though.

Right in front of us.

The doors swing open, and more mercenaries pour out.

Oh, come on. How many people did the Director hire? This is getting absurd.

These mercenaries are armed with heavy-duty tranquilizers, and they come out firing.

I try to dodge, but it's all happening too fast, and there's nowhere to hide. Beside me, Cy is raising his arm to try and protect us, but it won't be enough.

I brace myself, but by some fluke, none of them hit me.

They all hit Cy.

I expect Cy to shake it off—after all, he's a vampire, he's got superhealing. But he's also blocked me from getting burned by an explosion, which probably took a lot of healing energy, and now he's been pelted with no less than eight tranq darts—again, probably throwing himself between me and danger because he knows he can recover and I can't.

But this time it's too much, and he stumbles, swaying for a heartbeat before falling to his knees.

Oh no.

He looks at me, his eyes bleary, and tries to say something, but instead, his eyes roll up and he slowly keels over, crumpling to the pavement, unconscious.

Another group of mercenaries bursts from an alley, and even though it's against everything that I want, even though I hate myself for doing it, even though I wish there were another option—

I do exactly what Cy tried to tell me to do.

I run.

25

My feet pound the pavement as I run, a small, nimble form weaving through the dark night. Behind me, the crunch of boots and heavy breathing of the mercenaries gets farther and farther away as I speed away from my pursuers.

And from Cy and Priya.

The Friends were only supposed to be after me. And yet somehow, I'm still free and both my allies—the only two people in the world who I care about and who care about me—have been captured by the Friends.

For the first time in a long time, I'm completely alone.

Ever since I arrived in Newham, I've always had someone on my side. First it was my aunt, and then it was the Director and the whole Friends of the Restful Soul organization— even if they turned out to be evil, I didn't know that at the time. Through them, Priya came into my life, and then more recently, Cy.

Even when my world was falling apart, I lost my home and was being hunted by assassins—I still had Cy and Priya.

Now, I have no one.

For years, I've been conditioned to want that. To strive for isolation, to cut myself off from the world.

I can see it now, so clearly it hurts. The way I was trained to love the isolation of my tiny coffin room. The way I struggled to connect with others, my wariness and fear of them becoming Nightmares keeping me at a distance from anyone who could have helped me.

Isolation kept me safe. That's what the Friends wanted me to believe.

But the truth is they wanted me isolated so that no one would come save me when they finally decided to turn me into a monster.

It seems ironic, that in the time it's taken me to fully understand what they've done to me, and to understand that actually, I don't want to be alone, they finally manage to take away the people I care most about.

And now I am alone.

Finally, the sounds of pursuit die away, and I burst into a major thoroughfare. I mix easily into the bustling crowd, blending into the rush hour of people getting off their evening shifts or starting their night shifts. A steady stream of commuters comes up from the subway, and even more filter into the stores and buildings towering around the station entrance.

A woman dressed like a banana hands out flyers for a comedy show, and a man preaches on the street corner about how the age of Nightmares is over, so now the age of Dreams can begin. On the opposite corner, another preacher roars that hell has come to earth in the form of Nightmares, and that all people who turn into Nightmares are sinners and should be stoned like the Bible demands.

Pretty sure the Bible predates the people-turning-into-Nightmares phenomenon by a few thousand years, but I'm not about to get in a fight with a religious zealot on a street corner.

Though I do really want to punch someone.

I duck into a late-night café. The air is warm, and I rub my arms, realizing how cold I was outside. The nice thing about cafés is that no one talks to you. It's like an unwritten rule that everyone ignores everyone, and so I can sit there, blending into the people, surrounded by human shields, and not have to actually interact with anyone.

I look down at my trembling hands as the events of the evening come crashing down on me.

What am I going to do?

All my life, I've relied on others to save me. Cy rescued me from drowning after the boat explosion. Priya rescued me when the Mayor showed up at our coffee date today. When Cy and I were trapped by Nightmare Defense, I summoned the Nightmare Phantom to rescue both of us.

My whole life, I've leaned on my friends to save me. I'm small and weak and not terribly good at anything. I wasn't even smart enough to complete high school, and I'm not strong enough to fight anyone—not that I've ever been brave enough to try.

Without the people around me, I'm nothing.

But now, all those powerful people who I've learned to rely on are out of the picture. They've all been captured. They all need saving.

And I'm the only one left to do it.

I take a trembling breath. I'm terrified. I can't possibly do this, just small, weak me, up against a cult, a monster, an institution. I'm so scared of even the thought of trying to do this daunting rescue mission on my own that I can't breathe.

I'm so scared it hurts.

I could run. I could leave my friends, take Cy's money now that he's out of the picture, and vanish. I could be safe, and hide, and let whatever happens, happen. I could disappear, a wealthy woman, maybe even pay someone to turn me into a Nightmare that's hard to kill. Isn't that what I wanted?

I thought it was. And in many ways, it still is. I still want the safety of not being weak and breakable. I still want the financial security of having my own money.

But I want my friends back more.

So even though I'm so scared I can't stop shaking, even though my heart is beating faster than a rabbit's on cocaine, even though I'm small and weak and fragile—

—I'm not going to let it stop me from saving the people who matter to me.

26

Once decided, there's only one course of action left to me. I have to find out where the Friends are holding Cy and Priya. And I only know of one person who knows that information.

All I have to do is convince her to tell me.

Which, knowing Cindy, is going to be a challenge.

I still have her phone number in my pocket from when Cy passed it to me, and I'm lucky that she picks up immediately when I call, and is happy to meet up in the middle of the night. She must really want the information I'm claiming to have.

It's kind of a shame I lied about having any of the information she wants.

I take the time before our meeting to gather a few supplies, arm myself, and prepare for what's likely going to be a terrifying battle ahead.

If I fail, Cy and Priya will remain imprisoned and I'll have my mind destroyed and then be turned into a monster.

No pressure.

I show up ten minutes early to the meeting, which is at one of the few Newham landmarks I've never actually seen up close before.

The Nightmare Monument.

In the center is a giant crater in the ground, about half a city block long. A century ago, it was the site of a famous church, a Newham landmark featured more often on postcards than even the clock tower. Now it's known as being Newham's first mass-scale Nightmare-related tragedy.

No one knows who became the Nightmare. All that's known is that one Sunday, the church was packed with parishioners, listening to a long morning sermon, and one of them fell asleep.

And they became living magma.

The ground melted beneath them and the church melted above them as the magma burned and consumed the world around it. Firefighters rushed to the scene to put out the flames and cool the lava, only to be consumed by the heat.

The event happened in late fall, which, in Newham, is much colder than it has any right to be. And so the lava eventually cooled and hardened, creating a crater where once there was a church, like a meteorite had struck it.

The city could have rebuilt, turned it into condominiums or something. But instead, they made a monument, a memorial to everyone who died in that Nightmare attack. The crater is surrounded by tall stone walls etched with the names of the victims. Since then, more names have been added. Tradition states that the name of anyone who dies from a Nightmare attack is carved on the walls.

The problem is, too many people have died.

So now the stone slabs are covered in names, and people have chiseled names in the margins and on the backs and sides, in the aisles between other names and sometimes even on top of names.

I approach one of the stone tablets, and it looms above me, gray and foreboding.

My fingers run over name after name, the letters etched in the stone, remembered here in permanence even as the rest of the world forgets them. Ruby's name isn't on here. She didn't die in Newham, and this memorial is only for Newham's Nightmare victims.

There's something haunting about that, the idea that all these names are from only one city, one small piece of a giant planet, and that every city in the world must have its own monument, and even if they don't, their numbers must be just as bad.

It hammers home the magnitude of the consequences of trapping the Nightmare Phantom in dreams. Nightmares have always been so ubiquitous it's hard to remember there was a time before them. But now, staring at walls full of names, it hits me, the sheer scope of it.

It also hits me that however much the Nightmare Phantom says he's a victim, a prisoner trapped in a cage, he's also the one who did this. He's responsible for all these deaths.

And now, trapped in dreams again, he's going to be responsible for even more.

I stare at the names, hundreds of thousands, an unimaginable number of people whose lives have been destroyed. And I realize that ever since the Nightmare Phantom was recaptured, I've been thinking selfishly. I've been thinking how it affects me, how it means the Friends are going to try and kidnap me, and yes, that's important and immediately critical.

But I haven't been thinking about what it will do to the world.

The Nightmare Phantom is a creature of chaos. I saw that today, when he weaponized a gang to fight his enemy for him. He didn't have to do it like that, didn't have to make a T. rex, didn't have to destroy a whole city block, didn't need to have so many innocent victims caught up in the mess.

He did it because it entertained him. Because he finds chaos fun.

But as terrible as what he set up today was, it's nothing compared to the damage he can do in dreams again. Trapping him there again has set the whole world up to continue its path of misery and violence.

For all his evil, he can do far more damage in his cage than out of it.

"Ness?"

I turn around. Cindy stands with her shoulders tucked in, face half hidden by a dark red scarf. Her black bobbed hair has been slicked to create fake waves around her face, and her trousers and waistcoat are immaculately pressed, this time a deep red over a white oxford shirt.

"Cindy," I reply.

"Took you long enough to call."

"I've been busy."

"So I've heard." She rubs her temples. "Did you really think it was a good idea to go after the Director?"

"Well, sitting around waiting to be kidnapped seemed like a poor choice too. It was bad options all around." I raise an eyebrow. "Unless you'd care to share a better plan?"

"I'd have changed my name, bought a new identity, and been on the next train out, to be honest," she says.

"Sounds expensive," I say.

"It would be," she concedes.

"Also sounds like you have experience with that."

Which she obviously does. After all, one can't be going undercover in the Friends of the Restful Soul using their real name.

She brushes this comment aside. "All right, let's get to the point."

Oh, what a dodge. Looks like I might have come a little too close to the truth.

"So, what do you know about the assassination last month and who was targeting me?" Cindy asks.

"Quite a bit actually. Starting with you. Cindy Lim—or should I say Charlotte Kang?"

Cindy freezes, her whole body stilling.

"I don't know what you're talking about," she says stiffly.

"Oh, I think you do." I pull out a crumpled newspaper, the same edition that I'd been looking at in Cy's apartment. "You know, I almost didn't notice. It took me a while. I don't usually read the tabloids and I haven't been following the missing Koval heir story that closely."

I flip past pages of the Koval family in glamorous shots, mostly pictures of Clarence Koval, who died last year under mysterious circumstances—which were definitely that his second wife, Marissa, murdered him for his fortune.

Finally I stop at a photo from some expensive event from last year. The photo features the missing Koval heir, Dorothy Koval, laughing at something the girl beside her, dressed in equivalent splendor, is saying. Dorothy has her head back, golden hair pouring around her, and the girl across from her has perfectly styled black hair and heavy makeup, her eye-shadow so glittery even in the black-and-white photo, and a sparkling dress.

The girl in the sparkles is Cindy.

"I've seen all these pictures a hundred times in the news," I tell her. "But I never really looked at them, not really." I pull the picture back and read the caption. "'Billionaire heiress Dorothy Koval enjoys Newham's anniversary with glittering socialite Charlotte Kang.'"

I fold the paper closed.

Cindy pauses a moment before seeming to realize I'm waiting for her to react. She lifts her hand in a *move it along* gesture. "And?"

I blink, startled. That isn't the response I thought I'd get.

"I came here to hear what you know about the assassination attempt on me," she tells me, arms crossed. "Not to see you point at newspaper clippings and throw around whatever you think you've figured out yourself."

"So you don't deny it then," I cut in.

"Of course I don't deny it." She snorts. "That would be rather dumb of me when it's blatantly my face."

"You told me you worked for a newspaper," I point out, trying to wrest control of this situation back.

"I do." She taps the paper. "Doesn't it say there? I *own* the paper."

Oh. Oh wow.

She's really, *really* rich.

Which, I suppose, I should have figured what with her hanging out with the Koval heir and all that. But it's terrifying to hear her say it, to admit to being *that* rich.

"Then why," I ask her, "are you pretending to be one of the Friends? Trying to sneak close to the Director? Don't you have, I don't know, staff for this?"

Her lips tighten. "If you want things done right, you should always do them yourself."

I can't argue with that. I also have severe trust issues.

Though, given how much money Cindy seems to have and she's still doing this solo, I feel like her trust issues must be way worse than mine.

"Ness." Cindy steps forward. "I came here to find out what you know, not play twenty questions. Who ordered the hit on me, and what do you know about it?"

"All I know is that Charlie Chambers arranged the hit using the power and influence of Nightmare Defense," I tell her. "The hit was structured around your mail run, and other people were lured onto that specific boat because you were there."

Cindy is quiet for a moment, before she makes a disbelieving sound. "That's it?! That's all you know?"

"That's it."

"Unbelievable," she mutters. "You tricked me into helping you escape."

"You shouldn't need to be tricked into doing the right thing," I tell her.

"Why did you even call me here?"

I smile at her insincerely. "I need help getting into the building where the Friends keep their prisoners."

"No."

"Cindy—"

"No, Ness." Cindy shakes her head, her voice strained. "I'm so close to finding out what happened to her, I can't—I can't risk it all now. Not when I'm so close."

I'm quiet for a heartbeat before I repeat, "Her?"

Cindy stills. "Nothing that matters to you."

I think back to the gala with the Director and Marissa Koval, and how chummy they were. I think of the picture of Cindy, laughing with Dorothy Koval, heir to the Koval empire. An heir who's missing.

"Marissa gave Dorothy Koval to the Friends, didn't she?" I say. "And you're trying to find out what happened."

264

Cindy purses her lips. "Like I said, none of your business."

"Cindy," I tell her, trying to pull her heartstrings. "The Friends kidnapped Priya."

She looks away. "I'm sorry."

"I can't leave her there," I press. "You know how much I care for Priya. I have to save her."

"I—"

"I swear, if you help me do this, I'll do anything I can to find out what happened to Dorothy." I step toward her. "I'll have Priya help. Hell, Priya will hold down the Director and we can all take turns ripping his limbs off until he gives us an answer."

Cindy's mouth quirks at that. "That sounds like you."

I'm not sure if I should be insulted by that, given that I've never actually ripped anyone's limbs off before.

Well, not intentionally.

"Cindy"—I lean in—"you've been undercover long enough. You're smart, and you're good at this. If you haven't found out what happened yet, then you need to try a new tactic."

"A torture tactic?" Cindy remarks dryly.

"We can try blackmail. I like blackmail."

"I'm sure you do," she remarks. "Just like I'm sure if I don't say yes to this request, you're going to try and blackmail me into accepting it."

Ouch. She knows me way too well.

I clear my throat. "I'm hoping it won't come to that."

Cindy's lips are pressed into a thin line. "Were you born this awful or did you learn it?"

"I think it's a gift," I tell her proudly.

"You would," she mutters.

She's quiet for a long time before she finally says, "All right."

"You'll take me?" I say, surprised she gave in so easily.

"Well, you're Ness the Mess," she points out. "Everything you touch ends up in utter disaster. I can use the distraction from whatever chaos you're causing to finally break into some of the sealed-off areas and see if I can find evidence of what happened to Dorothy."

Wow. What high esteem she holds me in.

"So I'm a distraction," I say flatly.

She smiles winningly at me. "It's what you do best."

27

Cindy and I take the subway all the way to the end of the line, deep in the southern part of the city. We have to do some interesting transfers to avoid going through the central station, which still has a dead T. rex collapsed in it.

The subways are only moderately crowded in the middle of the night, maybe twenty people in a car instead of a hundred. A bearded man in neon pink leggings and a spiked leather jacket is passed out drunk across one of the benches, and the person across from him keeps staring at him with eyes that are slitted sideways like a goat's. They're covered almost completely in a voluminous trench coat, only a sliver of face peeking out, showcasing a long blue tongue darting out to lick dry, cracked lips. The goat eyes glance toward us occasionally, as though waiting for us to get off the train so they can eat the drunk.

When we reach our stop, Cindy smacks the drunk on his head with her bag on the way out. He yelps, sitting up quickly, confusion and fear in his eyes, and the goat-eyed Nightmare casts us both a glance full of hatred for the lost meal as the drunk stumbles off the train.

We leave the subway, and the tension in my body is so bad I feel like a wooden puppet, movements jerky and stiff with fear. We're in the warehouse district, massive buildings dotting the grimy landscape near the shipping routes. It's not an area I come to often, and the last time I was here wasn't exactly a great time.

This is where Nightmare Defense brought Cy and me when they kidnapped us.

I shudder as I think back to that long drive in their truck, the smooth glass and steel cages, the way Cy's flesh sloughed off his skin from the silver in the handcuffs. I still remember the way Charlie Chambers smiled as the gas filled my cage, sending me into dreams.

And to the Nightmare Phantom.

I bow my head. I thought, when I freed him, when I watched him annihilate the entirety of Nightmare Defense by turning them into cockroaches and screaming babies, that I was doing something terrible. Not something I regretted, because I never regret anything that keeps me alive. But something terrible nonetheless.

But now, I think putting him back was even more terrible.

It's a thought, crystal clear—I don't think he should be back there. I've rescued him before, can I rescue him again? Should I try?

I don't know. I don't think now is the time to think about it either.

Right now, I have to save Priya and Cy.

I can't always save everyone. Perhaps I can't save *anyone*. I'm one small person against a great big world full of lots of awful, very powerful people. I may be armed, but I'm not Priya, proficient with every weapon she's ever encountered. I'm not Cy, who can heal from bullet wounds. I'm not even terribly smart, I'm no super genius with elaborate plans.

I'm just me. That hasn't changed, not really.

What's changed is that this time I'm going to try.

Cindy leads us through the towering, boxy buildings, and I wonder who else is using buildings in this area for kidnapping. Nightmare Defense was, and the Friends are—maybe the whole warehouse district is dotted with secret bases. It is an ideal area for it. Very little foot traffic, large enclosed spaces, no one questioning deliveries at odd times.

When I think about it like that, I can't help but wonder if the whole district was designed for criminals to abuse.

Finally, we stop in front of a massive warehouse much like all the others. It's made of cement, and it looks more like a bomb shelter than a building. The door is the only spot of color, and it's a faded pastel blue, the same color as the uniform waistcoat Friends of the Restful Soul disciples wear.

Cindy heads to the door and pulls out a key ring. She unlocks lock after lock, going all the way up the door, until finally it swings open, and she tucks her keys away.

She steps through the door and looks back at me, eyebrow raised. "Coming?"

I take a deep breath, tighten my hand on the pepper spray in my belt, and follow her.

The door leads into a long hallway that seems to go along one side of the building. Its whitewashed walls and floors give it a strange feeling of flatness, like a blank piece of paper, and make it hard to judge distance.

On one side are doors, and on the other, a wall covered in elaborate portraits of the various saints of the Friends of the Restful Soul. They look down on us as we walk past. Irving, with his long dramatic beard, appears a dozen times, as does Magdalena, her expression as judgy as ever. The other two saints appear less often, so clearly whoever decorated the building had a favorite saint or two.

"This way," Cindy says, opening one of the doors.

I follow her, cautious, always wary of betrayal. But the room is empty of people, which I suppose makes sense given how late it is. Cindy clicks the lights on, and my eyes widen as I look over hundreds of test tubes and beakers, long counters full of notes and papers, jars on the wall full of preserved organs, and blackboards everywhere with incomprehensible scribblings.

I've been in Newham long enough to know a mad scientist's lair when I see it.

"So the Director is a mad scientist too?" I ask.

"Are you surprised?"

"Not really," I admit. "But what's all this for?"

"Side hustle," Cindy says. "The Friends kidnap Nightmares and do the usual experiments on them. Trying to see if they can transfer magic and abilities between people."

Well, I suppose that explains why they were kidnapping other Nightmares. At least that's one question answered.

Cindy gestures to one table, where a pair of eyes float in a jar. "See there? Those come from a Nightmare with X-ray vision. They kidnapped him, cut out his eyes, and they've been trying to reattach them into someone else to see if the ability transfers."

I cringe in disgust. That's just gross.

"It didn't work, in case you were interested," Cindy says.

Why does everyone in this city have so many evil plots? Frankly, the whole mad scientist thing is just so blasé. There's so many of them in Newham, it's tiring.

"Has anything they've done worked?" I ask, more out of morbid curiosity than anything else.

Cindy snorts. "Not really. Mostly they've managed to create weird toxic shit that just mutates people in ways you really don't want to be mutated. I saw one of their subjects grow antlers out of his brain from one of their experiments."

"Ew," I say, while trying to picture what that even looked like. Would they rip through the skull? Or would the subject just die from the pressure of having antlers in his *brain*?

"Yeah." Cindy nods. "And the creepy part is, they were trying to replicate another Nightmare who had super smell. It had nothing to do with antlers."

"I think we have different ideas of what the creepy part of that experiment was," I deadpan.

Cindy ignores me.

271

We exit through a door on the other side of the lab, which leads into a stairwell.

Cindy points down. "Bottom level is the prisoners. I don't have the key, so you're on your own getting in."

"And where are you going?" I ask.

"Elsewhere," she says, smiling. "When you inevitably set off the alarms, I'll be in place to take advantage of the distraction."

Charming.

"You're not going to speed that distraction along by reporting a break-in, are you?"

"Of course not," Cindy says. "Then there'd be questions about why I was here and how I knew you broke in. I can't have that."

I'm not sure I believe her, but this is the best I'm going to get. At least I'm in the building, and I know where the prisoners are held.

It will have to be enough.

I descend the stairs slowly, trying not to think of the last basement I descended into, with a gun at my back and Nightmare Defense planning to turn me into a monster. What is it with evil lairs and their basement prisons? Actually wait—what if all the warehouse buildings were designed with prisoner space beneath them? It would explain why I feel like I only ever hear about basement prisons, and both of the ones I've encountered have been in basements. Maybe these warehouses are all factories built by the same company. Prisoners in the basement, mad science laboratory on the main floor . . .

272

I reach the bottom of the stairwell and am faced with a large metal door identical to the one in Nightmare Defense.

Yeah, this place is a carbon copy of Nightmare Defense.

On the bright side, that means I know where everything is, and I probably won't get lost. On the bad side, it means I know exactly how impenetrable these doors are. And even though I brought a gun, I don't think I can shoot the door handle off.

I wish I had Cy's strength right about now. I could just rip the door off its hinges.

But I only have myself and my own ingenuity, and I approach the metal door carefully. The walls are concrete, so I can't go through them without some explosives. The door is metal, and it's got a keyhole, which I dutifully attempt to pick, to no avail.

I stand back, considering.

Then I realize—the Friends have already given me a way to break in.

I hurry back up to the lab, looking through jars of chemicals, their labels clear and bright. I grab three different bottles, all of them with the word "acid" after the chemical name.

I return to the basement, careful not to drop any of my glass containers. I swiped a pair of gloves from the lab too, though I'm not sure they'll help if I drip acid on myself, but they make me feel better.

I pull the first acid out.

I open the jar, and then oh so carefully tip the acid into

the door lock. It spills anyway, dripping down the front of the door, and I'm not sure how much actually gets into the keyhole itself.

I close the jar and wait a moment. The streaks of acid on the front of the steel door are changing the color of the metal, making it look almost rusty. I push at the door, but the locking mechanism is still in place.

Hmm. Maybe I should try splashing the acid in between the door and the wall, let it melt the lock itself.

It's worth a try, and I repeat my experiment with my second jar of acid, pouring some in the keyhole, but this time I also try and pour some in the tiny gap between door and wall. I'm only moderately successful.

This acid is looking much more promising though. It's sizzling against the metal, especially the already damaged parts. I think the acids might be combining and doing something, because the metal is eroding, like a parasite is eating it.

I probably should have thought that combining chemicals would produce different reactions and been more careful— after all, what if I'd accidentally made something explode? I'm not sure how I'd have been careful, since my chemistry knowledge is limited. I should probably fix that. I'll add it to the long list of things I need to learn.

I press the door, and this time, it swings open with ease.

I grin. Success.

"Thank you, unpronounceably named acids," I tell the jars. "I don't know which of you did it, but good job."

I take one of the jars with me, in case I can't get into the cages to break people out, and leave the other two at the door.

Stepping through the door is like walking back in time. The cages are identical to those in Nightmare Defense. Cage doors line each side of the hall, with glass panels in the front so that one can see what's inside, lined by steel, with steel coating the inside of the cages as well. They look almost futuristic, like what I see in films that imagine people living in space.

Some of the cells are filled. Some aren't. Some have Nightmares. Some have regular humans.

I'm in the right place.

I walk down the hall quickly, looking in cages, trying to find a familiar face, they have to be here, I saw them taken, I have to find them, I—

There she is.

Priya lies in one of the cages, fast asleep, her breathing steady and even. Her expression is creased a little, like she's having a thought in her sleep.

Or a dream.

My heart leaps into my throat, and I bang on the glass, hoping to wake Priya up. I don't want her to become a Nightmare—she could become anything. She could become small and weak and powerless like me. She could become something so inhuman it can't communicate with people anymore, or she could disappear, become a ghost or a microbe or—

She's not waking up. They've probably gassed her.

I look around, trying to remember where the release button was in Nightmare Defense, but I don't recall ever seeing it used. The Nightmare Phantom broke me out of my cage with a much more direct route.

But there has to be a way to get her out. If I could just—

There.

To the side of the cage is a discreet black panel, and I lift the top of it to reveal a release button. I press it.

With a hiss of releasing pressure, the door slides open.

I dart inside immediately, grab Priya under her armpits, and drag her out of the metal box and into the hallway. Out here, the air is hopefully clear of any sleeping chemicals, and I'm not in danger of ending up locked in the box with her.

"Priya," I say, tapping her face gently. "Wake up."

She stirs groggily.

I let out a massive sigh of relief. She's okay. She's going to be okay. We're both going to be okay.

"Stay here," I say. "I'm going to find Cy."

Priya just groans slightly in response, her eyes fluttering open and then quickly closing.

I race to the end of the hall, searching for Cy, looking in cage after cage. Finally, I get to the end, and I stop, breathing heavily, staring at the empty final cage, occupied by nothing but air.

Cy isn't here.

But that's impossible. I saw him kidnapped. I saw—

Back the way I came, I hear Priya yell in rage.

I spin around, freezing for a moment, my instinct when I hear a yell to run away. But I've nowhere to run, and I didn't come this far just to abandon Priya. I head toward Priya's shouts.

The Director is standing in the hall, glaring down at Priya. He's grabbed her by the hair with one claw and is dragging her back into her cage. Normally, Priya would be able to crush him in an instant, but she's groggy and drugged and can't even stand yet, never mind fight.

The Director looks up when he sees me, and his face twists in disgust. "I should have known the warning alarm was caused by you. How did you even get in here?"

Warning alarm? Did I set something off when I opened Priya's door? Or did Cindy decide I wasn't making enough of a mess and decide to help me along?

It doesn't matter.

I step forward, pulling my pepper spray from my belt. "Let her go."

"All right." He laughs, then tosses the groggy Priya the rest of the way into her cage. Once she's inside, the door slides closed, locking her back in.

I grind my teeth. "Step away from the cage."

"Or what? You won't really use that on me, will you? Come on, Ness," he says patiently. "The rest of the night guards will be here in a few minutes. You don't have a chance. Just give up. You're not a fighter."

No. I'm not.

But I want to be.

I'm done running. I'm done letting this snake oil salesman manipulate me and tell me who I am, and who I should be. I'm tired of hiding from my problems and letting others rescue me.

This time, I'm going to rescue myself.

So I raise my pepper spray up and say, "You don't know anything about me."

His eyes widen.

And I spray him right in those wide, yellow eyes.

28

The Director screams as the pepper burns his eyes.

He claws at his face, trying to rub the burn out, but I keep spraying, and now it's all over his claws too, so he's only rubbing more in. Tears stream down his scales, and he howls in agony.

He stumbles forward, and I pick up the jar of acid I left by Priya's cage in case I needed to melt it open.

"Don't make me use the acid too," I tell him, my voice cold. "Because I absolutely will."

He stops crawling toward me and just folds over in pain.

My breathing is coming hard.

This isn't the first time I fought back against the Director. I hit him with a drawer in a confrontation where he threatened Priya with a gun, but it's the first time I've stood my ground afterward. It's the first time I've stood up to him, and I haven't hesitated or second-guessed myself. I knew I could take him down, and I did.

It's a strange rush that fills me, this confidence. The knowledge that I didn't need to be strong, or magical, or invulnerable. After all, Priya isn't a superhero—she's just bold, and brave. And I've been putting her in the same category as Cy, someone supernaturally skilled, a place I could never reach, but that's not true.

Strength, power, it's not about being physically strong. Look at Cy, he's much stronger than me, and he was still captured.

Real strength is about your mind. It's about making a plan, and being brave enough to carry it out, even knowing the risks. It's about being bold when the occasion calls for it.

Strength comes from the mind, not the body.

Which is why places like the Friends focus so hard on destroying the mind. Ruin the mind, and no matter how powerful the body, the person can't act.

The Director wails again, still clawing at his red, bloodshot eyes. The can of pepper spray says not to use for prolonged periods on eyes, and that's exactly what I did. I wonder if I've permanently blinded him. That should bother me, but it doesn't.

I did it to save Priya. And I'd do it again.

I step past the Director, still crouched over clawing his face, to the door lock for Priya's cage. I unlock it and reach in, hauling Priya's arm over my shoulder. She's heavy, and a lot taller than me, so it's incredibly awkward to drag her out of the cage like this, but it's not like I have many other options.

"Priya." I eye her worriedly. "Priya, can you speak?"

"Can," she slurs, her eyes fluttering from the drugs.

"Do you know where they took Cy?" I ask.

She shakes her head. "Didn't take Cy." Her brow furrows. "Did something happen to Cy?"

Cy's not here.

I suspected as much when I looked through the cages, but I hadn't wanted to believe it, because he was supposed to be here, I was supposed to rescue him dramatically. But the Friends didn't kidnap him.

Which means someone *else* did.

I groan. Can't I just deal with one kidnapper at a time?

I gently lean Priya against the wall to get her bearings, and then walk over to the Director.

He's kneeling on the floor, gasping in pain.

"Help me get to the lab," he begs. "I need to cleanse this."

"Hmmm." I consider. "Maybe if you answer some questions."

He looks up at me, and oh god, that is a nasty sight, scales peeling off, eyes swollen and red and oozy.

"After you get me there," he says.

"No. Now." I cross my arms. "Or I'll drag you into a cage and leave you in there to go blind."

He grits his teeth. "What do you want to know?"

"I want to know"—my voice is low and steady—"what you planned to turn me into."

He's quiet for a long moment, probably thinking about how if he tells me, it will likely ruin his plans for me forever. Because once I know, I can take steps to make sure that I'm more afraid of something else, can preemptively counter whatever mind manipulation he plans to do.

"Ness," he says slowly. "I'm sure—"

"Don't lie," I snap. "I can tell you were building up to a lie. I know when you're lying."

I mean, I don't actually, not for sure. Nothing's ever for sure.

The Director rolls his eyes. "You're so dramatic."

"I think I'm entitled, given everything." I put my hands on my hips. "So, what was it?"

The Director looks at me a long moment, his expression somehow faded with age, and I wonder how long he's been running this cult. He looks at me with something approaching gentleness, a fond, grandfatherly emotion, even though I've just permanently scarred him. It's weird. I don't like it.

"It's not what you're thinking," he finally says. "You were never merchandise, Ness."

I snort, trying to cover the way those words clench painfully around my chest, that stupid wish my heart has for all this to still be a misunderstanding, even after everything. Even after I had to break in here to rescue my kidnapped best friend.

How is it, after everything I've learned about the Friends, everything they've done to me, I still want so desperately to believe that their promises to me were true? Why do I so wish to go back to the lie?

"Please," I say, voice scraping a little. "Like I'd believe that."

"I'm telling the truth." He shifts and I hold up my pepper spray threateningly. He stops moving.

"Fine." I don't believe him. He's a liar. But I have to ask. "What did you want me to become?"

The Director narrows his reddened eyes. "We wanted you to be afraid of becoming a Nightmare, so that when you went into the dream, that's what you'd become."

"A Nightmare?" I ask, baffled.

"No—a Nightmare Phantom. A creature that turns others into Nightmares." He looks up at me and his gaze is steady and cool. "We wanted you to be the new Nightmare Phantom."

I stare at him blankly.

Me? The new Nightmare Phantom?

For a moment I can't quite comprehend it—they planned to turn me into a Nightmare Phantom. A monster who could morph anyone into their nightmares, feared by everyone in the world. Someone indestructible, who bullets bounce off. Someone powerful, who could command the price of hiring them, turn their enemies into cockroaches.

"What the hell?" I whisper.

"Now, Ness—"

"Why didn't you tell me!" I lean forward, expression intense, voice rising. "I'd have signed up years ago!"

He stares at me, green snout twitching. "What?"

"Become powerful? Indestructible? Able to protect myself against the world?" I stare at the Director, abjectly betrayed.

"That isn't a Nightmare. It's a Dream!"

The Director blinks owlishly. "Um, well, yes, I hadn't thought of it that way."

How much easier would life in Newham be if I wasn't on the verge of getting murdered all the time? If instead of being the powerless nobody, I was the monster?

Isn't that the entire reason I'd made a deal with the Nightmare Phantom?

And all this time, the possibility had been so close I could have touched it.

"You understand," the Director says, "telling you would have completely changed your fears. It wouldn't have worked."

He's right. It wouldn't have worked. I wouldn't have been nearly as afraid as I'd have needed to be. I'd have been much too excited—I wouldn't have developed the kind of fear the Nightmare Phantom would have zeroed in on.

"It's too late now, of course," the Director says. "The chance has passed."

I almost regret it. Almost wish that wasn't the case. Almost wish that I could change my own mind. Almost wish I could go back in time and let the Friends kidnap me.

Because I want that power. I want it more than I've ever wanted anything. With power like that, I could finally be safe.

But it's gone.

Like most of the dreams I've had, like most of my chances at power, it's snatched out of reach before I even knew how close it was.

I try to tell myself that this is better. The Friends would have kept me in a cage too, their own personal monster. And I probably would have been happy for it, locked in my tiny room, afraid of the world even though I was all-powerful.

No. Power means nothing if my mind is so broken I can't use it to face my fears.

It's better to be brave than powerful.

Because powerful people can still be manipulated with fear, can still be locked away in cages of their own minds. I would never have been happy there, even as powerful as I would have been.

I don't know if I'm happy now, per se. But I *am* better off. I'm not isolated, and I'm experiencing life, instead of hiding from it. And that's worth something.

I take a deep breath.

"Well, thanks for the answers. I think it's time I'm going now," I tell him, turning away.

"Wait, you're supposed to take me to the lab!" The Director crawls after me, his eyes now so swollen they're completely shut and he can't see.

I adjust Priya's arm over my shoulder and she leans against me, but she's standing better now. She's still looking pretty dizzy though.

"Sorry, Director, but I took a leaf from your book." I look back at him, and smile. "I lied."

He reaches after me, but I ignore him, hauling Priya to the exit.

At the door, a small control panel faces the room. I pause

when I see it, and then I reach forward to the button that reads "Open all cages."

I may be braver now. I may be capable of saving myself.

But I've never been good at performing the killing blow myself. And I see no reason I should start now.

A buzz runs through the room.

And every door opens.

The last thing I hear as I slip out of the prison is the sound of the Director screaming in agony as his dozens of enraged prisoners descend on him en masse.

29

The Director of the Friends of the Restful Soul is gone.

In dark, dramatic penny novels, the heroes always feel terribly guilty after they kill someone, like there's a stain on their soul. They hate themselves, they cry, they seek absolution for the terrible things they've done, even knowing it will forever weigh on their minds.

In lighter ones, they feel a sense of accomplishment, of righteous justice in defeating the villain. There's no reflection on life taken, only on the goal accomplished, the evil defeated.

I don't feel either of those things.

I expect to feel *some* sort of sorrow or regret, given he was part of my life for so long. That lingering sadness for the life I thought I'd had. I also expect to feel some catharsis, given that this means all the drama with the Friends is finally over.

But I don't know that I feel anything at all. Maybe it's shock, maybe it hasn't sunk in yet, and later on I'll have lots of feelings, replay his final screams over and over, knowing that even if it wasn't my fingers that clawed his heart out, it was my hand that released the people who did, my hand that doused him in the pepper spray that prevented him from fighting back.

But right now, in this moment, I don't feel anything at all.

Maybe I'm a worse person than I thought.

Climbing the stairs seems to help wake Priya up a bit more. I can't haul her up all by myself, so she's leaning on me and taking the steps by herself. I think the blood flow and bit of exercise are clearing the drugs from her system, because by the time we reach the top of the stairwell, she's mostly walking on her own.

Which I'm grateful for, since even though I promised myself I'd do some weight lifting after the last time I had to haul an injured friend out of a prison basement, I didn't. I did no lifting. None. My muscles are as wobbly and sad as ever.

"Ugh." Priya rubs her forehead as we come out the stairwell and back into the mad scientist lab. "I feel like shit."

"That'll be the drugs."

"Can't believe he tried to turn me into a Nightmare," she mutters.

"I can," I say, voice flat. "That is what they do."

"But to me?" Priya seems to take this as a personal offense. "And I was just supposed to be an experiment to see if it worked again, since the Nightmare Phantom is back in dreams." She scowls. "I'm worth more than an experiment. I should be the star!"

"I really feel like that is not the part you should be angry about here," I inform her dryly.

She snorts. "Fine, probably."

I hesitate. "Did you dream?"

"Sure did. Never dreamed before. It's weird as hell. You know it feels so real? It's eerie."

I laugh. "Sure is." I hesitate. "You're not changed though?"

"Don't think so," she says. Then hesitates. "I did see . . ."

I still. "What?"

She looks at me as though she wants to say something, then smiles, shaking her head. "Nothing. It was just a dream. Nonsense built out of our subconscious, right?"

"Right," I agree, suddenly uneasy. "Did you see something?"

"Don't worry about it. I'm still me, yeah? Not a Nightmare." She grins wickedly. "Though I wouldn't have minded having some cool wings or claws or something."

I snort-laugh. "If only it were that predictable."

I joke, but honestly, I'm more relieved than I can express. Whatever strange thing she dreamed, it wasn't a nightmare. Not every dream is a nightmare, after all. She got lucky.

"Come on," I tell her. "Let's get out of here."

"Get out? Are you kidding me? And leave this place to continue on? They kidnapped me! They tried to kidnap you!" Priya puts her hands on her hips. "Oh no. I'm not leaving until this place is ash and dust."

I blink. "Oh." I clear my throat. "I kind of have to rescue Cy."

Priya grimaces, but nods to herself. "I suppose you need my help?"

I open my mouth to tell her yes, of course I need her help. But then I pause, and really consider what the best use of Priya's time and energy is.

"No," I tell her. "I can handle it on my own. If you want to stay here and burn this place to the ground, that sounds lovely."

Priya raises an eyebrow. "You've got it on your own?"

"I rescued you on my own, didn't I?"

"So you did." She grins. "Go on then. Go save your pretty vampire." She stretches, slow and languid, looking at the laboratory tools around us and smiling. "I've got some anger to work out here."

"Have fun," I tell her, then pause. "And maybe don't accidentally blow up Cindy. She's in here somewhere breaking into locked rooms."

Priya seems surprised. "She's how you found me, isn't she?"

"Yeah."

"I'm shocked she helped," Priya says.

"Me too," I admit. "But she had her own reasons."

And as much as Cindy and I clash personality wise, I

do hope she finds out what happened to Dorothy Koval. If Cindy is willing to go this far to find her, then she must mean a lot. I respect that kind of loyalty to the people you care about.

Besides, Cindy isn't a bad person. She's probably a better one than me.

Even if we'll likely never get along.

Priya looks over the chemicals on the wall and a slow, anticipatory smile spreads across her face. I have a feeling she, unlike me, knows chemistry.

"Have fun destroying everything the Friends worked for," I tell her.

"Oh, I will," she says, eyes alight.

As much as the Friends have hurt me, I don't want to annihilate the Friends the way Priya does. I just want to hide and avoid the things that hurt. I think her way is probably healthier—there's action and closure and all that. My way is just pretending the problem doesn't exist if I can't see it.

But today, I have an excuse for leaving the destruction part to Priya.

So as Priya starts smashing lab equipment and mixing chemicals to break into locked rooms and make sure that this place can never be a cage again, I slip away, up the long hall of saints looking down at me, and back out into the city.

The sun is rising over Newham. I'm exhausted beyond measure, I haven't slept in almost a day, and I'm still bruised from all my fights. But I don't go home, I don't rest, I don't give in to my own exhaustion. I get back on the subway, and I head uptown.

I've figured out where Cy is.

And I'm going to save him.

30

Dawn has come and gone, and the sky is patterned pink and orange by the time I return to the Château Newham. I had to stop by and pick up a few things on the way—I've never been more glad for Newham's moniker of "the city that never sleeps" as I have been strolling into a photography shop at the crack of dawn.

I don't even want to think about why they're open that late. Or that early, depending on your definition.

The hotel hasn't changed in the time since my disastrous attempt at napkinning the Mayor. It still oozes pretension, and I stroll up to the front desk with ease. I don't recognize the woman manning it, which means I probably can't play the "I work here too" card, especially since I think I've been fired.

So instead I haul my purchases up to the front desk and say, "I have a delivery."

The woman, who'd been reading a book in Chinese at the counter before I arrived, smiles and puts it down, carefully straightening her already perfectly straight tie.

"Sure, who's it for?"

I tell her, and then wait while she checks the ledger. She pauses when she finds the name, confirming my first, second, and third suspicions.

"Yes, of course. I'll call one of the bellhops over to bring it up."

"I'd appreciate it."

The bellhop is called over, and I gratefully unload my heavy burden onto his cart, which is even fancier than I thought, with golden arches at head height, presumably for hanging ball gowns on so they don't get wrinkled.

"We can take it from here," the desk clerk says.

"I'm supposed to ensure delivery," I say.

She shakes her head. "Not here. They don't let us do that. You can get a signed receipt when the bellhop returns if you want."

I consider, then say casually, "How much to make sure I get up there too?"

The woman considers this carefully, looking over my clothes, and then shakes her head. "Nothing you could afford."

Ouch.

"Try me," I say, like I haven't already spent most of my savings on getting these absurdly heavy tubs of liquid I'm toting around.

She names a number. She's right. I can't afford it.

What kind of Newhamite am I, so poor I can't even afford bribes now? This is just embarrassing.

I empty my pockets, taking out the last remaining bit of my savings from this month. It's not even close to the amount she asked for.

The woman considers, then looks at my tubs of liquid. She leans forward and sniffs, then wrinkles her nose. She considers me with narrow eyes, and I'm pretty sure she's figured out my whole plan.

"All right," she says, and gives me the room number.

I'm surprised, but I'm not going to look a gift horse in the mouth. "Thanks."

She hesitates and says, "Be careful."

I nod, my expression solemn. I suspect I know why she agreed to tell me.

All I say is "I will."

I drag my cart to the elevator and push the button for the fourth floor, my foot tapping an impatient rhythm on the overly plush carpet as it rises.

Finally, I'm disgorged into a hallway that looks like it was painted with money. The walls are a rich gold, the carpet the color of cut rubies, and polished white marble side tables with attractive flower arrangements sit against the wall in the spaces between each doorway.

I wheel my cart down the hall until I reach the door I'm looking for.

There's nothing unusual about it; it's a beautifully finished mahogany door like every other one on the hall.

I really hope I'm right about this.

There are two huge, heavy tubs sitting on the cart. One of them isn't full anymore, because I filled the water gun at my belt with the liquid in it. I pick up one of the tubs, carefully removing the lid and balancing it on my hip, trying not to let the liquid slosh out.

I take a deep breath. All right. Here goes nothing.

I knock on the door.

I wait a moment, then another, then knock again.

Finally, the door opens.

The man standing there looks to be around thirty. He's white and blond, his thick hair slicked down into a professional-looking part, and wearing a three-piece suit. He's got a sharp jaw and heavy-lidded eyes that are a bright, familiar green.

"Who the hell are you?" he asks, clearly irritated by the interruption.

I hold up my water gun, filled with silver nitrate.

"I'm a friend of your son's."

And then I spray him.

There are a great many different types of vampire Nightmares.

Ones who can fly, ones who are allergic to garlic, ones who can control your mind, ones who are basically blood-sucking zombies. A great many different people have had vampire nightmares over the years, and each of them has put their own spin on the myth. And since one of the commonalities across the board with vampires is that they can propagate themselves, a lot of people have been turned into vampires, increasing fear of them, causing more people to have night-mares. Which has led to a lot of different strains.

Despite the fact that Cy actually had a nightmare to become a vampire, and wasn't turned, he and his father are the same type—he became his father after all.

And that type has several weaknesses of varying power.

But the most useful one is silver.

Silver, of course, is expensive. Silver bullets are available, but they're expensive too, and anyway, I have absolutely no idea how to aim a gun—I'd probably just shoot myself. And silver cuffs are great, but getting them on would be a prob-lem.

But there is one way to get silver in large, less horrifically expensive quantities.

Photography shops.

In order to develop photos, one needs a mixture of silver nitrate. It's a liquid, and it comes in large tins.

And you know what else are cheap?

Water guns.

So I spray the hell out of Cy's father. I don't need great aim, I just need to hit him somewhere.

He screams.

He collapses, howling, the flesh literally melting off his bones. Even though I aimed for his chest—the largest target—droplets splash onto his face and scald him. His eye dribbles into ooze and exposes the bone socket beneath, even as the majority of the liquid eats away at his shoulder and chest, dripping down his arm in painful red rivulets.

He's on his knees, one hand limp as the acid burns through muscle and tendon, destroying his ability to use that arm. Until he heals, that is.

So I don't give him the opportunity.

I pour an entire tub of silver nitrate on him.

Flesh sloughs right off bone, leaving little more than a skeleton behind, but he's still screaming, still melting, still alive, even in that horrific state. But it'll take him a while to heal and take his vengeance on me, which is all I wanted, so I don't mind that he's not dead yet.

He's not mine to kill, after all. Though I will if I have to.

I calmly reload my water gun from the other tub.

I step over the screaming, writhing monster in the doorway and into the hotel room. My shoes squelch in a puddle of melted flesh and silver nitrate. Ew.

The room is stunning. It's a whole suite, complete with living room, lounge, and a separate bedroom. The bedroom has a massive canopied bed, and the thick, heavy curtains are drawn. All the furniture has elaborate carvings in the wood, dragon claw feet and wooden filigree. I could sell one piece of furniture in here for a month of rent.

I take a few more steps in, giving me a glimpse of yet another room connected to this one, a small servants' quarters if I had to guess from the size and much plainer accoutrements.

Chained to the radiator in the corner of that room is Cy.

"Ness!" he cries, or I think that's what he says. It's hard to tell, since he's gagged. His dark hair is a mess, and it falls over his forehead and into his eyes, which are wide and hopeful.

Relief slams through me, so powerful my knees feel weak. He's here. He's alive. He's okay.

I stumble over to him, falling to my knees beside him to rip the gag from his face. He tries to hold still for me to get it off, but can't help wincing from my touch.

Where my fingers brushed his cheek, his skin has sizzled, a vicious red burn mark blooming.

I pull my hand back quickly. I must have spilled some silver nitrate on it. "Sorry."

"Don't worry about it," he says, his voice a little hoarse.

I look at his cuffs. I'm not sure what metal they're made of, but they must be something strong to keep a vampire contained, especially since he has no burn marks on his wrists, which means there's no silver in them.

"Where are the keys?" I ask.

"On the dresser."

I fetch them, quickly checking on his father at the door on the way back. The flesh is starting to rebuild itself, muscles knitting back together. It's absolutely disgusting to watch the muscles bubble and form over that skeleton, but now that he has his muscles back, he's starting to crawl my way, a pink blob of skinned monster. I'm sure he's planning to eat me since all that damage made him hungry.

I spray him with some more silver nitrate from my water gun, and he screams, a horrible wailing sound. Looks like his vocal cords re-formed.

I spray him again, and this time it's silent. No more vocal cords.

That's better.

I head back to Cy, unlocking his cuffs as carefully as I can. I'm absolutely covered in silver nitrate spray, but he grits his teeth against the pain, even as little red welts appear where my fingers inevitably brush his wrists. I try to move quickly, minimizing the exposure.

Finally, he's unlocked, and I step back from him.

He rubs his wrists, which are already healing, and looks up at me. "How did you find me?"

"I thought the Friends of the Restful Soul got you at first," I admit. "But after I broke in there to save Priya and realized you weren't there . . . well, it wasn't much of a stretch."

I shrug. "Anyone can hire people in a dark van to kidnap someone. And given that they came prepared with enough tranqs to take down a vampire and completely ignored me, the target was obviously you."

He nods along as I speak, using one of his free hands to attempt to fix the mess of his hair. Because obviously that's what's important here.

"Then it was a question of who would want to kidnap you." I give him a self-deprecating grin. "Lots of people want to kidnap me, but you? I can only really think of one—and he had a movie premiere in town this week."

I smile wickedly at him. "And where would someone that rich stay in town except here?"

Cy grins back, his eyes lowered in that bedroom look that always makes my face flush and my heart do uncomfortable flips. "My hero."

"Well." Yep, I'm flushing. That look is too powerful. "I figured after all the rescuing you've done for me, I ought to return the favor."

He's about to respond when a crash behind me makes us both spin around.

Cy's father is crawling toward us, teeth bared on his still half-melted face. His arms, pink with folding muscle, end in clawed fingernails, and his mouth is open, teeth glistening in salvia.

I spray him with the silver nitrate again.

"Did you want to put those chains on him?" I ask, trying to pretend that the image of a half-melted vampire crawling toward me with murderous intent doesn't bother me.

Just another day in Newham, after all.

"We can shove him in the bathroom to melt less messily in the tub?" I suggest.

Cy winces. "Yeah. Sure."

Cy gets to his feet slowly, wincing in pain and stiffness. After a moment of rolling his shoulders, he seems to recover, and his movements get smoother and more languid, back to normal.

Damn, I want that vampire healing.

Cy takes the chains and carefully clips them onto his melting father, tightening the cuffs so that they go right around the bone. His father's flesh will have to heal around the cuffs.

The sound of sizzling returns, but Cy ignores the red burns blooming on his hands as he binds his gasping, struggling father. He moves quickly, and in moments, his father is chained, and Cy is hauling him across the room, trailing a horrible ooze of melted flesh and skin on the pristine carpet.

Cy drags him into the bathroom and hooks the other ends of the cuffs around a metal loop welded into the floor. I'm not sure what it's for, and I don't ask.

Finally, confident his father is secure, Cy closes the bathroom door, locking him inside.

He leans his back against the door, resting the back of his head against the wood.

"What was he planning?" I ask.

Cy's eyes are still closed. "I don't know."

"Kill you?"

"Maybe," he says, then admits, "or maybe something worse."

I shiver. I don't want to think about what those worse options might be.

I hesitate. "You're going to have to figure out what to do with him."

Cy winces. "I know."

It's pretty obvious to me that there's only one thing you can do if you want to stop someone like Cy's father. The man is rich beyond words, which means that he can bribe his way out of any charge. He's also nearly impossible to kill, and just as hard to imprison, both because of the money and because of his vampire strength, speed, and healing.

What can you possibly do to stop someone the law can't touch? Someone who can't be controlled by any normal method?

But Cy doesn't want to hear that the only way to stop his father is to kill him. He doesn't want to be a murderer, and if I'm being honest, *I* don't want him becoming a murderer either.

I resist the urge to put my hand on Cy's shoulder to comfort him. I'm still covered in silver nitrate fumes, and I'm sure my touch would only hurt worse.

"We'll figure it out," I tell him, exhaustion from the past day weighing me down, making my eyes heavy and my body nauseous. Though that might be the smell of half-melted vampire.

I glance at the bed and take a deep breath. "But right now, I still have one more person to rescue."

31

My nightmare begins in darkness.

I know it's a nightmare and not just a dream, because I always have nightmares. When you're as scared as I am, with as much baggage as I have, anytime I dream it becomes a nightmare.

This time will be no different.

The question is only what form the nightmare will take.

The only two times I've ever dreamed, it's been of my sister, transformed into a giant spider. I dreamed of the way her long, hairy leg would creep around the door. I dreamed of the feel of her heavy steps approaching. I dreamed of the sound of her eating my father, crunching and slurping on his bones while I hid, hands over my mouth, small and trapped in the tiny space under the sink, hidden away from the world.

Over and over, I dreamed of that moment in my life, unable to move beyond it.

Not tonight.

Tonight, I'm alone. I stand in the living room of the house I grew up in, a tiny little rural home I shared with my father and sister. The floor is coated with blood. It drips off the walls and the sink, raining from the ceiling and dripping onto my clothes.

But no bodies. My father isn't lying where he died, and there's no sign of my sister.

The windows are open though, and outside, I can smell the charred scent of burning hair, and I know, without knowing how, that they're burning my sister's body. That they chopped up her giant spider form and set it all on fire, just like they did in real life. Now she's burning, and the smoke chokes me, making me cough.

Blood from the ceiling drips into my mouth.

I spit it out and stumble forward. I need to get out of here. I slosh through the blood, which has risen higher, up to my ankles now. Shivering, I pick up the pace, splashing around the corner and into—

—I'm standing in a hallway in the Friends of the Restful Soul's central building. The walls are exposed brick, and the doors are old and warped. Portraits of various saints hang along the empty hall, and I look around, waiting for one of the disciples to appear, but I'm alone.

The hairs stand up on the back of my neck, and I step forward, then again, and soon I'm running, racing for my safe place, the only place in the world that made me feel safe for so many years.

My tiny little coffin room.

I burst through the door and it's just as I left it. The bed is made, neat pastel blue blanket draped across crisp sheets. I close the door behind me and crawl onto the bed. Here, alone in the dark, I'm safe. I'm finally safe.

Something sloshes.

I open my eyes, and the ceiling is dripping blood, and I sit up, and the blood is on the floor too, the level rising slowly, burbling and glooping, almost like it's on the verge of boiling.

I have to get out of here before I drown.

I try the door, but it's locked. I rattle it, trying to escape, but the blood is rising higher, and it's up to my hips now.

No—the blood isn't rising.

The room is shrinking.

The walls are coming down, toward me, making the space tinier and tinier, and soon I'm cramped, curled up tightly, in the same position I was in when I hid in the cupboard under the sink and listened to my sister eat our father. I'm hearing him scream again, and the blood is up to my mouth and I've got my hands covering my head trying to protect it from the ceiling bearing down on me.

I scream, calling for Cy, for Priya, for anyone.

No one comes. I'm alone, and no one is coming to rescue me.

The walls grow tighter and tighter around me, squeezing, cracking, and breaking my bones like my sister did my father's, my safe space revealed for what it truly is: a prison that's slowly been crushing me, squishing me flat until my soul is stretched thin and malleable, easy to shape into what other people want.

306

I'm screaming, but my voice is gone, crushed out of me, I need help, someone help me, I'm all alone, and I don't want to be alone, I never wanted to be alone, I was tricked—

Suddenly, the pressure is gone.

I gasp, sucking in choked breaths, and look down at myself. All my limbs are still attached and uncrushed. I'm okay. Everything's okay.

"I didn't expect to see you again so soon."

I turn around and face the Nightmare Phantom.

His appearance hasn't changed in the dream. He's still got the spider-silk thin hair, silvery white, and the black, endless eyes. The only difference is that here, his clothes seem more mutable, like they're made from smoke shaped into a shirt rather than actual fabric.

"Can't a girl come for a visit?" I say casually, trying to calm my racing heart, still in panic mode after the nightmare.

"Of course," he agrees. He tilts his head to one side. "But surely that's not why you're here."

I take a deep breath. "I'm here to rescue you."

He stares at me, puzzled, as if he's not sure he heard me right.

"Rescue me?" he says, his tone as confused as his face.

"You don't want to be here, do you?" I ask, gesturing at the chasm of dark around us. "That's what you told me."

"No," he admits easily. "I don't."

"So?" I say. "I'm here to rescue you."

"But . . ." He hesitates. I've never seen him look so confused.

He clearly can't believe anyone would come for him.

Which, I mean, given the absolute catastrophe his sheer existence is, doesn't surprise me.

"You don't need to act so surprised." I cross my arms. "The world was absolute shit while you were trapped in dreams. I see no reason it should go back to that."

He blinks at me slowly, as though he's still struggling to understand what I'm saying.

"Ness," he says slowly, his sharp teeth glinting. "I've seen your deepest, darkest fears."

"Thanks for the reminder." I snort.

His mouth quirks. "I'd like to think I know you reasonably well. If you know a person's fears, you know their essence."

"Is there a point to this?" I ask.

"The point is," he says, "you're not an altruistic person."

I blink slowly. "You're gonna have to use smaller words. I didn't go to school much."

"You don't do things for the greater good," he clarifies. "You do things for yourself."

I shake my head. "That makes absolutely no sense."

"How so?"

"Well, if something is good for everyone, then obviously it's good for me too," I explain patiently.

He opens his mouth, then closes it.

"Nightmares popping up everywhere sucks," I tell him flatly. "And you've fucked up the whole world for the last century. I'd rather you cause your devastation locally, so that

I can be somewhere else, rather than everywhere all at once."

The Nightmare Phantom stares at me a long moment, then tips his head back and laughs. His hair glitters even though there's no light to reflect off it, and his smoky, swirling clothes whirl in strange patterns.

"Ness," he says, smiling wide. "You know, you just might be one of my favorite people."

"That's nice," I tell him. "The feeling isn't mutual."

"But you're still going to rescue me?"

"Sure am."

He shakes his head. "You're a very strange person."

"Right back at you," I say.

Around us, the world is dark, but for a moment, I think I glimpse something in the depths, a shadow that reminds me of the shape of my little room, so small, so tiny, so contained.

I hesitate, and then decide to go for it.

"I've been wondering something," I say as I stroll through the darkness. My feet make no sound, and there's no real sense of movement, which is unsettling.

"Oh?"

"Why?" I ask, looking up at him. "Why risk yourself by having such a dramatic confrontation with the Mayor?"

"I told you—"

"It's fun, yes, I know." I tip my head to one side, unconsciously mirroring him. "But you're not an idiot. You have to know that it was smarter to do this the sneaky way, and you still went with the flashy route."

His smile falls.

"What is it," I ask him, "about chaos that appeals to you so much?"

He smiles back, his voice light. "I couldn't say. It's just a part of me."

"Is it?" I ask. I lick my lips, and then say, "Or is it simply that you replicate nightmares in the real world?"

He frowns. "What do you mean?"

"For a long time," I say, my hands falling to my sides, "I only ever felt safe in small, contained spaces. It was a security thing."

The world around us re-forms, and we're both standing in my tiny room at the Friends of the Restful Soul. We can barely fit, and the Nightmare Phantom looks around with his eyebrows raised, examining it with curiosity.

"After I left the Friends," I say, "I learned they'd been messing with my head. And I assumed that they made me love my room, that they wanted me to crave isolation, that they were preparing me for the cage they planned to lock me in, so that I would never leave."

The world around us changes and morphs, and suddenly, we're back in my childhood home. It's empty except for us.

"But I don't think that's true anymore," I tell him, my voice sad. I walk over to the tiny cupboard under the sink and crouch to open it, showing a small, dark space that the grown-up me would never fit in. "I think I did it to myself. I think, even though it was the worst moment of my life, even though I was so scared I never really recovered, this little box, this feeling of being contained, became a safety blanket for me."

I rise, turning back to him. "I hadn't quite made the connection before I saw my nightmare today. Then it all became so clear. I was going back to the point of my greatest fear, replaying it in every aspect of my life."

I step toward him. "I'm not a psychologist or a brain expert. I don't know the ins and outs of the mind."

I'm standing right in front of him, an inch away, so close I can see that his skin has no texture at all, it's smooth like porcelain, all the fine details and signs of humanity long worn away.

"But I do know that what you did, creating that chaotic, insane scene in the Central Plaza"—my voice lowered—"looked very much like a nightmare."

He stiffens.

"I think," I tell him, "that you were subconsciously recreating a nightmare. I can't speak to why—perhaps part of you wanted the Mayor to live through what you had. Perhaps nightmares are all you can communicate through anymore. Perhaps it's none of those things.

"But"—I raise a finger—"it was a nightmare. *Your* nightmare. And it wasn't done to you, you did it to yourself. You brought your own trauma into the real world."

He stares at me with those inky black eyes, his expression perfectly still, so still I have no idea what he's thinking.

Finally, he inclines his head slightly. "Perhaps you're right."

The world around us vanishes.

This time, we're standing in space, but all around us are bubbles, huge, massive, world-size bubbles. They smash into each other, no space in between, impossible to escape. Through their transparent surfaces, I can see details, monsters and murderers, blood on the walls, nude people fleeing from their coworkers.

Nightmares.

And then I realize that we're already in a bubble. My bubble. We're in my nightmare.

But we're surrounded by others, all of them pressed toward us, as though trying to crush and pop my bubble and absorb us into theirs. There's no space to exist outside of the nightmares, they're infinite, endless, and the pressure of them all seems massive, like all that's keeping me from being crushed alive is this tiny layer of bubble.

"Do you like it?" the Nightmare Phantom asks from beside me.

"Not really."

"Me neither," he says. "But I can't remember much else anymore."

He'd mentioned that before. But now, seeing the sheer massiveness of it, seeing whole worlds of terror waiting to press down and crush me, I truly feel the weight of it.

"Maybe I did try to bring the nightmare to the real world," he says, considering. "But chaos is all I know, and all I am."

"But chaos isn't just nightmares," I tell him. "My closest friend, Priya, she loves chaos. Thrives off it. She hunts Nightmares and monsters."

I look up at him. "The difference is that she isn't *creating* the chaos. She's stopping the monsters that already exist. She's using her love of chaos to make the world a better place."

The Nightmare Phantom looks out at the bubbles of nightmares surrounding us, and smiles slightly. "Are you saying I should fight my own creations?"

"There's more to chaos than Nightmares. We have mad scientists and human trafficking rings and assassination companies—this is Newham." I grin slightly. "You know there's literally a vigilante group called the Chaos League dedicated to bringing chaos to the villains of Newham?"

He raises his eyebrows. "Is there?"

"There is," I tell him. "They're not very effective but"—I shrug—"Newham has so many insane monsters, it's hard to make a dent. It's a lifetime's work." I glance sideways at him. "Even for someone as powerful as you."

He laughs. "I see what you're trying to do."

"Is it working?"

He considers this carefully. "Perhaps. I'm thinking about it."

"That's all I hoped for," I tell him, because it is. I can't control his actions, and frankly, I don't want to try. That sounds exhausting and also like it would backfire.

But even if I make him think twice before causing another disaster like what happened at Newham Square, I'll count that as a win.

He turns to me. "So, how do you plan to rescue me?"

"Isn't it obvious?" I say, spreading my hands to either side.

313

"You're going to change me into something that can pull you out of dreams."

He watches me carefully. "You understand, my control in dreams is not what it is outside of them. I can't always predict the consequences of my changes."

I grimace. This is the part of my plan I'm not so much a fan of. "I know."

"And if I do this, even if I get out," he says, "I won't be able to change you again. This will be it."

"I know," I repeat, voice low.

I wish it didn't have to be like this, of course. I'd love to be invulnerable and have superhealing and all those other things I initially wanted. I'd love to walk down the street and not be afraid.

But changing my body to fit the world I was in was always a patch, a bandage on a festering wound. It would hide the problem and trick me into thinking it was solved, when in reality, the wound was still eating me.

I don't need to change my body to feel safe. I need to change my *mind*.

And it's going to be a long, hard road. I know that. I'm so afraid, all the time. But today, I've shown myself that if I don't let my fear stop me, I can be just as incredible as Priya or Cy.

I will never be fearless, but I *can* be brave.

And that's more important.

"I understand." I take a deep breath. "But it's okay. I'd rather use this change to save you from here."

And the world, I guess. But he's right, that sounds a little too heroic, and we all know I'm not exactly a hero. I'm doing this for my own future safety, not anyone else's. It's an investment in my lifespan.

He looks at me a long moment, and then his eyes soften a little.

"All right then." He approaches me, leaning forward and examining me. "I need strong fears to work with. You're a lucid dreamer, so you should be able to somewhat control things—what can you make yourself absolutely terrified of on command?"

"What can I? More like what *can't* I?" I put my hand on my hip and grin. "I'm afraid of *everything.* You think I can't give myself a panic attack over the smallest shit? It's practically my superpower."

He blinks, then laughs. The sound echoes in the dark space around us for a moment before vanishing in an instant.

He smiles at me, and I'm shocked to see that his teeth are no longer sharp. They're blunt and human, and his smile is just that, a smile. If I didn't know better, I'd say it looked almost genuine.

He steps toward me and explains what he's going to do.

I listen, and when he's done, I can't help but smile back at him.

32

I wake.

For a moment, I'm disoriented, my mind still trapped in the endless darkness. Part of me expects to wake in my small coffin room with the Friends, my little haven that was nothing more than a tiny prison in my mind.

It takes at least a minute before I fully register the opulent surroundings and heavy, drawn curtains, and remember that I'm in a hotel room. And whose hotel room I'm in.

I sit up slowly, and blink the sleep from my eyes.

"Ness." Cy rises from where he's sitting by the bathroom door. I can't tell if he was talking with his father through the door or just guarding him to make sure he couldn't get out.

"Hey." I rub my eyes and blink myself awake.

I get off the bed carefully, my body stiff and aching. I look down at my hands. They look the same, pale and chapped. I stumble over to the full-length mirror on the other side of the room and examine myself top to bottom, but nothing is out of the ordinary with the reflection except that Cy isn't in it. He doesn't show up in silver-backed mirrors.

I stare out at myself, and sure, my hair's a bit messier than usual, and I have bags under my eyes even though I just slept. But I'm still *me*.

I let out a long breath of relief. The Nightmare Phantom kept his promise.

Which, when I think about it, shouldn't actually surprise me. The Nightmare Phantom has never once lied to me, or broken his promises. He's been extremely up front and honest about exactly who and what he is, and what he'll do, and he's stuck to that.

He might be the most honest person in Newham.

Which is just weird to think about, given the sheer amount of evil he's done. I suppose there's no real reason honesty and morality should necessarily go together, it just seems like it.

Cy clears his throat, eyeing me with worry. "I don't see the Nightmare Phantom."

"No," I tell him. "You wouldn't. Not yet." I take a deep breath. "Let's see if this works."

I stand there and hold out my hand, focusing my mind—

—and a brick drops into my outstretched palm.

I stumble slightly under the sudden weight, and nearly drop the brick on my foot, but I regain my balance in time. I heft the brick, feeling the solidity and weight of it. I hold it up to the lamp and turn it over. There, on the underside, is the little etching of a bat I did while I was bored one night in my tiny, cramped room at the Friends.

It worked. It really worked.

I don't know what I'm feeling right now. Relief, certainly,

but also a strange, other feeling. It's a combination of sadness and loss, as though I've given something precious up for this power, even though all I've given up is my ability to claim I'm human, which, who cares about *that*?

Cy's eyes widen. "What just . . ."

I take a deep breath. I need to make sure it's reliable. That it works more than once, though I don't know why it wouldn't.

I hold out my hand. This time, a pistol appears in it. The same pistol that the Mayor nearly blew my head off with yesterday.

"It works," I whisper, still unable to believe it, even though the evidence is right in front of me.

Cy runs a hand through his hair. "Are you going to explain what's happening now?"

I turn over the pistol in my hand, feeling the slickness of the metal. "The Nightmare Phantom said he was going to try and change me so that I could summon the things I was afraid of."

Cy blinks, his expression startled. "The things you fear?"

"I'm a Nightmare now," I tell him. "And my great superpower is that I can make things I'm terrified of appear in front of me."

Which, when you think about it, is kind of a shitty superpower. After all, who wants to be able to summon what they fear?

But that's why he could do it. It wouldn't be a Nightmare if it was something the person wanted.

However, much like any curse, it can also be a gift.

I hold out the gun. "I'm scared of being shot, so I can summon a gun." I heft the brick. "I'm scared of the small room the Friends conditioned me to love, so I can summon a piece of it."

"That is . . ." Cy considers carefully. "I was going to say that's a terrible power, but now that I'm thinking about it, it actually seems useful."

"That was the idea." I laugh. "I just need to see if I can summon people now."

"People?" he asks.

I stare at him, hold out my hand, and—

Cy vanishes and reappears in front of me.

Right in front of me.

Like, nose to nose.

We both jerk backward, because wow, that is *way* too close, holy shit, I'm still covered in silver nitrate, being that close to me is probably toxic for him right now.

He yelps as he stumbles back. "Some warning next time!"

I let out a long breath, final test confirmed. "It works on people too."

Cy straightens his waistcoat and looks up at me with serious eyes.

"Ness," he says slowly.

"Hmm?" I put the brick and gun on a table.

"Ness," he says again, and his voice is concerned enough I look at him, really look at him, at the concern in his eyes, the hurt in the tentative way he speaks. "Are you afraid of me?"

Oh.

I did not think this whole thing through.

I open my mouth to deny it, but I mean, given what just happened, that's obviously a lie.

I flush and look away. "I—not like that. Not the way you're thinking."

"Then like what?" he whispers.

"Cy, you know me. I'm afraid of everything."

He doesn't look convinced.

"I'm afraid of you kicking me out when I have no savings," I tell him, my voice soft and low. "Even though I know you wouldn't be that cruel, a part of me is afraid of it."

"I—"

"I'm afraid of you getting tired of me living with you," I interrupt. "I'm afraid that I'll start feeling pressured to offer you blood for rent, even if I don't want to."

He's silent, just listening now.

"I'm afraid of our future." I give him a sardonic smile. "I'm afraid that all these random fears will eat at me until I do something dumb and ruin our relationship. And I couldn't bear that."

He's quiet a long moment, brow furrowed.

"Ness," he says slowly. "I'm not going to kick you out."

"I know," I tell him. "But someday you might get tired of me mooching—"

"No, you don't get it." He shakes his head. "You're misunderstanding something basic here."

"What do you mean?"

"I don't *want* you to move out," he says. "I want you to *stay*."

To . . . stay?

I frown, not sure I'm understanding him correctly. "Wait. You *want* a roommate that doesn't pay?"

He snorts. "What a way to put it. But yes."

I can't even fathom this. Who *wants* something like that?

"Why?" I ask, completely bewildered.

He blinks at me, confused. "You don't know?"

I shake my head. Clearly, he thinks this is something obvious, but I'm either clueless or dumb, because it's just not clicking for me.

He sighs, running a hand through his hair. "Ness . . . before you came, I was absolutely, pathetically lonely."

I blink, startled. I *did* actually know that.

"I was going out to parties every night just to meet people. Just to *be* with people, even for a little while." He looks at me with his bright green eyes. "Don't get me wrong, I love parties. I do. I'm an extrovert, you know. I always have been. I need people in my life. But I need more than shallow one-night relationships."

He leans his head back. "Everything's been so complicated since I came to Newham. I'm in a new city, I don't have any connections from before. And now I'm a vampire, which makes befriending people even *more* complicated. People think I want blood more than companionship." He grimaces. "They don't understand I need *both*."

He looks at me right in the eye. "I *like* having someone around. I *like* living with people. And I like living with *you*."

I stare at him, flabbergasted. "Me? What on earth is so good about living with *me*?"

He rolls his eyes. "Do I need to make a list?"

"Maybe."

"Fine." He holds up a hand and starts counting things off. "You treat me like a normal human, not a bloodsucking Nightmare. You're funny. You make me laugh all the time. You listen to me, and I always come out of hard conversations with you feeling better about myself and my life."

He holds my gaze, his eyes gentle. "Ness, don't you get it?"

He reaches over, as though to cup my face, but his hands stop just shy of my skin.

"You make me *happy*."

I can't even form a response. All I can do is sit here, mouth hanging open like a drunk fish.

"So no," he says, his voice intense. "If you're asking me about my own selfish desires, then I don't want you to leave." His eyes are so green they seem to glow. "I want you to stay."

I'm floored.

I've always seen myself as a burden, a mooch living off Cy's charity. I've been so obsessed with making sure I can be independent, that I can stand on my own two feet without needing to lean on Cy, that I never stopped to consider that Cy wanted something completely different.

Cy isn't like me. He doesn't need to hide in a closet alone

322

for days when he's tired. He likes people. He likes having people around all the time. He *wanted* someone to share his home with.

He wanted me.

I don't even know how to handle this information.

I bow my head. "I had no idea. I thought I was a burden all this time."

"Never," he whispers, leaning forward so our faces are nearly touching. "Ness, I never saw you as a burden. I *like* having you stay with me. And if that ever changes, I'll *tell* you." He snort-laughs. "Honestly, I don't think I could find a better roommate if I tried. You live in a *closet*."

A laugh coughs its way out. "I suppose I do."

He grins, and my chest tightens, because god, it feels good to be wanted, to know that at least *some* of my anxieties really were all in my head.

"I don't want to leave," I tell him quietly.

He blinks. "You don't? But I thought . . ."

"I thought so too." I turn away from him. "I was so convinced that if I could just make it work, if I could just earn enough money to live in my own closet, that would make me happy. But I don't think it will. I've been realizing that what I was imagining wasn't reality. I was picturing the dark little room I had in the Friends, somewhere away from the world, and I . . . I don't think that's actually what I want. I think that's what my mind tricked me into thinking was safe."

I pause for a moment before admitting, "I've dreamed for

so long of my own space. But when I realized why I was so obsessed with it, I had to ask if that was something I really wanted anymore. And it wasn't."

My lips quirk into a slight smile. "I thought it would hurt, when I realized that dream wasn't what I wanted anymore, but actually, it was kind of freeing."

He's silent, listening, his face so intent, his eyes so green.

"The truth is"—my face is flushing beet red as I say—"I like living with you too."

Cy looks like he's been told he can look at the sun without burning to ash—disbelieving yet hopeful. "Really?"

"Really," I tell him. "And I haven't been able to admit that to myself, because I've been afraid."

"Afraid of what?"

I look him square in the eye. "I've been afraid that I'm becoming completely dependent on you."

He blinks, startled.

"Every time I've been powerless, someone's taken advantage of me. I trust you more than anyone in the world, but fear like that doesn't go away overnight," I explain. "I'm afraid that you're going to ask me for something"—we both know what that something is—"and I'm going to be too scared to say no. I'm scared even if I want to say yes, I'll doubt myself because I won't be sure if I really want something, or if I just subconsciously want to keep you happy."

Shock, then hurt crosses his face.

"Have I, even once, asked you for *anything*?" he asks.

"No," I tell him firmly. "You haven't done anything

wrong. But you could, and that's scary."

He takes a deep breath, then lets it out.

"You're right. I can see why that would be scary." He raises his eyes to mine. "So let's take it off the table. If being bitten scares you, I'll never ask, and you don't *ever* need to feel like you should offer."

I look up at him, at his serious green eyes, his earnest expression.

The easy choice would be to agree. To confirm that it's out, not on the table, now or ever.

But I don't think that's the *right* choice. Avoiding something just because it's scary or difficult or could go wrong has pretty much never panned out for me. Especially since, in this case, I don't actually *mind* the whole biting thing.

I just don't want to feel pressured into it.

It's an important difference.

"No," I say, my voice small but steady.

"No?" He frowns slightly, confused.

"You can ask," I finally say, my heart beating so loud I'm sure he can hear it. "But if I say no, you can't push."

He blinks, staring at me. "Wait, what?"

I flush. "Was I unclear?"

"No, no, I just—I wasn't expecting that." He stares at my neon red face. "I thought—" He looks down. "I thought I hurt you. Last time. You got so weird about it afterward, I was sure it had been a terrible experience for you."

I shake my head. "It wasn't a terrible experience."

"You're not just saying that?"

"If it was, I'd just say I'd prefer it to never happen again, wouldn't I?"

He's watching me carefully. "Then why did you get so weird?"

My flush comes back, full force.

"Oh my god," he whispers, a smile pulling at his lips. "You *liked* it."

I cover my burning face with my hands. "I was just embarrassed!"

He's laughing, leaning back and laugh-crying. "Oh my god, do you know how much I was afraid you hated me after that? You were all avoidant about even mentioning the vampire thing and I straight up thought it hurt like hell and you didn't want to mention it because you didn't want to make me feel bad."

Oh god, somehow that's even more embarrassing.

We're such a pair of idiots, both assuming the absolute worst.

"I didn't hate it," I finally admit.

That's all he's getting from me.

He leans in, and his face is so close, his eyes all bedroomy and pretty as he murmurs, "Well, then, can I bite you again?"

"Right now?"

"Yes."

"No."

The words are out of my mouth instantly, so fast it takes my brain a moment to catch up.

Part of me wants to start making excuses—I'm still

covered with silver nitrate, he'd probably burn his face off if he tried to bite me.

But I force myself to remain quiet. Because I don't need a reason to say no. I don't need an excuse.

No can just be no.

"All right," Cy says, and that's the end of it. "So, what's next?"

Something inside me relaxes at his words, at how easily he's taking the no, how completely and totally he doesn't care about this rejection.

I hadn't realized until this moment that I needed this too—I needed to feel confident that *I* would say no. I needed to know that I wouldn't feel the need to make excuses for it. I needed to see that his wants wouldn't somehow subsume my own.

And I needed to see that Cy would take that no with grace and good humor.

"Hey, Cy," I say.

"Yeah?"

"I just wanted you to know." I smile up at him, my heart so full of warmth it feels like it might burst. "You make me happy too."

33

Three hours later, I'm standing in a warehouse on the edge of town. It's filled with trucks, buses, bulldozers, and all sorts of other city vehicles that have been parked for the night. The overhead lights flicker, and the orangey light they cast barely moves the shadows that lurk throughout the building.

Which is why I summoned myself a nice large flashlight. All I had to do was think about how terrifying it would be to be bashed over the head with one and, voilà, flashlight.

I kind of like this power. For once, my fear is actually helping me.

In front of me is a large metal coffin. Not just a box, a *coffin*, in full coffin shape, even though a box would have done just fine, really. But Newham villains always have to be extra, even when they're taking the practical, non-chaotic way out.

The Nightmare Phantom stands beside me. Bringing him out of dreams was as easy as a thought, and he came out looking exactly the way I left him.

And I do mean exactly.

His clothes are now that strange misty fabric that looks more like smoke, eerie and otherworldly. They seem to function the same as normal clothes, since at one point he rolled his sleeves up to avoid getting them messy. But I'm not actually sure he can take them off or if they're just a part of his body now. If they are, does that mean he's technically naked?

Ugh. Why is my brain like this?

I suppose I should be grateful that his clothes came out with him at all, but I'd be lying if I said that the way they shifted and swirled didn't creep me out a little.

But then again, most things about the Nightmare Phantom creep me out.

"Is everything ready?" I ask.

"I believe so," he says, his voice crisp.

His teeth flash as he speaks—still sharp. That moment where they were normal in dreams must have passed by the time I brought him out. I have to admit, I'm weirdly relieved that didn't change. I've gotten too used to the sharklike teeth that the human teeth looked weird on him.

I hand him the napkin launcher. "Then I guess you better get in position."

He stares at it a long moment with his strange black eyes. I'd found it in Cy's father's hotel room. He'd taken it with him when he kidnapped Cy. I figured it would be better to reuse it than to make a new one.

Since, you know, they're made from people.

But I'm trying not to think about that.

He takes the napkin launcher from me and walks around

to the other side of the metal coffin. He positions himself against the truck there, standing at an angle where I can't quite see him, just the end of the napkin launcher.

It's time.

Sweat sticks my clothes to my back, and I rub my hand nervously. Part of me thinks I'm insane for doing this, because there's so many ways that this could go wrong, and in most of them, I don't survive.

But if I don't do this, we'll be caught in a loop, where the Nightmare Phantom is forever getting trapped. And I won't always be here to free him.

I'm tired of the world being so shitty. And right now, I have the power to change it.

So I'm going to.

Even if I'm terrified out of my skin.

Which is why, even though my arm shakes, and my hand is sticky with sweat, I'm here now. And I'm not going to back down.

I take a deep breath, and raise my hand over the coffin. I want to close my eyes to concentrate, but I'm way too scared to actually do it, given who I'm about to summon, so I end up doing a weird squinty thing while I focus my mind on my fears.

The Mayor appears.

She's dressed in her usual black tuxedo, with white shirt peeking out beneath, and her lipstick is as red as freshly spilled blood. The pristine look is only somewhat marred by several droplets of actual blood that stain her white shirt and spatter across her cheek, but they're still fresh red enough to match the theme, not yet faded into a dried, unflattering brown.

"—make the smart decision to reelect me—"

She stops, mid-speech.

I step back from her, scuttling backward until I'm out of her reach—and out of the firing range.

Thud.

The Mayor hears the sound, but she's not fast enough to react to it, and the napkin that the Nightmare Phantom has fired lands on the back of her head, tangling in her long black hair. An area where she can't see it.

And if she can't see it, she can't send it away.

Her eyes widen, and her hands reach back to claw at the napkin, but it's untouchable, like steel. It seesaws its way around her head, crawling over her cheek.

She pulls out a gun and tries to shoot it, but the bullet bounces off. I duck, hands covering my head in case the bullet ricochets.

The Mayor empties a whole clip of bullets, but it doesn't faze the napkin, which crawls, slowly, patiently, into her mouth. Her head tips back as she tries to scream, but it's choking her, and her fingernails trace lines on her face and throat, as though she can rip through her own skin and pry it out.

Then the napkin bursts from her eye sockets in a spray of blood.

Her eyeballs tumble across the cement and roll toward me,

and I kick them away. They roll a few feet before hitting a sewer grate and falling down, washing away.

The napkin now covers her whole body like a blanket, wrapping tight until she looks like a dead body swaddled in a rug. She squirms beneath the napkin, thrashing and jerking, the spasms of a desperate monster trying to get out of a prison.

The Nightmare Phantom walks up and casually pushes the Mayor over, into the steel coffin.

The Mayor falls with a thud, and muffled shouts rise from within the coffin.

"I can't believe she's still alive in that," I say.

"Like I said, she's invulnerable to most things. This won't kill her." His smile widens. "And I wouldn't want it to. No, she's going to suffer just as much as I have."

He strolls over to the truck he hid behind when firing the napkin launcher. He pauses at the driver's-side door and looks back at the black-wrapped prisoner in the coffin.

"Any final words?" he asks her.

The bundle of napkin stops squirming, and after a moment a muffled "fuck you" comes out.

"Wonderful," the Nightmare Phantom says, and then he climbs into the truck and starts it.

I peer into the coffin, and I'm just close enough to hear the words, angry and bitter.

"It should have been me."

I want to ask what should have been her, what she's talking about, but it's too late. The truck has started, the drum on top is whirling.

The cement starts pouring into the coffin.

The thick gray mixture glops over the struggling form of the bound Mayor, piling on like a murderous ice cream cone. The Nightmare Phantom steps down from the truck and grabs the napkin launcher, using it to reach into the coffin and spread the cement more evenly, filling in the empty spaces of the coffin, smoothing it so that it reaches every corner.

Finally, the whole coffin is filled, and he ducks back into the truck to turn the cement off.

The top of the cement ripples slightly, the Mayor clearly struggling still beneath the weight of it, knowing that once it dries she won't be able to move ever again.

But all that wet cement is heavy, and while the Mayor may be indestructible, she doesn't have titanic strength. Maybe she should have bargained for it in the last century, but too late now.

Slowly, the ripples begin to fade, the surface of the filled coffin smoothing out.

The Nightmare Phantom comes to stand beside me, both of us watching the cement as it dries. It's oddly calming, watching it slowly harden and solidify. Both meditative because of its simplicity, and relaxing because it means that I'm finally free from one more monster that's been hunting me.

"That was"—the Nightmare Phantom considers—"unexpectedly easy."

"It was," I agree.

"I feel," he says slowly, "like I should have taken your

advice about keeping things simple from the start."

"Yes," I say. "You should have."

"Though I must say," he says, head tipped to the side, hair glittering in the light as he watches me with considering eyes, "your power isn't to be underestimated."

I know, I just *know*, that now he's thinking about how easy it would be for me to summon him just as I did the Mayor. Trap him exactly like we did to his enemy.

I don't know if there's anything I could say to convince him I wouldn't do that—that, frankly, I'd like to never do anything like this again. I'd be happy to never use this power for anything except stealing ice cream for the rest of my life.

But I don't know if he'd believe me.

And right now, if he decided to kill me, to get rid of a possible future danger, there's not much I could do to stop him.

Sure, I could summon a gun or a rocket launcher or something like that, but what use would they be against someone with bulletproof skin?

Finally, the Nightmare Phantom turns away from me, and touches the cement, his fingers light on the smooth surface. They leave a small imprint, a fingerprint absent the whorls and swoops the rest of us have.

"How long, do you think, to dry?" he asks.

I let out a silent breath of relief, and some of the tension in my shoulders loosens. I'm okay—for now.

"I'm not sure," I tell him. "Give it a little bit longer."

"Very well."

He's silent, and I shift my feet, unsettled by the quiet. I

don't like giving him an opportunity to think, to reconsider getting rid of me before I can cause him problems in the future.

"What will you do now?" I ask him.

"Hmm." He smiles, wide and sharp. "I'm still deciding."

Whatever he's deciding on, his expression says he's looking forward to it.

"Did you think about what I told you," I ask carefully, not liking the hungry anticipation in his smile, "in dreams?"

"I did," he says, and tilts his head up to the light. "I still am."

I think that's all I'm going to get from him, so I drop the subject. I hope that whatever his plans are, they don't destroy the city. Again.

Eventually, the cement dries, and we cover the coffin with a steel cap. It takes us another ten minutes to weld it on, trapping the Mayor inside forever.

The Nightmare Phantom dusts his hands off. "Next step, Newham Harbor."

I shudder.

It seems fitting punishment that after everything the Mayor did, she ends up trapped in a cement coffin for the next century or three, unable to eat or drink, unable to die, only able to exist in the dark, completely isolated from the rest of the world, her only company her own mind.

It's a torture just as cruel as the one she devised for the Nightmare Phantom.

I'm not sure I should approve of things like that, but

honestly, I don't even care about the methods as much as I do about the results. And the result of this is that one of Newham's most violent, powerful villains will be gone.

As the Nightmare Phantom walks away, the coffin over his shoulder, I wonder what the world will be like now, and how it'll change with the Mayor gone, and him free.

Maybe, finally, we'll all have a chance at something better.

Or maybe it'll crash and burn like the war the Nightmare Phantom spoke about. Maybe humans are always doomed to have awful lives full of awful people with too much power.

I guess I'll find out.

I look up to the flickering orange light overhead, and smile. I'm looking forward to seeing where the world goes. Because no matter what happens, things are going to be different.

34

It's several hours before the Lantern Man restaurant's illicit speakeasy opens for the evening, and I'm sitting on a barstool across from Estelle while one of the new hires sweeps the floor and puts the chairs out for the evening. I run my finger over the smooth surface of the bar, worn down over the years from use. It's a totally different feel from the polished surface of the bar at the fancy job I had for all of five seconds before it blew up in my face.

"I admit," Estelle says, leaning an elbow on the counter and resting her chin on it, "I didn't expect to see you back here."

"Me neither," I confess, looking up at her.

"So, you want your old job back?" Estelle asks matter-of-factly.

I shake my head. "No—I want a new job."

Her eyebrows rise. "Oh?"

I take a deep breath, in and out. I've got this. True, I don't have the powers I wanted from the Nightmare Phantom. I'm not indestructible. I'm not strong. I'm not powerful in any of the ways that I've always defined power.

But that doesn't mean what I *do* have can't be useful.

"I've been Nightmared," I tell Estelle.

She winces. "My condolences."

I shake my head. "It's not a bad one, all things considered."

"Oh?"

I hold out my hand, palm up, demonstrating that it's empty. Then I focus, picturing the pistol Estelle always keeps tucked in her boot, handle worn and barrel starting to rust, but still functioning like clockwork. The one she pulls out when things get truly dire.

The pistol appears in my hand, so suddenly and with enough weight that I nearly drop it.

Estelle jerks back when it appears, an instinctive response to sudden change from too much time working in a bar where shoot-outs are a common occurrence.

She catches herself quickly though, leaning in to peer at the pistol. She reaches down into her boot and fumbles for a moment, realizing that yes, I've taken the actual pistol, not made a copy.

"That's mine," she finally says.

"Yep."

"You can summon weapons?" Her voice is curious, and a little thoughtful, and her brows are furrowed. She's seeing the potential benefits of this ability as well.

"If I know they're there, I can," I tell her. "Which means

in a shoot-out, I could summon all the guns to me."

Estelle's lips purse in thought. A stray red curl bounces from her bun and trails down the side of her face. "That's a useful power."

"I think so."

"Can you summon other things?" she asks.

"Only dangerous things."

Estelle considers this for a long moment. "There's a lot more profitable jobs you could get with an ability like this."

"Probably," I admit. "But I have to find them first." I wrinkle my nose. "And I don't want to work for the gangs, which clears out at least half the highest-paying jobs."

Estelle raises an eyebrow. "Why not work for a gang? The pay is great." Her expression shifts to something deeply unimpressed. "Don't tell me it's *morals*."

She says "morals" like it's a dirty word. I don't blame her—morals are one of those things only rich people have the luxury of worrying about.

I snort and shake my head. "Nah, just practicality. I don't want any job that puts a target on my back. I've had enough of that for a lifetime."

Estelle's expression relaxes. "That's true. The better you do your job the more a rival gang will want to get rid of you."

"Exactly."

I hand her pistol back, and she examines it for a moment, checking to make sure nothing's changed, before tucking it back in her boot.

"So?" I ask. "What do you say? I bet a bouncer like me

could cut down casualties a lot. The minute a gunfight breaks out, they're all weaponless. Less murder means better profits for the speakeasy itself."

She laughs. "But less bodies to pickpocket."

I snort. "We'll have to find another way to get tips."

"We will." Estelle smiles. "But sure. We can do a trial period."

We spend a few minutes hammering out salary details—as someone with a unique skill, I feel I should be paid more, and Estelle agrees. We barter a bit before we settle on an amount, subject to the owner's approval, which we're both confident will be granted.

We shake on it, and I agree to start tomorrow.

I already have plans later tonight.

Outside, the city is thriving, crowds pressing through the streets, a sea of people, all of them hurrying from one place to another, none of them stopping. Autos honk and the smell of exhaust and sewers greets me. On the other side of the street, a man leans out a fifth-story window, trying to grab a piece of laundry that's blown onto his neighbor's balcony, and a few floors up, a giant slug lies in a sun chair with sunglasses on his face, as though he can get a tan when there's this much smog between him and the sun.

"Paper, ma'am?"

I look down at the paperboy, and I'm about to tell him no when I see the headline of the paper. I take the proffered paper.

MISSING KOVAL HEIR FOUND!

The picture on the front page shows the Mayor's pet pterodactyl.

I stare at the picture of the pterodactyl for a long moment, then look down to the caption, and yep, that's Dorothy Koval right there.

Well, that's awkward. Apparently, Priya and I flew on the back of the richest person in Newham, which I feel like might make her angry at us. But then again, we also took that drugged collar off her, so maybe she'll actually be grateful. Maybe we'll even get a reward.

Or Priya will, at least.

I skim the article, but it doesn't say much, except that the pterodactyl is communicating via Morse code, and that reconstructive surgery is scheduled in the hopes that she'll be able to produce human language again. At the bottom of the article, it mentions that Marissa Koval has mysteriously vanished. The article writer is uncertain if she's fled to avoid punishment for selling the Koval heir to a cult that turned her into a dinosaur, or if Dorothy the pterodactyl ate her.

I'm betting on the latter.

"You gonna buy that?" the paperboy asks in irritation.

I hand it back. "No."

He stalks away in a huff. I look up at the smoggy sky. I'm glad Cindy managed to find her friend, after everything she did. Even if said friend is a dinosaur now.

Better a dinosaur than dead.

"Sorry I'm late," says a familiar voice. "How did the meeting with Estelle go?"

I turn to Priya. She's washed and changed since I last saw her, and there's no sign on her pristine red-and-gold waistcoat and black shirt that she'd been kidnapped yesterday and spent the night destroying everything the Friends of the Restful Soul owned.

"Fine," I tell her. "I got the job."

Priya bumps my shoulder companionably. "I knew you would."

I bump her back. "And how did it go burning down the Friends' building?"

Priya grins, and she falls into step with me as we walk, telling me in excruciating detail all the devastation she wrought on the Friends' evil lab. She apparently recruited the other prisoners to help her. Once everything was destroyed beyond fixing, they all used their just-whipped-up-in-the-evil-lab acids to break into three other warehouses in the area, all of which, to the surprise of absolutely no one, turned out to be evil headquarters of various gangs, monsters, and mad scientists.

"All of them had basement prisons. Some of them were even worse than—" Priya shakes her head. "The important part is we released the prisoners and destroyed everything in the buildings."

She flashes me a grin. "I'm meeting up with some of the other prisoners tonight and we're going to break into some more buildings in the warehouse district and cause as much chaos as possible, before the supervillains all get wind of what we're doing and clear out their shady dealings."

I shake my head in disbelief. Destroying one evil organization clearly wasn't enough. Trust Priya to be an overachiever.

"It sounds like you're having fun," I say.

"I am!" Priya grins at me. "This is what I always wanted to do. Fight monsters, save people. This is what Nightmare Defense was *supposed* to be."

The truth of what it actually *was* hangs between us: a kidnapping, murderous organization that hadn't even managed to be fighting Nightmares for the past month.

She takes a long, sad breath. "You were right. About letting dreams go."

I'm silent, waiting.

"I decided to leave Nightmare Defense," Priya says. "It's not what I hoped it would be, and now that the Nightmare Phantom is out, I think it's done for good. I'm sure he'll still make Nightmares, but it won't be on that scale. Nightmare Defense will probably die soon, or get merged with Newham Police." She makes a disgusted expression. "And I've no interest in joining the Newham Police. I want to *fight* monsters not *be* one."

I snort-laugh at that. "I don't blame you."

"Fighting the Friends last night"—Priya hesitates, frowning, as though trying to find the right words—"it made me remember what I really love. Fighting *real* monsters. I want to keep doing that."

"Did you find a job that does that?" I ask. "Or are you

gonna go vigilante in your spare time while you work at a coffee shop?"

Priya grins at me. "I actually have a job interview lined up for tonight. One that would let me bring all the chaos to the monsters in this city for good pay and benefits."

I raise one eyebrow in skepticism. "Sounds ideal."

"It does." She winks at me, clearly understanding my skepticism. "We'll see if it's too good to be true. If it is, I guess I'll just have one more villain to take down."

I laugh and link my arm through Priya's as we walk. Priya's smile is open and wide as she tells me all her plans for the future, and I smile back at her, glad that she's finally shed the idea of who she had to be, and embraced the possibilities of who she could become.

35

That evening, after the sun has set and the cover of night has once again wrapped Newham in its cloak, I sit in a taxi with Cy. A massive box sits in the trunk, coated with silver on the inside, steel on the outside. Cy had it special-delivered to the hotel while I was out. These sorts of things are ready to order in a city like Newham.

Well, vampires are probably a global problem at this point, so I imagine they're ready to order in a number of places, just like many other common dangerous Nightmare containment tools.

The taxi jerks and spasms occasionally. It's hard to tell if we've gone over a pothole or if Cy's father is trying to escape, kicking at the walls of his prison.

The driver is unfazed to find us transporting a prisoner in a trunk. He asks no questions and shows no concern, which really makes me wonder what Newham cabbies must see in their lives. It's not the first time I've wondered this, but every time I get in a taxi I'm reminded that this must be the most insane job in the city.

Before we left, we could hear the muffled curses of Cy's father through the steel box, but sitting in the cab itself, we're far enough from the trunk that I can't hear them anymore. Cy, from his pained expression, still can. I don't envy his hearing.

The cabbie lets us off at Victoria Park, and Cy tips him handsomely.

Cy hauls the steel box over one shoulder, and we wind through the dark park. I lead the way, since Cy hasn't been there before.

"Are you sure about this?" I ask him.

He looks determined, but his voice is full of pain. "I am. There's no other way."

I just nod. If he's settled, then that's enough for me.

We're the only ones in the park this late. Or, if we aren't, whoever else is here stays well away, probably seeing Cy toting a massive steel box on his shoulder like it's nothing. I'd stay away if I were them too. Things that strong are often very dangerous—especially when they're out late at night.

Finally, I stop, and turn to face Cy. "This is it."

Cy silently puts the box down. He takes care not to jostle it as he lowers it to the ground, which I think is far more consideration than his father deserves, but I don't tell him that.

"You have to take him out for this to work," I finally say, my voice gentle.

"I know." He grimaces. "I'm just . . . bracing myself."

I reach over and take his hand, squeezing gently, just letting him know I'm here, with him. He squeezes back.

Then he opens the box.

His father falls out.

The man is still half melted from all the silver, and his face is a mass of missing cartilage and constantly re-forming muscle. His fangs look massive and sharp because his lips have melted around them, and his eyes shine malevolently out of bone sockets. They're an electric green, an almost identical color to Cy's.

He looks at me with what can only be described as raw hunger.

I shudder and shuffle back, well out of reach.

Cy is wearing gloves, so even though his father is coated in silver, Cy doesn't burn as he holds his father back from escaping.

"You going to kill me?" his father says, his jaw coming unhinged because all the muscles have melted around it. "Your own flesh and blood?"

"Don't give me that," Cy whispers, his voice harsh. "You killed my mother."

Cy's father scowls, his face rippling as flesh re-forms, a smooth layer over the muscles, making him look almost human again. "Cy, we've been over this, it was—"

"Enough," Cy interrupts. "I'm done."

His father glares up at him. "Excuse me?"

"I'm done listening to your lies and excuses," Cy says. "You've been preaching your bullshit my whole life, and quite frankly, I've heard enough of it."

Cy leans forward, his face inches from his father's.

"I want you to know," Cy says, his voice cold, "that when you're gone, I'm going to take over your film business. And I'm going to spend all your money tearing down everything you've built and exposing you for what you are."

Cy's voice lowers to a hiss. "Within a decade, the world will call you a monster. Your legacy will be disgust and revulsion."

Leaning back, Cy's eyes are piercingly green in the dark. "You taught me the power of film. You showed me how you can shape people's perceptions with stories to nudge them into believing what you want them to. Now I'm going to use those same tools to make films that show your stories for what they are—a monster making excuses for his crimes."

As he speaks, I think of my own mind, and how it was warped by the stories it's been told. The story of how my sister slaughtered my father—and how later, I learned that she did it to save me and herself. The story I told myself that hiding away from the world would keep me safe—and how now I see that was just isolation.

We are surrounded with stories, in media, in our lives. How we perceive them shapes the way we see the world. For a long time, I've accepted the worst stories, swallowed them whole.

But now I wonder if I can tell my own stories, tell myself a story. I can tell myself I'm brave, and clever, and good at learning from my mistakes. And maybe, if I tell it to myself enough, I'll believe it as much as I've believed the other,

348

malicious stories told to me over the years.

Believe it enough that it becomes truth.

"Cy—"

"Goodbye, Father," Cy says.

Then, Cy shoves the rotting monster backward, into the turtle pond.

When I'd met the Nightmare Phantom here and first seen the pond full of turtles that had once been people, I'd thought it a terrible fate. Simply touching the water turns people into small helpless amphibians, all of them trapped in a tiny pool of water. It sounded like torture.

Now I think it's kind of useful.

The moment Cy's father touches the water, he begins to shrink, body warping and twisting. His flesh fades to yellow, then to green as he becomes smaller and smaller. His bones crunch and pop as they re-form, and I wince at the sound, because it reminds me too much of my own father's bones, popping as my sister snapped them like twigs.

It will always be a sound I associate with fear, with the death of the only parent I ever really knew. And while I know, objectively, my father wasn't a good person—though not as evil as Cy's—the memories are still tinged with pain. I don't think that will ever change, no matter how much I understand about that night, and how far away I move from the terrified child who hid through her father's death.

I close my eyes and take a deep breath, let the memory wash over me—and then gently, tenderly, push it away. I'm stepping away from the power that memory held over me. It might take a lifetime, but that's okay. I'm taking it one day at a time.

When I open my eyes, Cy's father is gone.

A tiny green turtle floats where he stood.

The turtle swims angrily to the edge of the pond and snaps at us, its tiny, powerless mouth nipping ineffectively at Cy's shoes. I kneel down beside it, and it opens its mouth, showcasing tiny little turtle fangs, completely powerless.

Cy's father will never hurt anyone again.

Cy shudders beside me, and I put my hand on his shoulder.

"It's over," I reassure him. "It's okay. He'll have a happy life as a turtle."

His voice is thick. "You think?"

"Sure," I tell him, even though I'm not sure how happy a turtle's life is. "It's better than being dead, isn't it?"

He leans against me. "Yeah."

"You did the right thing, Cy," I tell him, reaching up to turn his face to mine. "You made the world a better place, and you did it in the kindest way you could think of."

He bows his head, a single strand of hair falling from his perfectly slicked part and over his forehead. "I still feel awful though."

"Why?"

"I guess"—he considers—"part of me feels like I should have done something like this years ago. Maybe my mother would still be alive."

"You were a child," I insist. "Stop putting expectations on

someone who had no way of meeting them."

He lets out a breath. "Yeah, you're right."

"Of course I am," I tell him firmly. Then I sober. "Were you serious about taking over his film business?"

"Yeah," he says, raising his head. "I am. I'm going to try and fix the damage he's done to the world. I mean, I'm the one inheriting all the money he made hurting people—I'd feel complicit in his crimes if I didn't use it to try and fix what he's done."

I nod slowly. I can understand that.

"It might take time to get going," he admits. "I'm not sure how long after someone goes missing they're declared dead. I don't know what the inheritance laws are like." He grins wryly. "I should probably look into that."

"Probably," I agree, smiling. I bite my lip. "Will you leave Newham then? Go back home?"

He blinks, clearly startled. "What?"

"Well, to run the business . . ."

"No." He shakes his head. "Definitely not. I'm not going back to that house. I don't even know if I could ever live in that part of the country again. There are too many bad memories there." Something pained crosses his expression. "I might have to go for a visit occasionally, but I'm staying in Newham."

My shoulders slump in relief. "Oh, all right."

He looks at me a long moment, and says, "You know, you could come with me, if you're interested. When I visit my father's house. I could use the company."

"Oh." I haven't left Newham since I came here at eleven, except for a brief visit to Palton Island. "I suppose I could go for a few days. See a new place."

I can't even imagine what it would be like. Whenever I picture cities, they all look like Newham. Newham, but with more sun. Newham, but with a green river. Newham, but with different villains.

Maybe it's time to broaden my knowledge a little. See how the rest of the world lives.

He grins, bright and vibrant. "I can't wait to show you everything."

"I thought it was all bad memories," I say, eyebrows rising.

He links his arm through mine, and we stroll away from the turtle pond, arm in arm. "Well, that's why you're coming. To create new memories. Better memories."

"Hmm," I say, and I can't help the smile that warms my face. "So what kind of places would you take me?"

His voice rises in excitement as he tells me about beaches and ice cream, about streets full of stars and dreams. I smile as I listen, because for the first time in my life, instead of feeling like I'm living through a nightmare, I feel like I'm walking toward a dream, one that the two of us will share together.

EPILOGUE

On the other side of Newham, in the towering Mayoral Palace, a new Mayor has just been inaugurated.

He's just finished his speech, and the camera crew are packing up. It will air tomorrow, bright and early. Unlike his predecessor, the new Mayor won't be doing public speeches with reporters—he's learned from her mistakes.

And, perhaps, from his own.

"Sir," says an aide. "You've got that interview now?"

"That's right," the new Mayor says, smiling, his teeth wide and sharp. "I can't be late."

As he walks the halls, the light glints on his hair, ethereal and silver. His eyes, endlessly black, survey the people who run to and fro, trying to make all the alterations to the Mayoral Palace he's requested.

He wants all traces of the previous Mayor scrubbed from the building.

Now that he's in charge, things are going to change around here.

He steps into the interview room, and the young woman waiting there rises. She's tall, with dark hair that has a turquoise ombré, and far too many weapons on her belt.

"Thank you for joining me," he says, gesturing for her to sit.

"How could I refuse?" she asks, but her eyes are sharp and her smile is anticipatory. She's ready for a fight—whether it will be with him or against him, she hasn't decided yet.

He smiles back at her. He knew, the moment he saw her nightmare, that she'd be perfect for what he wants to do.

He sits down across from her, and leans in, his hands clasped together.

"Priya," the Nightmare Phantom says, his voice low and full of excitement for all the chaos to come. "How would you like to change the world?"

And Priya, sitting across from him, slowly smiles.

Far above the two of them, a pterodactyl soars across the sky, silhouetted against the moon. It screeches a challenge into the night, a sound that echoes between the towering buildings like jagged teeth. It sounds as if the city itself is roaring.

Tonight, an era has ended, and a new one has begun. Only time will tell whether it's a better or worse one.

One thing is certain—the City of Nightmares will never be the same.

ACKNOWLEDGMENTS

Here we are, at the end of another book! I hope you've had fun.

Writing this book was a lot of fun, but also a big challenge. I had so much I wanted to do in this world with these characters, and it just couldn't all fit in one book! Hopefully one day I'll have a chance to revisit the world and tell more of these characters' stories. But for now, I hope you've all enjoyed Ness's adventures.

I want to give a big thanks to the teams at Clarion Books in the US and Hodderscape in the UK. Special thanks on the US side to Liz for all her insightful feedback, and on the UK side to Molly for always going above and beyond. I'm so grateful for everything both my incredible teams have done for this series. And a huge thank-you to everyone at Fairy-Loot who worked on a stunning special edition for *City of Nightmares*!

Big thanks as well to Suzie, Jim, and the foreign rights team at New Leaf! I also want to thank Ella, who read this book in like a week so I could get an outside opinion, and Natasha, who picked out all the issues in the book so I could fix them.

As always, I want to thank my incredibly supportive friends and family, who have been an anchor in the stormy seas of the publishing industry. I'm very lucky to have good people in my life.

And finally, a huge thanks to my readers of the first book who kept going and read the second! I hope you'll continue on to whatever comes next.

.